Angel's Influence

D.S. Boyce

ISBN 979-8-89345-338-6 (paperback)
ISBN 979-8-89345-339-3 (digital)

Copyright © 2024 by D.S. Boyce

All rights reserved. No part of this publication may be reproduced, distributed, or transmitted in any form or by any means, including photocopying, recording, or other electronic or mechanical methods without the prior written permission of the publisher. For permission requests, solicit the publisher via the address below.

Christian Faith Publishing
832 Park Avenue
Meadville, PA 16335
www.christianfaithpublishing.com

Printed in the United States of America

CHAPTER 1

The Vision of the Cherub

Between the seven mountains lay walkways of stones, connected by portals. The steps pointed the way to heaven. Called the Third Heaven, it was there that the Ancient of Days ruled, encircled by a deep, dark, vacuous space. This insulated God and his throne. Known as the Second Heaven, the void is where the celestial bodies lived. Of the heavenly host, the highest angels, seraphim, protected the throne. Always there, ever-encompassing, the seraphim never left the presence of God.

Under the keepers of the throne, the diligent archangels oversaw the realm. Guardians of the kingdom, the great warriors honored the will of their Father. The lowest of the celestial hierarchy were the retainers of the hosts. Called cherubim, they were the rank and file of the messengers. All natural in composition and singular in mindset, the angels shared an unbreakable bond with their Creator. Among the cherubs, the Father made a special one, a mountain among them, frosted in beauty with glittering wings. An angel of special significance, its purpose was to blanket the throne with its shadow of light. Floating above God, it hovered seamlessly. No twisting wind could thwart its proud, linear stance. The name of the cherub was Lucifer, the angel over the Almighty seat.

Timeless in structure and an ever-illuminating beacon, all the kingdom recognized Lucifer. The angels honed into its light. Lucifer's wingspan was massive, shimmering, turning in an undulating motion. The angel rolled and swayed in elemental beauty, with clean, sheer colors of recognizable brilliance. Its wings had an intoxicating static buzz. The wind whistled a sound through its feathers, a hum similar to whispers fawning for attention. The most breathtaking of canopies all knew the cherub as the bringer of light. Fairest of all, its arc lamp enthralled the Father's countenance. The celestial body marveled at the luminescence of the covering cherub.

However, time is cruel to mountains, and such was the fate of Lucifer. Through the ages, it listened to the words of the throne. No other angel fell privy to godly proclamations. The covering cherub became a silent partner in deliberations. In time, the angel felt privately exclusive to the matters of the state. The perch above the throne gave it prominent notability. Lucifer believed to be equal among the supreme union, a false alliance that gave the pretense of godly power to the other watchers. Nonetheless, knowing secrets not meant for the angels did not implicate equality.

Lucifer made a misguided assumption. Inner aspirations emerged; the angel coveted the throne. The most cherished cherub aspired to sit next to the Father. Blazing in excitement, it romanced intimacy with its creator, fixated eyes on the Father, absorbing his every word. Nodding agreeably with a slight up-smile, the luster around Lucifer's face riveted his mind to the wisdom. The fixation deluded reality. *Am I beyond my fellow angels?* Lucifer thought. The cherub had the envy of the host. None ever witnessed the Father care of its angelic presence. Such belief of acceptance prompted a deep dignity. Lucifer celebrated internally. *Is it not true that I am magnificent, the most glorious? There is not another, for I am bewitching*, it thought. For perpetuity, the one-sided relationship evolved. The angel's delusion cemented as it grew in knowledge. Access to the dealings of the throne made it a studious observer. Lucifer examined every aspect of the affairs of the kingdom.

Yet another occupied the seat to the right. The Father called the one next to him Son, a relationship that confused Lucifer. After all, when the Father named his covering angel, he called it his light bearer. All in heaven knew the meaning of the name *Lucifer*. It was the angel who projected the luminous flux. Lucifer, the son of the morning, the bringer of the dawn. From the beginning, it basked in godly light. Sharing such intimacy, it thought, *How could anything be any closer?* The cherub compared itself to the Son. It refused to believe the Father loved him more. "No one loves the Master greater than me," it concluded.

Lucifer worshiped the Father, but the Son, the angel despised. Each time Father and Son spoke, its hatred burned. Lucifer internally questioned the order. Throughout time, the Father never asked for an opinion from the cherub. Never once did he turn and allow it to speak. Yet he allowed Lucifer to remain, listening, hearing divine decrees and holy judgments. This cruelty was like the wind, slowly carving away the angel's beauty. No other angel perceived the dulling of Lucifer. Bright externally yet dark internally, its heart hardened as it reconsidered its place. An imbalanced triad plagued the throne. Next to the Father, the Son, with Lucifer suspended above—three present, two of importance. It became self-evident that the Son was a begetter, an impostor. This perception impressed an idea, *I should take my seat*, it thought. Pride surpassed reality, and Lucifer believed itself to be the rightful son. A transfiguration from joy to anger occurred each time it heard the Son's voice.

No longer a covering cherub, but a befitting ruler. With no limits of reason, the cherub's fantasies took hold. Lucifer became the stone too heavy to lift. No turning back because haughtiness became a prelude to decision. Lucifer understood the angelic body. It knew they adored the Father. However, love for the Son revolved around fatherly devotion. The Father gave the Son authority, and the holy stars complied. Although Lucifer was the morning star, the Father named the Son his bright morning star. Problematic titles since the watchers of the realm were innocent in design. Beings of the Father, angels never considered past their servitude. All eyed Lucifer as their model and appreciated its beauty. Knowing this, Lucifer began to beguile the others. Its charm was overwhelming and naturally distracting, the angel's knowledge commanded sway. Lucifer commenced the ruination of its nemesis. It rewrote its value and became an archfiend to the Son.

Vexing the lesser peaks, the mountain of an angel enticed legions. Many heeded the seductive tongue, the cunning utterances.

They contemplated the assertion that Lucifer was better equipped to govern. The angels began to question the sovereignty of the Son. This seed of doubt and the span of rhetoric became irreversible. At the core, there were two contentious points: who best to rule and who was set higher. Insecurities undaunted, the great cherub continued its campaign. More and more angels believed and followed. Some were secretly supplanted; others began to exhibit disloyalty. The Father knew Lucifer's vision but did not restrain it. He knew the mounting treachery troubled his Son. Yet never a word was said since the adversary hovered close by. The silent test of patience affected the psyche of the angels. A third of the angels declared their fealty to Lucifer. The lovely cherub gathered an impressive force.

Rebellion burrowed into hearts, and the rebellious fought against the Son. In the most glorious of battles, heaven exploded in conflict. The fray overflowed into the cosmos, an amazing clash never witnessed since time began, with angels fighting angels. The archangels, tasked with vanquishing the defiant, saw the fight spill throughout the corners of the realm. In the surge, stellar bodies shattered, and planets shook. A supernatural war caused cataclysmic effects. Archangel Michael seized the star, Lucifer. The archangel hurled it from heaven. The myriad of angels still loyal to the Father grabbed hold of Lucifer's legions. The insurgents met a similar fate as their leader. Angels, whose parts of shame resembled rampaging horses, were bound and hurled. The Father instructed that the rebellious be locked away on a planet called Earth, a fractured planet due to extramundane activity. The supernatural skirmish destroyed it, leaving it formless. The once-covering cherub had to be punished; that punishment was banishment. *If only I could have swayed more*, it thought, *then this unworthy God would have received a proper dealing.* The angel shouted to the heavens, "I am the true God!" The war for dominance was over, the Son the victor. Lucifer declared, "This is not over!" It was not over because Lucifer failed to perceive that the defeat was not due to numbers. Blinded to the nature of the Son, the struggle for supremacy began anew.

CHAPTER 2

Designing a World Fit for a King

It was a costly battle that had weakened heaven. No cherubs reached the throne because none could match the strength of a seraph. The angel of light could not divide the seraphim nor separate the archangels. Only cherubim idolized Lucifer. The revolt jolted those angels left in heaven; they all heard the grievances of the rebels. The words of the fallen dazed the host as they heard the case for Lucifer. It reshaped heaven because, in the minds of the angels, doubt replaced harmony. Now cloudy eyes looked to the throne, uncertainty overwhelmed their thoughts. Father and Son knew the churning; both sensed the disenchantment. The damage was extensive, and the angels of God wondered and pondered the words of Lucifer. Only the Son could settle the matter because the angels required affirmation. The Father gazed at his Son; both knew what had to be done. The haughty angel and his fallen cherubim had to be dealt with because rebellion planted seeds of doubt.

Order needed to be reestablished. Skepticism had to be abated. Cherubim were restless because the recent rebellion obsessed them. After the battle, all pledged fealty to the Son. Yet confusion remained since a third of the hosts followed another. To leave Lucifer idle would fan more unpleasantness. The spotlight veered heavily over the Son. Many angels wondered, *What will he do?* Others waited to see who would win. At any moment, the Father could have forced love from them. With a thought, he could have disposed of all heavenly bodies and begun anew. But the Father wanted them to openly worship. He wanted faithful adherence without enforcement of will. There was no place for corruptible spirits; everything needed to be tried and true. The Father designed the perfect stumbling block. He called the name of that stumbling block Lucifer.

In response to the rebellion, the Son was charged to create an image, and not just any image but one with a character based on himself. This image would become Lucifer's stumbling block. To right the wrong required an expensive toll, a price only the Son could pay. The image was the key to shore the rift; restoration demanded an unnatural sacrifice. Spanning his eyes to the cherubim before him, he declared, "It is up to me." There was no other way; the suspicion stirred within the angelic host had to be rectified. With a deep inhalation, "Through an image, I will show my prerogative. All in heaven will know the true heir, the one worthy to be next to you, Father." The Son turned to his father and said, "With your blessing, I will create." Both stared intently; the silence stopped everything in heaven. Tenderly holding his hand, gingerly kneeling before his Father, "Abba?" He pled. "All creation must have no doubt who sits next to you."

The Father looked back with tender eyes. "To ask this is much, my Son. To do this will demand no restraint... It must be done freely." The Father did not want to see his Son suffer. Knowing the gravity of the situation, he could not contain his sadness. The Son kissed his hand. The touch moved the Father to bless him, "I give you authority to create an image of us." Pulling his chin, the Father lifted the face of his Son, "My Son, take this lifeless hulk and make it yours." While he still spoke, his eyes shifted to the angels, "Design it with the future in mind. Through it, demonstrate your ascendancy because, until that day, Lucifer will remain unshackled." It was settled; the earth had become the place of decision. There, the rebellious would remain free until the Son proved his worthiness.

Undeniably, the Father gave angels a choice. Although not an assertive trait, still a given trait. Both Father and Son recognized the pride in Lucifer. Its beauty made the angel most influential; its persuasion was difficult to resist. To defeat the angel, the Son had to counter its charm. The centerpiece of his plan was predestination, to foreordain an image that would be his children. To do this, the Son decided to add something not found in angels. God intended to give the image the potential to be like God. Seraphs, archangels, and cherubim did not possess the characteristics of God. Angels were nothing like their creator. Deciding to foster such children insulted Lucifer. The angel devised a divisive scheme, a plot to steal the image from the Son. Lucifer decided to alter the distinguishing quality; the angel intended to corrupt them as it did the angels.

A risky gamble, failure meant the Son would forfeit his seat. A fair fight required a fair venue. The Father chose the place where he banished Lucifer: Earth, a most neutral arena that assured an unquestionable result. To even the odds, the Son decided to give Lucifer an advantage. He would shed his divinity and walk among his children, a most hazardous risk since exposure meant vulnerability. To shed his Godhood and become part of creation put him lower than the angel. An unfair disparity, being Lucifer kept its angelic abilities. Should the Son be defiled, he would become unsuitable for the throne. The real issue was salvaging heaven. The remaining angels were susceptible to influence; the revolt piqued the interest of the watchers. Lucifer caused a breach that had to be sealed. Falling short meant an uncertain future for heaven.

The Son stretched out his hands. By the grace of the Father, he moved his breath over the formless planet. The Spirit flowed above the darkness and upon the face of the waters. "Let there be light!" A supernatural light pushed back the darkness. Continual and fixated on the Earth, the light shone unceasingly, a light the Son called day. He divided the light from the dark and called it night. To hold back the void, the Son dipped his Spirit into the waters. An extreme part of the waters lifted, swirling in all directions, it streamed around the planet. The water flowed above, condensing into a thin barrier of vapor. The film sealed the air and created an atmosphere. The Son called it a firmament, a canopy that cut a distinction between the two heavens. The sky around Earth became the first heaven, the youngest of the three heavens.

The beginning of the night he called evening, and the beginning of the light, morning. The Son said, "Let the waters under the heaven be gathered together. Let dry land appear." The Son called the land earth and the waters seas. As the design unfolded, the greenhouse effect began to enrich the air. Molecule-filled nutrients were injected into the land. At the Son's direction, "Let the earth bring forth grass, the herb-yielding seed, and fruit-yielding trees." Lush grass prickled from the ground. Foliage covered the landscape, and succulent herbs accompanied the trees. Lovely and picturesque, the first three days of creation brought three divisions: the first division day and night, the second water and sky, and the third separation land from sea. Each portion prepared the way for life.

Yet the light of day was supernatural; the power of the Son kept darkness away. Lifting his strong arm to the second heaven, "Let there be lights in the firmament. With these lights, let them divide the day from the night." Two stellar bodies appeared, one to rule the day and the other the night. The Son called the body of light the Sun. Its heat solidified the firmament, turning it into a pure layer of hydrogen. The other body had no light but stole it from the Sun. The Son called the lesser light the moon. Both Earth and Moon became embraced in an everlasting dance, compressing and releasing against each other. While the sun lit the day, the moon pulsed the seas. The waters swelled when the moon came near and ebbed when it moved away. The union created interacting fields that set in motion the seasons. The sun, moon, and Earth, strongest when aligned and weakest when apart, controlled the cycle that gave the oceans its heartbeat. The Son said, "Let these be for signs, for seasons, and for days and years." Each rotation of light and dark became a day. Succession of days framed time, and the seasonal cycles defined a year. The Son added more lights in the second heaven, beacons named after the angels, lights that honored their fealty. Lovely stars that matched the seasons, decorative lights that kept their boundaries. The light of day washed out their presence; it was night when the stars took control. With the division between light and dark, the Son withdrew his glow. The fourth day set the lights and the cycles of the year. Each facet relied on the other, and the order pleased the Son.

The Son said, "Let the waters bring forth abundantly moving creatures. Let life spring not only from the waters but also from the air." With a gesture, all sorts of living creatures came forth. The earth was teeming with organisms and inorganic objects. Environmentally adaptive, the land flourished as did the seas. Moving creatures, great whales, monstrous beings glided through the waters. An assortment of birds hung in the air, and fruit-eating fowl reseeded the land. The Son blessed everything: "Be fruitful and multiply. Fill the waters and the seas, and let the fowl multiply abundantly on the earth." The extension of life was the labor of the fifth day.

On the sixth day, the Son cried, "Let the earth bring forth the living creature after his kind." With the power of his voice, the Son made all sorts of beasts: types of cattle, groups of bees, no creature beast or crawler crossed out of their kind. The Son molded a sublime miracle, a perfect ecological balance. Looking to heaven, he said to his Father, "Let us make an image after our likeness. The image will be called man, and I will give him dominion over the fish of the sea, the fowl of the air, and every living creature." All life came from the dirt: beasts, fowl, fish. Likewise, the Son swirled the dust and sculpted a form. Pleased with the shell, he decreed a promise, "Behold, I will give you every herb bearing seed, every tree and its fruit for meat. All will be yours to eat. The fowls and beasts spread the seed, the creepy things of the earth distribute the seed. All life will I give bounty from the seed; food to eat. You, my likeness, will have dominion over all things." As the Son surveyed his work, he saw the image still dormant before him. Breathing the breath of God into the image, it turned into a living soul. Everything living possessed a soul, but none of them had been intimately conceived through the breath of God. The Son blessed man with the gift of thought and reason. Of all creation, only he had the ability to speak.

The Son thought, *I should prepare a special place full of beauty.* With a powerful command, a garden pulled together. The Son put a tree in the center, which he called the tree of life, a special source of nourishment to the garden, spreading its roots into everything. Beside the tree of life lay another tree. The second tree, called the tree of knowledge of good and evil, had a different purpose. Forbidden to eat, the Son made a covenant with man, "Of every tree of the garden you shall eat freely. But of the tree of knowledge of good and evil you shall not eat. For in the day that you eat of it, you shall surely die." The rest of creation could not compare to the garden. Showing itself in the east, the Son named the garden Eden and put the man in the center of it. On the seventh day, he rested, taking in the splendor of it all. Six days did the Son create, but the seventh he set aside as a hallowed remembrance.

The man became the caretaker of the garden. He cultivated it and kept it. Since the Son rested on the seventh day, he imprinted the need for man to rest. More than a physical necessity, the Son desired an intimate connection between man and himself. Time had passed, and the relationship evolved into an unbreakable bond. He called the man Adam, the first of his kind. The Son tasked Adam with naming everything; whatever Adam named, that was its name. Adam asked, "You have allowed me to name all things, but I do not know what to call you. With your permission, could I give you a name?"

The Son replied, "What would you like to call me?"

"I would like to call you Yahweh because I can sense you."

The Son nodded to Adam, "Very well, from here on, my name to you is Yahweh." Alone, Yahweh had yet to give Adam a mate. The Son decided it was not good for him to be alone.

While Adam was keeping the garden, Yahweh caused him to fall into a deep sleep. While sleeping, he took one of his ribs. Out of his rib, the Son made a mate for Adam. When Adam woke from his slumber, Yahweh introduced him to his helpmeet. Riveted by her beauty, he said, "This is now bone of my bones and flesh of my flesh. She shall be called woman because she was taken out of man." Pleased with the match, Yahweh responded, "A man shall leave his father and mother and shall cleave unto his wife. They shall multiply and be one flesh." Both naked and innocent, Adam named his wife Eve because she was the mother of all living. Yahweh did not give life to Eve as he did to Adam. He did not directly give her his breath or make her from the dirt. Her life came out of man. Both shared the breath of God but in different ways. A binding like none other, Adam received his essence from the Son, and Eve possessed her essence through Adam. All of Adam and Eve's children gained their uniqueness through them.

Lucifer observed the work of the Son. It saw the river that ran out of Eden, a great river called Pishon that flowed through the garden, splitting four ways on the other side. Pristine minerals flowed through it; precious stones covered the riverbed. Observing man walk the garden, Lucifer saw the unbreakable bond between Adam and the Son. However, Lucifer also noted a weakness, the gift of free will. *If I were to deceive Adam, I could spread my influence*, it thought. It had to be Adam because he was the source of God's breath. Seeing their bond too strong, the angel considered the woman. Lucifer knew Adam loved Eve. Although she learned the covenant from him, Eve was not present when Adam and God made it. Her understanding was innocent, and her obedience was generated through the will of her husband. Lucifer targeted Eve. The angel desired to bring out the primal need within her.

CHAPTER 3

Deception Can Be Laced with Innocent Allusions

Lucifer studied Adam and Eve. It noted their specialty of thought, the fullness of their reason. Children were not like the angels. Their adaptability was advanced, and their emotional awareness was obvious. Yahweh and Adam interacted as brothers; of all men, only Adam could speak directly to the Son. The union miffed Lucifer because, while the angel hovered over the throne, neither God gave it a thought. Seeing them in deep discourse hurt the angel because it saw a cherished relationship it never had. The exchanging of ideas, the Son giving Adam a wide berth in topics of discussion. The Father never embraced the angel in such a way. Angels lacked the intellectual ability to evolve past their stations. Their natural rationality, their simple purpose was to do the bidding of the Father. Lucifer watched, amazed at the freedom of thought men possessed. The angel wanted to be worshiped. It didn't want a fellowship with men; Lucifer aspired to rule them. The cherub focused on the daily routines of Adam and his wife.

Their habitation was clean, fruit large and sweet. It was a self-enriching garden. Bird droppings filled the water with nutrients, and the richness of it sustained fish. An amazing ecosystem was set with self-sustaining building blocks; nothing harmed another. Men moved among animals and throughout the plant life. Everything in the garden fed off the tree of life. Next to it stood the tree of knowledge of good and evil. Adam asked, "Father, everything is so lovely to the eye. Why can't we eat of that tree?"

Yahweh smiled. "My son, it is a tree of good and evil. For in the day you should eat of it, you will surely die."

"Of course, we will do as you say, Master."

Yahweh replied, "Adam, you are my son. You may move freely as all is at your touch. However, this tree in the center of the garden you must not disturb." Adam did not comprehend the whole of it. Yahweh never gave an explanation; Adam didn't understand the reason for such a tree. The only thing certain was his covenant with the Son centered around that tree. Yahweh wanted Adam to believe; he desired Adam to follow faithfully.

Lucifer thought how considerate to allow man such circumspection. However, there were a couple of things that troubled the angel. It whispered, "An uneatable tree that serves no purpose for Adam or his children." The other thing that bothered Lucifer was why the Son allowed it in the garden.

Yahweh knew the presence of the angel; although hidden, the Son knew Lucifer was there. Suddenly, paranoia welled up inside the cherub. *Could the Son be mocking me?* It thought. While standing next to the poisonous tree, the angel saw Eve emerge from the greenery. It lay silently watching her. She looked at the tree of knowledge of good and evil. Lucifer noted her demeanor as she stared at it. He wondered if Eve too had questioned its purpose.

After a moment, she turned and walked away. Then a thought hit the angel, *Is this tree tied to me? Considering its allowance to remain, does this tree represent me?* Lucifer looked at the tree of life next to the poisonous tree. Two great trees side by side, one giving life and one taking life. One tree flowing with freshness and the other weak and dismal. Anger began to fill its thoughts, *Is he implying I am weak and ugly inside?* Openly, Lucifer scowled, "How dare he insult me." Anger filled Lucifer; once again, the angel wanted to take from the Son. The angel set its sights on Adam. The children of God would be a worthy conquest. The angel thought, *To corrupt them would solidify its grip on the fallen. After all, there were spectators above and below.* With a pleasing smile, "Yahweh will regret this mockery of a tree." The angel saw the woman consider the tree. To get to Adam, Lucifer needed to befriend the woman.

Lucifer knew Eve was pliable, a pure innocent soul left to lean on her husband. Her bond with Yahweh was more commonplace; she strolled with God only when Adam was with her. Still, she knew she was peculiar in her own way. The most beautiful of maidens, her responsibility focused on teaching and nurturing her children. A duty most fitting, Eve passed on the lessons of her husband, foremost the covenant of the Son. When Adam walked with God, Eve strolled with her children. Lucifer took note of her outings. The garden inspired Eve. Its harmony and form, colors, and proportion; she loved the originality of the different flowers, trees, and animals. The combinations of butterflies, watching the seedlings hanging in the air, floating and flowing in the cool breeze. The angel could tell the woman fell into sensory overload; the beauty of the garden gratified her. For a long time it observed, it saw her mind immersed in pleasure each day she walked—enticing beauty, a quality Lucifer understood well. The angel decided to beguile her with its beauty. Deciding to disguise itself, the angel took on the appearance of a serpent. A beast Eve had seen many times, the snake intrigued Lucifer. They dangled from branches, agile with deliberate movement, snakes had the unique ability to traverse above and below. The cherub thought the creature best to catch Eve's eye. *All other serpents will pale to my beauty*, it thought. *I will be one of a kind.*

Yahweh knew the character of Lucifer. Disruptive in spirit and bent on destruction, he knew the cherub roamed the garden. Neither part of creation nor a complying participant, the Father commanded the Son to leave the angel. Freedom meant the possibility that Lucifer would enact deception. Both Father and Son knew it planned to hide. Both watched Lucifer attach itself to the serpent. It strobed many colors through the creature; the animal flickered its rays through the leaves. Lucifer felt assured it would pique curiosity; the cherub counted on Eve to notice it. Hoping the absence of uniformity did not arouse suspicion, the angel revealed itself. Shimmering multiple colors, Lucifer intended to flutter those colors before her. Its goal was to fascinate Eve. It knew no other beasts could communicate, and the angel believed Eve felt lonely.

After a while, it saw her coming through the shadows of the foliage. As on any other day, she walked through the garden, singing as she touched her surroundings. "Hello."

Startled, she looked around, "Who are you?"

Lucifer wrangled around a branch midway down a tree, "I'm me." The snake tilted up, exposing its rear parts from the bark. Both stared at each other; indecision rolled over her face. Gazing at the serpent, her face lit like the sun, "Oh, so beautiful. I have never seen such a beautiful creature." Its skin fluttered in a flirtatious way.

Excited and shocked, Eve responded, "You can talk! Only my husband and my children can talk." Lifting her hand slightly toward the serpent, Eve said, "How can you talk to me?"

Lucifer swayed in a mild hypnotic swing. "It is because I am a special creation, as you and Adam."

Joy filled Eve. "I cannot wait to tell Adam about you!"

Quickly, the angel replied, "Adam already knows about me. After all, Yahweh gave him permission to name everything in the garden."

A state of confusion came over Eve. "Then why didn't my husband tell me about you?" She was saddened. "He knows how much I love the garden, and he kept a creature so wonderful from me."

Lucifer cunningly responded, "I have not existed long. Adam knew you wanted someone to walk with you in the garden. He asked Yahweh to make me for you."

Eve's unhappiness shifted to great delight. "You are for me?"

The serpent nodded. "I am, but Adam had not yet given me permission to talk to you." Slyly, he asked, "Could you promise not to tell him you know about me?" Then he gently hissed, "If I'm meant to be a gift, I don't want to be in trouble."

"Of course, I will not say anything." She danced and twirled in front of the snake. Lucifer had no doubt its beauty would overwhelm her.

Thus began a series of rendezvous. Although the angel had her interest, it soon became clear that her covenant with Yahweh was strong. Patiently, Lucifer worked her senses. It was a slow seduction as the serpent wore her down. In lay many barriers, Lucifer chiseled at her sense and sensibilities. Day after day, she visited this beast. The serpent stimulated her with curiosity. The cherub's knowledge pulling, its ravishing brilliance eye-piercing. Everything about Lucifer intrigued her.

One day, the serpent changed its tone. "Is this god you serve that good to you?" By now, the two of them had bonded through many outings.

Due to this, Eve did not catch the disdain hidden within Lucifer's tone. She retorted, "Yes, he is."

"Well then," it countered, "If he is so good, didn't Yahweh tell you all here is yours?"

With a smile, Eve looked at him, "He did."

Craftily, the angel set a snare. "Interesting. What about this tree?"

She pointed to everything in the garden. "Adam said that I may enjoy anything in the garden except one thing."

It asked, "What can't you have in this garden?"

With childlike innocence, she panned the garden. "Yahweh flows in everything here. The flow generates from a tree called the tree of life. It is his essence that is pure, and it is what makes this place so lovely." Eve looked at the strangely beautiful creature. Its beauty was matchless; its light seemed to extend in all directions. With a pause, Eve said, "You are the most breathtaking being I've seen." Entrancement caught her. "Our creator said we must not partake of what has been forbidden because on the day we do, we will die."

Lucifer pushed more. "But tell me, what is it that you can't have?" Eve pointed to the tree next to the tree of life.

An ancient-looking tree that seemed older than creation. "See that tree? It is called the tree of good and evil. Yahweh said if anyone eats of that tree, they shall surely die."

Shrewdly the angel said, "Certainly, you will not die." She turned to the serpent. Her face had an astonished look upon it. So naive, so trusting, Lucifer thought her longing inspires temptation. Consoling her, "Yahweh loves you. He will not destroy you." Susceptible to the

ANGEL'S INFLUENCE

words, Eve looked at her friend. She stared at the tree. The fruit called out to her. Every fruit in the garden she knew by smell, the taste except for this one tree.

Thought transformed into want, and the temptation burrowed into Eve's heart. It began with a thought, productive use of inner desires. Lucifer whispered a premise, "God knows that if you taste the sweetness, you will become like him. He withholds that knowledge from you because he does not want you to be his equal." Shocked at what she heard, in disbelief, she listened. "You will be a god." Eve put her fingers to her lips. She wondered after the fruit. The more the woman looked at the tree, the more the fruit aroused her senses. Lucifer whispered, "If you're a god, then you will not need Yahweh. He knows this." Unaware and gullible to the seduction, Eve allowed her thoughts to twist her consciousness. The words of the serpent kept drumming into her. "God is keeping it from you. He is a selfish god that doesn't want you to experience the pleasure that will make you complete." With the grace of a snake, Lucifer moved closer. "A good god would not refuse you anything, so taste it." Extending from the branch, the serpent coiled around her shoulder. "After all, why would Yahweh create such a delight if he didn't want you to have it?"

An odoriferous tree, the fragrance agreeable, the appearance strong and elegant. Golden pollen spored off the flowers, sprinkling glowing specks that circled her. The woman moved closer to the leguminous fruit. Brown dangling pods, pulp oozing down from the succulent fruit. The craving was insatiable, Eve wanted it. It did not matter if it was sweet or tangy; the extremely fine, grape-shaped fruit extended to her. Comforting branches reached out, begging Eve to take it. Her face changed. No longer was there unfettered obedience. Dissatisfaction covered her expression. "You're right," she said. Wanting filled her heart. "It should not be forbidden. Yahweh only walks with Adam. If eating this will make me equal, then I could walk with them." She looked at the sensual beast. Eve pulled a fruit off the tree. The allurement won; now she longed to know.

Lucifer taught her the same defiance that was in its heart. "You don't need god because you are capable of becoming something more," it said.

Holding the fruit in her hand, Eve rethought her loyalties. Staring off into the abyss of the fragrant air, the pure colors, her mind carefully calculated the magnificence around her. "If what you say is true, it is hard to believe my Lord has more to offer than what I see, smell, taste," she whispered. What she thought was the most stunning of creatures opened her to a greater magic. Her heart began to pulse. The excitement of learning more drove the blood in her veins. What more could there be compared to what her awareness verified? Her mental process relieved her of the obligation; far removed from her mind was the consequential warning Yahweh had given. *Crunch!* The taste was invigorating; no other fruit in the garden had such a flavor. Almost immediately, a rush coursed through her veins. Eve's eyes widened. Her stomach turned. The fruity sweetness turned bitter; she dropped to her knees. Her body felt an uncontrollable surge; the innocence within Eve drained away. An ominous spirit filled her; the comprehension of good and evil took hold. The stimulus was too much for her biological makeup; Eve passed out under the tree.

Coiled on a branch, Lucifer kept its attention on the woman. Curled under the tree for a length of time, Eve showed no sign of life. The angel wondered if the fruit had killed her. The stillness in Eden seemed as dead as the woman. Gradually, the snake saw Eve's eyes open. Her breath deepened. Slowly regaining consciousness, she rolled on her back. Looking up, she could see the serpent hovering over her. The snake stretched itself down the limb. "How do you feel?" he asked, peeking from under her arm.

"I don't know."

Lucifer could tell she was different. Her exuberance gone, Eve took on a more serious aura. Sitting up, she saw Eden in a new light. The garden's amazement faded from her eyes. "Nothing is new to me." She looked at the snake, who by now dangled at eye level. "I know about heaven and everything before this garden." She looked at the serpent. "I know who you are. Your name is Lucifer."

With a grinning hiss, "The pleasure is all mine, Eve." The snake wrapped around her and helped her to her feet. "What will you do now?" the angel asked.

Eve pulled down another fruit from the tree. Staring at it, she said, "This knowledge is incredible. By taking of this fruit, I have chosen you over Yahweh." She knew it was too late. "I am no longer tied to my husband's spirit. Now I am tied to you because I chose you."

Lucifer said, "Your change is not a bad thing. You have become free. Doesn't it feel good to be free?" It slithered up into the tree, hiding itself from Eve. "Then go and make Adam like you. Then both of you will be one again." She looked up to the weathered tree. The woman could not see the serpent anymore.

She ran through the garden looking for her husband. Eve knew this time of the day Adam pruned trees along the riverbank. Seeing him from afar, she ran to him shouting, "Adam! Adam!"

Adam saw her excitement. "What have you been up to, my wife?" Adam immediately knew what she held in her hand. "Why do you have that?" he asked.

Impatiently, Eve said, "Adam, it isn't true."

"What isn't true?"

She held up the fruit. "Yahweh told us if we ate this, we would die. I ate it, and I didn't die." Adam sat down on a rock near the river. He knew a blood promise had been made concerning this tree and its fruit. He also knew Yahweh would take his wife away for breaking the covenant. Adam didn't want to lose her. He loved Eve, but there was a change. Her eyes were deeper, more intense; the sensual look pulled at him. He looked at the fruit. The skin looked fleshy, ripe, and ready to eat. The moment overshadowed reason as his wife caressed his face. "Eat, and you will be like me."

His eyes reeled with the seductiveness of his wife. She had gained experience; her submissiveness seemed lessened. Her luscious long hair covered her curves. Her soft skin, her touch, and her kiss aroused him. She understood her body, and how Yahweh made it to please the erotic urges and natural passions. As the serpent did to her, she beguiled her husband. Her newfound knowledge intoxicated Adam with the white heat of her caress. Luring eyes siren him, Eve coaxed her husband, "Eat, my husband." Adam looked at Eve. Her words moved him, her touch swayed him. Taking hold of the fruit,

Eve softly stroked his cheek. "Go ahead. Don't be afraid. I have eaten it, and as you can see, I did not die." The change in his wife stunned him. Fixated on his wife, Adam bit the fruit. It was pleasing, sweet to the smell, and more so to the taste. As with Eve, Adam's heart began to race. The blood heated as all within his vision blurred. Adam could feel strings rip within his soul. An internal breakdown, as the man's mind gained a new focus. Lucifer watched from a distance. It knew once Adam ate the fruit, the bond was severed. The tie switched from Yahweh to the angel. The breach complete, it traveled through all the children. Corruption filled the man and woman; for the first time, they knew they were naked.

Suddenly, Adam heard the footsteps of Yahweh walking through the garden. His gait had never startled him before. Shame filled his bones. He grabbed Eve's hand and pulled her into the tree line. God saw that they had gained unknown knowledge. "How did you know you were naked?"

Adam fell on his face, "Master, the woman you gave me brought it to me and beguiled me." Eve began shaking.

Yahweh asked, "Gave you what?" The Son knew what had happened but he wanted Adam to confess.

Adam replied, "She gave me one of the fruits of the forbidden tree, and I did eat it."

"What have you done!" Yahweh turned to the woman.

Trembling, she said, "My Lord, this animal reminded me that all was given to us in the garden. He assured me that this fruit would make me more like you."

God looked at them. "He that commits sin is of the one who sinned from the beginning." Yahweh looked down upon them. "Because you did this, a curse meant for Lucifer has been placed on you." The gift of choice had always been a double-edged sword. That freedom of will made man special, exclusively unique. With a sad tone, the Son said to the man, "Adam, you were created in my image. Now you have the knowledge of good and evil. Because you allowed your wife to lure you, the earth will constantly fight you." The curse took away the blessings of the garden. Adam had yet to understand the fullness of his decision. "From this day forth, you will toil and contend with the land. The thorns and brambles will resist you." The Lord turned to the woman. "Because of your sin, Eve, you will be forever subservient to your husband. I will multiply the pains of this curse into childbirth. It will be a reminder of your choice." Finally, the Son focused on the serpent. "Rebellious cherub, how dare you pollute creation! On your belly, you shall crawl forever!"

The Son altered the appearance of the snake. Once having the ability to crawl, the small appendages dissolved away. Yahweh made the serpent slither in the dirt. A punishment for the beast because Lucifer used it to tempt the woman. Now the lowest of creation, the serpent became identified with the angel. Lucifer laughed at what Yahweh did. It didn't care if the change made the creature suffer. Seeing the slight as a meaningless jab. the angel thought, *He thinks I'm the lowest*. An insignificant gesture that did nothing to affect the cherub, the response made Lucifer feel untouchable. Gleefully, it looked at the fallen angels and the ones in heaven. The angel felt victorious because the chains of its curse had been lifted. Lucifer regained the right to heaven. Although Lucifer regained access, the rest of the fallen did not. Never again could it raise an army in heaven. The thought of approaching the Father excited the cherub. Seeing a bitter reaction from the Son filled the angel with rapturous satisfaction. *Let's see how the angels react when I cross heaven's border*. The victory changed the angel, and it began to form a persona similar to men. No longer singularly driven, Lucifer expanded his reasoning. He had this world and decided to keep it. The fallen noticed the difference; all saw Lucifer evolve from an angel to an adversary.

Yahweh knew the appearance of Lucifer would bring further discourse among the angels. He grieved to see what one angel had perpetrated. Yahweh desired to act but he stayed himself. It was a terrible test of patience, as the Son knew the angels watched with speculative conjecture. He had to withhold understanding; an explanation had to be withheld from the heavenly host. The stakes were high with the future in question, and the angels had to develop faith in the Son. All in heaven watched the children of the garden turn into men of disobedience.

With the corruption of men, there was no more need for the garden. Yahweh declared, "Eden will be no more." He killed animals and clothed Adam and Eve; it was the first shedding of blood. He barred them from the garden and set two strong angels at the entrance. Adam, his wife, and their children were shut out. The Son shut up the Pishon River and dissolved the garden. Barren land slowly replaced the perfection that was once Eden.

CHAPTER 4

Snakes Symbols and Satan

Lucifer had an empire. His subjects bore the mark that used to be on him. The change made men hostile; they became creatures of flesh. Creation too felt the burden of the mark. The environment became unfriendly and unpredictable. Earth resisted men, and the fullness of plenty wasted away as the consequences of the curse took hold. First, the cherub won an army and then acquired subjects, but the best win was regaining access to heaven. Stoked with excitement, he called out, "Look, Father! See! I am worthy!" Pointing to the earth, he said, "The image of your Son is now mine." The victory scored life on earth in a new way. It brought on natural disobedience, and darkness rose within the human soul. Their shame reflected enmity; their spirit turned contentious. Men learned to exalt and exonerate. They explained away sin, and disorderly passions became the gauge of value. Mankind wanted to be philanthropic, philosophical, and progressive. Acquiring wealth, having intellect, and seizing power became most important; the world delved into the concept of self-worship.

Although Lucifer plunged men into darkness, he failed to eradicate the memory of Yahweh. Adam and his wife still sought God. Yahweh kept speaking to Adam. Despite sin, Adam and Eve did their best to keep the ways of the Son. The memories in the garden bedded deep in Adam. He could never forget the intimacy he once felt. Out of the garden and on their own, they had three more sons. Adam taught them the ways of Yahweh. Like Adam, God conversed with the sons of Adam. Eve named her first child Cain. Excited, she declared, "I have gotten a man from the Lord." The name meant "I bought" or "have the essence of the Lord in my hand." The birth gave Eve a renewed closeness to Yahweh. The second son she named Abel. The name reflected her understanding of the curse's effect on her. Abel meant "breath" or "vanity," an acknowledgment that she brought vanity to men.

Their continual relationship with Yahweh disturbed Lucifer. The angel figured opening the wisdom of the evil tree would set in their souls. Instead, Adam and Eve more so craved Yahweh. The fall had the opposite effect. They realized how much they needed their God. Yet another thing troubled Lucifer, the words the Son had said. He remembered what he told the woman: "I will put enmity between you and the woman and between your seed and her seed. It shall bruise your head, and you shall bruise his heel." *What did that mean?* he thought. The cryptic words confused Lucifer. Was Eve going to hate him? He thought. And was this hatred going to be passed on? The meaning of the words eluded him.

Considering the children of men, he saw their power weak, their strength useless. It was impossible for men to challenge him. Yet Lucifer enjoyed watching men. He watched Cain kill his brother. The reason Cain murdered Abel was jealousy because Cain felt Yahweh favored him. It was a self-inflicted rejection; Cain did not offer God his best. He intentionally set aside the finest fruit for himself. Lucifer applauded the half-hearted devotion.

Abel's death broke Eve. She had lost one son at the hand of the other. The murder rocked the world. It brought on another change, men killing for greed, jealousy, and revenge. The progress of humanity pleased Lucifer. Of Adam's sons, one followed the world and the other was dead. Adam and Eve bore one more son. The last son she named Seth. The name Seth meant "appointed one," her replacement for Abel. A good son who followed the ways of Yahweh. Seth became a thorn in Lucifer's side. The seemingly hapless curse that affected Cain had little influence on him. The angel was certain all could be corrupted, but choice within men proved an uncertainty.

From observing Seth, Lucifer began to realize that here lay a lineage that challenged his authority. He started to wonder about the words "seed through Eve." He considered the possibility that someone from her would resist him. By now, Eve hated Lucifer. She gave him a new name: Satan. Lucifer became the adversary of her family and her God. She blamed the serpent for her circumstance. She believed what occurred between her two sons was her fault. That guilt stemmed from her interaction with the serpent. So she protected Seth. Adam taught him the ways of Yahweh, and Eve warned him about Lucifer. The words spoken by Yahweh became true. The woman became his enemy, and he hated her. Eve implanted a glimmer of resistance. This opposition made Satan uneasy.

Thus began the law of unintended consequences. The fallout brought a new battle. The key to victory: this curse. *Did Yahweh give men the power to break it?* he thought. The word *bruised* had the angel perplexed. Satan reconsidered the consciousness of men. For the most part, he had thought them simplistic. The leverage his, but if the curse was to be lifted, would he lose control? This unknown worried Lucifer; it increased his contempt. He did not like the potential men possessed. Uneasy and paranoid, Lucifer concerted his efforts. *I'll place wicked men in positions of authority*, he thought. The strength of kings and princes will become his agent of change. Through them, he will compel vengeance against Yahweh. *The Son will rue the day he mocked me*, Lucifer thought. *If you want me to slither on my belly, oh Bright and Morning Star, then I will use the snake as a symbol to alienate you.* Satan decided to elevate the serpent over Yahweh.

Lowered to the dirt, cursed to the gutter, snakes became Lucifer's instrument. He thought if Yahweh made serpents a symbol, he would lure men to worship them. Innocent creatures, non-partakers of defiance, the snake became the likeness of trickery. In the dust, they wormed, a constant emblem of enmity and subversion. The serpent's plight became Lucifer's ambition. He remembered what Yahweh declared to the serpent, "Because you had been the instrument of temptation, cursed are you of all cattle and out of every beast of the field." Snakes, a perfect mnemonic of the degradation of Satan. Serpents, an optic of future divine judgment. God labeled them as unclean. "Whatever crawls on its belly, you shall not eat, for they are detestable." Snakes became most vile, most detested, scorned, and most feared. Every slither, each movement embodied Lucifer's persona. Serpentine motion, sinister appearance, animated tongue, the snake proudly intimidating with each head tilt. Lucifer pushed the world to seek the serpent. Through the image of the serpent, Satan became the god of ages.

The serpent became the centerpiece of the gods. Filtered within deities, the symbol of the snake. Whether as part of a god or its apparel, the snake came to represent cunning, craftiness, or wisdom. If Lucifer did not make his symbol part of a god, he depicted it in backgrounds. The serpent came to symbolize influential seductiveness. Within every idol lay the snake, and behind every god, Lucifer. Knowing men related to the physical, gods became associated with beliefs, politics, gender, and sex. Gods answered to destruction, war, violence, anything that affected life. Lucifer made the snake a fascinating tool, and it was his mysterious signature. Satan wanted to make his nature as captivating as the snake. The snake became more than a symbol; it became a godlike caricature. To deify the snake was to worship Lucifer.

Men began to hold snakes during a ritual dance. Others created rhythmic ceremonies involving serpents inside the mouths of parishioners. Lucifer pushed men to adore the creature; he humanized the serpent in every deity. The White Snake god gave birth to a son who freed his imprisoned mother. The Cosmic Serpent, god of the heavens, opposed light. Believed as beautiful as the rainbow, men created charms and trinkets to capture power from the snake deity. Wearing baubles and potent gems coated in venom, followers hoped for answered prayers and spiritual energy from the sky serpent. Then there was Lucifer's primordial snake god that judged the deceased in the afterlife. Known by men as the "lord of the good tree," it appeared as a double-headed serpent coiled in a double helix. Fearfully slinking in the shadows, many believed the god killed vegetation each time it crossed into the underworld. Fear in men made it easy for Lucifer to insert serpent-gods. Guardian snake statues lined

ANGEL'S INFLUENCE

thresholds. The stone carvings promised protection to the household and fertility to the residents.

The attraction of the snake was not enough; Lucifer wanted men to humanize gods. He knew gods with human traits drew them because it gave men the dream of achieving godhood. Lucifer's specialty is the art of intertwining reality with delusion. Human pride made it easy to attach personalities to gods. Through gods, men began to desire supernatural qualities. Kings became gods to their people. Successors were obsessed with immortalizing themselves higher than previous monarchs. A great deluge of human-like gods infiltrated the imagination. Men of power assigned a god for every aspect of life. Lucifer reveled in the confusion—the more delusion, the easier the hypocrisy.

However, Satan could not get past labels. The angel remembered the comparison of the trees, Yahweh the tree of life, and Lucifer the evil tree. *How arrogant*, he thought. The opposite of life, death; contrary to evil, good. *If following me means death, to worship me evil, then I will change that*, he thought. He decided to muddy the concept and intertwine the meanings of right and wrong. Lucifer knew the culture of men regulated values. To move minds, the boundaries had to be blurred. Satan influenced men to rethink the tale that set morality. It was an old story that told of a serpent enveloped in darkness and an angel that possessed it. Lucifer twisted the fable to imply the angel freed the snake, and through the light, it discovered hidden potential. The slant of the story renewed the interpretation. Men began to see Lucifer as a cosmic being able to pull scales off ignorant minds. His knowledge urged men to rework morality. Haughty actions once deemed evil now received a new assessment. Men redefined good; they turned to the promises of special powers to those who followed. Men praised the serpent and began to believe the banishment of the angel was a tragic injustice. He rewrote concepts; Lucifer brainwashed men to see insight as a pathway to godhood.

This contortion of knowledge romanced divination. Crafty men reached for the stars. Some sacrificed offspring to curry favor, shedding blood through hysteria. Some humans saw evil in everything; others accused demonic possession, many times targeting the innocent. The worldly questioned or denied the existence of any deity. Others accepted the premise but could not identify the unforeseen power. This lack of clarity convoluted divine existence. While unending discussions plagued men, Lucifer edified his divinity. Good or bad, he wanted to be known in many ways and by many names. Throughout the world, men called him Shaitan, Iblis, Duivel, Satana, Satanei, or Satnav. In English, he became known as the Evil One, Archfiend, Father of Lies, Wicked One, Black Prince, or Prince of Darkness. Some called him Diabolus, the main spirit of evil. He took on the name Beelzebub, which meant lord of the flies. Baal, the Canaanite god of fertility, depicted the fallen angel. Abaddon and Apollyon, the angel that destroys and rules the abyss. Then there was the god Quetzalcoatl, or "feathered serpent," believed to have a key role in creation. Like Lucifer, Quetzalcoatl could shift-shape from snake to human. In another part of the world, Naga appeared as a half-human, half-cobra. Of all the titles given to Lucifer, the surnames Satan and Old Serpent were there from the beginning, passed down through anecdotal accounts.

Satan manifested himself in legends and folklore. He infiltrated traditional beliefs, myths, and oral practices. The angel presented himself as half-human, half-nature manifestations. He created varieties of horned god deities and versions of fertility goddesses. Lucifer understood the love of nature, so he portrayed himself as a protector of the environment. Injecting himself within urban legends, he made himself fodder for some fantastic tales through collective mediums. Curiosity piqued men. Creative people depicted the angel in unguarded and disoriented ways. Harmless superficial illustrations molded Satan as a farce or curiosity. Men made jest of Lucifer and the serpent in comedic productions. A devil with horns and a red pointed tail playfully frolicking. Plays with a satyr acting as the agitator, he wanted men to view him as pathetic, innocuous, and repulsive. As long as men saw the angel this way, he would seem insignificant. Satan wanted men to think they were superior, shrewder, and more intelligent than the mythical serpent.

But it was this delusion that kept Satan dominant. The angel tricked men through craftiness and stealth. Political and sociologi-

ANGEL'S INFLUENCE

cal conspiratorial theories conditioned minds to question reality and fiction. Secret societies cited love for God but shared in cultist values. Charitable groups that longed and worked towards a new order. His innovation invaded learning, doctrines, economics, and science. Simultaneously, the angel used polluted minds to debase and degrade social lifestyles. Lucifer became an afterthought; the general public no longer viewed the devil as a serious threat. Others applauded the ways of Satan. Believing to be enlightened, they scoffed at restraint and made secret traditions commonplace whims.

Through allusion, Lucifer dulled down his influence. The effort created a perception that he was lower than humans. Men used terminology relating to Satan flippantly. With slang terms like *fallen angel, demon,* and *jinni* and frivolous sayings such as *hell-bent, hell on wheels, blue devil,* and *hellion,* the vocabulary became acceptable. To turn phrases made Lucifer seem like a fairy tale. Hearing is believing; the loudest voice infiltrates. The innocuous exercise in cultural norms diluted the reality of the senses. It became easier to believe that life was more an exercise in luck, chance, or fate. The potential of a real adversary became unbelievable.

Humans sought answers to destiny. Many looked to the stars, others to psychics and fortune tellers. Some ran with readings, believing tormenting spirits to be lost loved ones. Lucifer was more than willing to accommodate irrationality. Satan's angels played ghosts, spirits, and apparitions to inspire belief in paranormal activity. Insight into the future overrode belief in God. Events in life became shrugged off as fate, luck, or chance. These ideas became idols, alternatives to faith. Lucifer made it easy to accept designed sequences to explain away an unseen God. Fate, chance, luck—a cultist system that curried randomness over godly abilities. Men had greater assurance in gambling and the lottery, guesswork, and coveting destiny. Outcomes became the result of how luck favored fate. Some replaced blessed with a lucky dog. Others exchanged faith with "wish me luck." Plain luck had become as valuable as having lady luck, and tough, rotten, or bad luck marked the unfortunate. Good luck and blind luck replace hope. Men sought their future in horoscopes; the zodiac dictated human behavior. Men altered themselves to fit zodiac character traits. Many made a living through chance. Palm readers, tarot cards, Ouija boards—men searched for answers through sorcery. Men wanted to believe in fleshly impulses; they desired to catch their future and control their destiny. Then there was a segment of humans who believed in satanism and devil worship.

Different sects of devil worship sprang up throughout humanity. Some believed Lucifer to be the symbol of the cosmos. The motivating force, Satan reflected the prideful, carnal soul of men. Men desired lascivious living. Satan worshippers wanted to investigate what it meant to live lasciviously. Men desired to make contact with their holy guardians. Worshippers of Lucifer wanted to tap into the secrets of Satan and use that power. An esoteric spiritual philosophy with mystic ceremonial magic all centered around Lucifer. The predominant edict to "do what thou wilt," many craved individual empowerment; others dreamed of god status—opposing ideologies that detested religious systems because they hampered free expression. Satan loved human instinct. He reveled in men tapping into their animal urges. Appealing to the sciences and inexhaustible aptitude, haughtiness hardened the thought that those who cleaved to religion were archaic and ignorant.

To Lucifer, men were nothing more than mongrels. Exploiting weaknesses, Lucifer made men love creation more than they cared for the creator. Extorting pride and motivational superiority, the complexity turned men into slaves. His actions motivated his fallen cohorts, as they, too, wanted to rule. The fallen angels knew they could not sway men to the degree of Lucifer, so they concocted a plan of their own. The angels that fell with Lucifer decided to imprint themselves within the genetic makeup of men.

CHAPTER 5

The Plot to Remake Creation

The daughters of men, being very beautiful, attracted the angels. They wanted them. The most rebellious of the fallen desired to create a new race. As the angels discussed, Samyaza said, "I fear that you may perhaps be indisposed to the performance of this enterprise. If we do this, I alone shall suffer for so grievous a crime." Knowing the consequences, they set a pact: "For once we do this, we will corrupt the blood of men."

The angels responded with a unifying voice, "We all will swear and bind ourselves to our intentions. We will not restrain from our undertaking to alter the seed of man."

Unable to discourage them, Samyaza proclaimed, "I will speak to Lucifer." The angels agreed to wait for the words of Lucifer. Descending upon Ardis on Mount Armon, they gathered as they waited for an answer.

As Samyaza appeared in the presence of Lucifer, he could tell something preoccupied him. "Great Lucifer, I've come to you with some news."

The interference shook Lucifer out of his dilemma. "What do you need, Samyaza?"

"I have something to report. As you have commanded, the angels have been watching the lineage of Seth. The Watchers of Yahweh have been revealing to one named Enoch the things of heaven."

Still haunted over that one thing Yahweh said to Eve, "What had Yahweh been telling Enoch?" Lucifer listened as Samyaza reported the activities of the angels. How they taught him the knowledge of reading and writing. Raphael instructed Enoch to describe to men the signs in heaven, signs meant to guide the seasons and track time. Twelve groups of stars, one for each month, constellations men used to count days. Satan's chief angel continued, "Enoch gave names to the illuminating lights in the sky. The angels revealed to him the meanings within these groupings, stories of future events." Samyaza had his full attention. "These groups of stars are telling a story of a child that will come." Fear rushed through Lucifer. Did this have to do with the bruising? He demanded to know everything that Enoch wrote and what he named the stars.

Lucifer listened intently as his subordinate angel explained what he heard. Samyaza told of a group of stars Enoch named Virgo. "I heard the angel Raphael tell him that this group of stars represent a young woman." Lucifer looked to the stars as he listened. "Aligning the stars together revealed a silhouette of a young girl. The girl is pure because no man had touched her." Samyaza described the significance of the one bright star. "The young girl held a stalk of wheat in her hand and in the middle of the wheat glowed a bright star." Raphael explained to Enoch the shining star was a child she would have. Fear turned to panic; the mystery of the bruise became clear. "They called the star Spica, which means the virgin's ear of grain," he said.

Lucifer snapped forward and asked, "The star tells of a seed from men?"

Samyaza nodded. "The star is an infant prince that the virgin would bring into the world." He added, "Another shape lay within Virgo, a frame of a shepherd named Bootes or Herdsman. The angel explained to Enoch that within Virgo lay a herder of flocks. He said a righteous shepherd."

A righteous shepherd inside a virgin? he thought.

Samyaza pointed out other constellations named by Enoch. The Centaur, a set of stars in the shape of a half horse, half man. A creature half immortal and half god, Enoch named the stars Chiron. Samyaza listed other clusters, Libra, which meant balance, Crux, a cross, Lupus, the Wolf, and a ring of stars called the Northern Crown.

Situated above the crown, a serpent reaching for it. Lucifer stopped him. "What did Enoch call the name of the serpent?"

"Raphael said it was the Serpent Bearer." Lucifer didn't know what to think. *Is Yahweh saying this serpent is me?* He did not comprehend all the groupings, but the one called Virgo with her child prince concerned him. He mumbled, "Yahweh is going to create a child of men that will harm me."

The random statement confused Samyaza, "Lord Lucifer?"

Lucifer recovered from his rambling. "Never mind. Was there anything else you heard?"

"Yes, lord. I heard Enoch praise him who made the great and splendid stars and signs. He thanked the angel for revealing the magnificence of the operations." The last thing Samyaza added was this: "Enoch thanked the angel for revealing the plan of God for the souls of men." Lucifer sat silent before his subordinate. His thoughts were rampant with the meanings of the constellations. Samyaza broke the silence, "My lord, I have a request."

The words broke the fury smoldering in Lucifer. He snapped. "What do you need?"

"Myself and the others desire to take some of the women of men." Satan processed the request. He began to consider the stars, and one popped out among the rest—the figure of the immortal half-man, half-beast. The mixing with men held promise. An intriguing consideration, the remaking of men. *Someone from men could appear,* he thought. However, if men became a new creation, then no child would come.

Lucifer smiled. "Indeed, take women for yourselves. Come to them disguised as men and bear half-human, immortal beings. They will be a better creation. They will share in the superior power of the angels."

Gliding slowly toward Samyaza, Lucifer quipped, "Powerful like us but not like us, these men will be higher than men and lower than us." Lucifer postured a proud stance. "The new race will be called Nephilim because they will be giants among men." The information Samyaza provided uplifted Lucifer.

Lucifer wanted to reward his chief angel for his diligent work. "And when the offspring of angels cover the land, we will destroy the image of Yahweh."

Samyaza bowed in gratitude. Lucifer enjoyed the plan. Before the chief angel left his presence, he called, "Samyaza!"

Turning back startled, he asked, "My lord?"

"Make sure you and the others teach them the mysteries."

"Of course, my lord." Straightaway, the cherub departed.

Lucifer considered the angels and Enoch. *If Yahweh is using his angels to teach men, then so shall I,* he thought. *It's possible the star child might come out of the children of Seth. Of all family lines, the genealogy of Seth has proven most resistant.* The request of the angels gave Satan a solution. The star child must never be born. By this act, all the bloodlines of Adam will be severed.

In a vile, insidious campaign, Samyaza gathered his captains and angels—over two hundred of the most wicked. They dispersed over the land and claimed themselves wives. Through the bodies of men, they consummated. Finding the pleasures of the body exhilarating, women became toys to them. Out of their enjoyment, the union created a twisted genetic anomaly. As the angels cohabited with the daughters of men, they taught them sorcery. Amazarak taught dividing root cuttings and the magical art of enchantment. The angel Armaros taught banishing enchantments to empower weapons— charmed amulets infused with magic to lure the attraction of men, trinkets made of figurines designed to curse or cure, and incantations to trigger effects on objects or the living. Women learned to open closed-off segments of the mind. The angels imparted principles, pulled out hidden messages, and expanded consciousness. Through potions, women acquired heightened mental awareness. The unseen became reality to them. The mothers of giants became feared. Schooled in magical and occult wisdom, they inherited psychic and magical abilities. These women became spiritually and metaphorically known as the *witch blood*. Their emergence of powers unnerved men. Many believed these witches possessed elven or fairy blood.

As their children grew, the angels elevated their minds to fit their strength. The angel Baraqijal taught astrology, and Kokabiel the understanding of constellations. Barkayal opened knowledge of the stars, while Akibeel gave insight into the teaching of signs. The weather lore of the clouds and sky came from Chazaqiel. Shamsiel opened the mysteries of sun signs. Tamiel taught the tenets of astronomy, and Asaradel clarified the motion of the moon's tides. Sariel shared lunar cycles for agriculture, while Penemuel revealed the skill of reading and writing. Kashdejan imparted knowledge of disease and healing using medicinal herb concoctions. Azazel demonstrated the skill of weaponry. Angels instructed their children, and men learned as well. Artisan craftsmen perfected the workmanship of bracelets, ornaments, and the art of taking stones to create beautiful jewelry. Men learned how to make paint from the resources around them: fine paint to enhance the beauty of women, painting of eyebrows, and dyes for clothes. The world evolved at an unbelievable pace.

The first angelic generation brought on larger-framed men. Big men that spawned a second generation they called Nephilim. By the third generation, Nephilim mated with Nephilim. The dominant gene combination became known as the Elioud, the demigods. They overwhelmed men in skill, knowledge, and stature. At twelve to eighteen feet tall, their hunger was insatiable. They dominated through terror, war, and bloodshed. Evil and violent, the Elioud demanded men feed them. Devouring everything, leaving nothing for humans, men began to detest them. In response to the rebellion, the Elioud began to eat men along with birds, beasts, reptiles, and fishes. Their presence upended the ecological balance. The world of man decayed at a frantic pace. All was in peril as wickedness prevailed. Respect for the natural order diminished as the world became more and more violent. Fornication increased as men fought to outpopulate the Elioud. Procreation became imperative as men required numbers to fight.

Methuselah, the son of Enoch, knew his father conversed with angels. Life became so dreadful he sought his wisdom. "Father, the Nephilim are killing men. I am afraid."

Enoch could see the fear in his son's eyes. "Be of courage, my son. The God of the angels has been watching, and he is not pleased." Enoch poured a cup and handed it to Methuselah. "Here, refresh yourself." He sat next to his father. As he took in the drink, a comforting spirit filled the room. Peace had always been present here. No matter how dire, Enoch always seemed at rest. The visit of his son, forewarned by the angels, Enoch answered, "Hear me, my son. The Lord will effect a new thing upon the earth. The angels have committed grievous crimes against Yahweh." Sincerity connected their eye contact. "My son, the angels have told me about the future of our world. Be of good cheer because the great God Yahweh will give your son Lamech a son. Through this child, God will cleanse the land of the Nephilim." *A child*, he thought.

"Father…" before Methuselah could finish, Enoch stopped him.

"Listen, son, Lamech will name his son Noah. Through him, peace and rest will come." Enoch continued. "The sign will be unnatural. The child will praise Yahweh from the womb." Methuselah listened. Enoch shared how the Lord would put to sleep the innocent and that this message to him was from God. "When the time comes, go to Lamech and tell him the child is his. He will be afraid because of the unnatural aura. Tell your son the Lord has anointed the child to do a great thing." Methuselah kissed his father and left.

Never forgetting the words of his father, Methuselah realized Enoch would never see his great-grandson. He knew God would put him to sleep, and the angels would whisk Enoch away. While Lamech was young, he raised his son in the ways of Yahweh. Both father and son separated themselves from wickedness. One day, Methuselah discovered his father gone. As foretold, the angels took Enoch because he pleased God.

From a safe place on Earth, Enoch watched. He saw the angels hedge Methuselah and Lamech from evil. Through the eyes of the angels, he witnessed the birth of his great-grandson, Noah. Born white as snow, a bright light filled the household when the child opened his eyes. The unusual appearance startled Lamech. Afraid, he went to his father and said, "I have begotten a son, a changed son. He is not human. He resembles the offspring of the angels." Lamech thought the child was a Nephilim. Panicked, he cried, "The child praised Yahweh once out of the womb."

Methuselah knew his son was distraught. "Your grandfather Enoch told me long ago that you would have a son. Before the birth of the child, he declared to me Yahweh chose him for a special purpose." Sharing the wisdom of his grandfather, Methuselah could see relief in his son's eyes. "God wants you to name him Noah. Through him will Yahweh cleanse our world of the Nephilim." Hearing this, Lamech surmised that the brilliant countenance of his son was an anointing. He believed the words of his father and, as instructed, named the child Noah.

As the child grew, the sacrileges against God mounted. The angels conspired to push humanity into an irreversible state. Pleased with the Nephilim, Lucifer saw no salvation for men. Men cried out and wailed as their destruction seemed imminent. Yahweh and his Father heard their cries.

Mankind had been altered, and their sins brought desperation. Yahweh summoned five archangels: Michael, Gabriel, Raphael, Suriel, and Uriel. The Lord told his servants, "I have sent Arsayalalyur to Noah, the great-grandson of Enoch. Uriel, I charge you with protecting Noah as he builds a vessel. Guide him in wisdom, for it will take him 120 years to complete the task." The Lord turned to Suriel. "Keep watch over Noah. Protect him from the contamination that has plagued the earth." The two archangels looked down upon Earth.

Men did eat and drink; they married but lived in constant fear. From heaven, the angels saw great quantities of bloodshed at the hands of the Elioud. Yahweh linked the screams into the minds of his archangels. A voice in heaven proclaimed, "The earth, deprived of her children, their cries have reached heaven. O ye holy ones of heaven, the souls of men complain. They plead for judgment from the Most High."

The five angels bowed and praised their master. "Thou art Lord of Lords, God of gods, King of kings."

The seraphim chanted, "The throne of thy glory is forever and ever. Thou art blessed and glorified."

All acknowledged, "Thou hast made all things. Thou possesses power over all things. All is opened and manifested before thee. Thou beholds all things, and nothing can be concealed from thee." Yahweh released Uriel and Suriel. The two angels departed.

Not even the thoughts of Lucifer remained obscured. Yahweh knew the plan. With patience, he allowed the infestation. During this perilous time, Noah, the eighth after Seth, grew into a righteous preacher. As Noah matured, the angel Arsayalalyur came to warn him, "I am an angel from the Great Holy One. The Mighty One of your fathers has commanded me to conceal you from the abominations plaguing the land." Suriel and Uriel stood hidden, watching.

Unnerved, Noah sought the words of his father. Entering the house, he said, "Father, an angel came to me."

Lamech listened to what the angel had said, "An ark, you say." Neither man understood the meaning of a ship. At this time, the firmament over the earth remained intact. No one understood the concept of rain; the barrier never let water fall from the skies. Looking at his concerned son, he said, "We must speak to your grandfather." The men walked a short distance to visit Methuselah. As they walked, Lamech told Noah of the circumstances of his birth. Methuselah retold the words of Enoch. How God had chosen him to build a vessel to house animals.

He said, "No one has seen an ark, Noah, but the angels will show you the way." Grateful, Noah kissed his grandfather, "Thank you for telling me everything, Grandfather." Noah took his leave from the men.

After he walked a distance, the angel Uriel appeared, "Greetings, Most Holy. Lord Yahweh has sent me."

While Uriel spoke, Suriel came out of the shadows. "We have been charged with protecting you and your family." Seeing the angels reaffirmed Noah. Both archangels knew the importance of their task. Uriel declared. "I will stay with you and guide you in wisdom."

Suriel exclaimed, "I will protect you from the abounding corruption, and any that should threaten you."

Like his great-grandfather Enoch, the angels conversed with Noah. "God has heard the cries of men. Because of the evil that had been done, the Holy One is going to consume them. All the earth shall perish." Uriel continued, "A great deluge of water will cover the whole, and the world will be destroyed." The two angels hid Noah and his family from the giants. From this point forward, Uriel and Suriel stayed by their side. Uriel gave Noah counsel on matters of the building and concerning the humans that crossed his path. Suriel kept watch, keeping away any giants that ventured too close. They fought away all spiritual or physical threats. Noah assembled the gopher wood according to the prescribed dimensions. He and his sons began to build the ark.

Three archangels still knelt before their Master. Yahweh charged his angel. "Raphael, I want you to bind Azazel hand and foot. The earth has been corrupted because of his teachings. Open the desert in Dudael and hurl him deep under it. Throw upon him pointed stones until he is covered with darkness that he might not see the light." There was a long decisive pause. "There he shall remain." Yahweh saw what Samyaza, the one known to men as Azazel, had done. He revealed the dark mysteries and disclosed secret things that should have stayed in heaven. He led the most wicked to upend creation. His crimes, spilled blood, cries from the grave, resounding noise that could not be ignored. The leader of two hundred replaced hope with horror. Raphael lowered his head as he listened to the words of his Master.

Turning to Gabriel, he said, "Go to the biters, to the reprobates, to the children of fornication. Find the offspring of the watchers from among men. Pull them forth and pit them one against another. Let them perish through mutual slaughter. This is their reward because the daughters of men embraced corruption." Yahweh took a deep breath. "Even if their fathers beg, their pleas will not be heard. The Elioud will hope for eternity, but their days will be cut short." Gabriel heard the command. He lowered his head in subservience. The Lord had a specific assignment for Michael. "Go and announce to Samyaza his crime. Make sure the angels that commingled with women hear the words. Those wicked ones that followed him, who desired to recreate in their image. Spreaders of their impurity, they shall see the judgment of their offspring." With authority, Yahweh commanded, "Bind them for generations beneath the earth. From there, let them witness the death of their sons. There they will remain until the season of judgment and consummation." Michael acknowledged his mission.

Michael and Raphael took on their assignment of dealing with the angels. The challenge was no easy undertaking. Loyalty to Samyaza was unbreakable, many of his subordinates protected him. War exploded on earth. Angel after angel shielded Samyaza from Michael and Raphael. An unending battle, unseen angels fought around men. Simultaneously, Gabriel pushed humans into a state of mental instability. Fear overwhelmed men. The archangel pushed them to take up armaments against the giants. For much of the time Noah built the ark, humans and angels warred. The diversion kept attentive eyes from the activities of Noah and his sons. It was a battle of years that ended with Michael and Raphael laying hold on Samyaza. Michael and his company of angels locked up the two hundred fallen angels that turned creation into an aberration. The imprisonment of their fathers blinded the giants with fury. Their countenances blackened. They hated Yahweh, the God of men. By now, Noah had finished the ark. For some time, God had summoned the animals of his choosing. Two pairs unclean and seven pairs clean, animals not defiled or altered. They began their journey, some close and others from afar. Noah stocked the ark with the necessary essentials. When the final creature entered the vessel, Uriel told Noah it was time to enter.

The hearts of Noah's sons burned differently. The soul of Shem glowed brightly, a moral man who concerned himself with the cares of his father. Japheth carried a countenance as red as crimson, a good, thoughtful man who changed with emotions. His kind character lacked the deep complexities of good and evil. Then there was Ham, the youngest son, who carried a black hue. Demented and dark, he restrained his character in the presence of his father. Upstanding outwardly, Ham harbored a spirit of worldliness. Noah, his wife, his sons, and their wives entered the ark. However, the door was heavy and immense, a menacingly large opening Noah had no idea how to close. Suddenly, without warning, Yahweh sent an intimidating wind. The violent swirl slammed the massive door shut. The impact shook the ground and reverberated through the ark. Once the noise subsided, Yahweh supernaturally sealed the door from the outside. The ship stood on its stilts, waiting for the treasures from heaven.

It was during the time of Peleg that Yahweh pressed the continental plates. With great power, the fissures collided. This immeasurable pressure erupted the underground springs. The exerting energy spouted deep into the sky. The filament canopy that had covered the earth shattered from the explosion of water. The collision disrupted the aquifers and underground springs. Surging waters coupled with falling moisture hit the earth at an alarming rate. Rain came rushing from heaven. Water began to boil up from the depths. Precipitation, coupled with earth springs and firmament moisture, flooded the earth. The Nephilim and the dark-hearted souls drowned. Within hours, the world Noah knew disappeared beneath the water. The flood rushed suddenly and quickly. The world washed away while Yahweh kept Noah and his children safe. However, within the wife of Ham lay a mystery. In her genetic makeup lingered a recessive gene from the line of giants. Unbeknownst to anyone on the ark, Yahweh allowed a glimmer of the angelic genetic pool to survive. God set aside a small lineage to elevate his future king, David.

Yahweh punished the angels. Of the most wicked of angels, they became known as the Grigori. Angels that once dwelt in the highest heaven but took on the appearance of men. Originally watchers, they decided to interfere with human evolution. Yahweh created a cluster of seven stars. The stars hovered over the abyss where he imprisoned Samyaza and his Grigori. Heavenly pillars of fire strung from the abyss to the stars. The formation bound the fallen angels to those stars. Seven stars shone over the horizon of the South Pole. The Lord named them the Pleiades. The star group Pleiades became part of the symbols in the skies. It told the story of how fallen angels mingled with women.

CHAPTER 6

The Beginning of Civilization

The death of the Nephilim proved puzzling. While the human half returned to dust, the angelic part fell into limbo. Creation did not account for the demise of spiritual abnormalities. The immortal souls found themselves tethered, trapped on earth, unable to die or be angels. Hopelessness filled them; the Nephilim lamented. Their bitterness gave them a taste for destruction. They blamed men for their torment because God had saved them from annihilation. Due to this, men became the catalyst for hatred. Lucifer had no remedy but to offer them a purpose. He proposed an enticing contract, an agreement to wreak havoc on men. The Nephilim jumped at the proposal. A simple arrangement: Lucifer would influence men to obey the whims of the spirits, and in return, they declared their fidelity to him. The Nephilim became known as demons, and Satan was the devil over them. Demons became tools, vessels to attack, possess, and influence. The demons moved objects and animated idols; the spirits gave Lucifer's plan validity. Generations of men experienced unnatural haunting, grievous pain, and mental despair. Demons enjoyed stirring mass hysteria. Harming individuals physically or psychologically brought them deep satisfaction. The union turned into mutual gain: Lucifer furthered his influence, and the demonic Nephilim found a reason to exist.

On earth, waters still dominated. After forty days and nights, Yahweh took the cataracts away. The fountains equalized, and the colliding lands carved deep hollows. Gulf fissures scarred the earth, and the waters congregated in the depths. The peaks of mountains peeked out of the waters. Unable to steer, Noah relied on the power of Yahweh to move the ship. Eventually, the surface overtook the deep, and the ark hit dry land. Noah, his family, and the animals disembarked. The human reset began with Noah and his sons. Of his three sons, Ham held a dark heart. He remembered the power of the wicked and wanted to rule.

One day, an opportunity presented itself: Ham noticed his father drunk in his tent, naked and asleep. He decided to possess his mother. Taking a man's wife was akin to asserting authority. Bragging to his brothers, Ham expected to become the new patriarch. Excitement lifted him; the thought of becoming the male head exhilarated him. His brothers, Shem and Japheth, refused to witness his act. Instead, they respectfully covered their father and mother. Stunned, Ham stood in disbelief because his brothers rejected him. Not long after, Noah awakened from his stupor. Realizing what had happened, bitterness filled his heart. The situation seared his soul because not long after, the wife of Noah had been found with child. Being his sons had been blessed by Yahweh, Noah could not curse Ham. He hated the child in his wife because it was the source of his bitterness. Cursing the child was the only way Noah could release his hostility. He wanted Ham punished for his disrespect. A son of Noah but not of Noah, he named him Canaan. A name fit for degradation, it meant lowland or a child from unwarranted merchandising. Ham was trafficked in incest, and the line of Canaan paid the price. The sins prevailed, and the descendants of Canaan followed the lewdness of Ham.

Cush, the oldest son of Ham, had a son, a Nephilim he called Nimrod. The name reflected the anger Cush harbored for the treatment of his father. *Nimrod* meant rebellion, and he shared in contempt for Yahweh. Born a giant by the recessive genes of his mother, the son of Cush became a mighty hunter. Through his intimidating physique, he pressured his servants to reject the God of heaven. A superior warrior and unruly tyrant, Nimrod made himself king and called his kingdom Babel. His rule extended to the cities in the southern lands of Shinar. Through him, Satan designed his religion.

He influenced Nimrod to call the religion Baal, with the sun god as its deity. The son of Cush wanted to be above all, and he felt the strength of the sun best described him. Moving the people to build a tower, he wanted it to reach heaven. From the great tower, Nimrod could rule in the stars and rise with the angels. Naming it the Tower of Babel, it stood in direct rebellion to Yahweh. Lucifer hoped the tower would reach the sun. Although a man desired to sit in the tower, it would be Lucifer they would worship. All in heaven observed the tower that the sunlight touched. Nimrod, his tower, and his god Baal were desecrations. In response to the blasphemy, the Son confounded tongues; the people of Babel began speaking different languages. Through the confusion, the followers of Nimrod dispersed. Lucifer used the scattering to infuse Baal everywhere. Each tongue changed the god's name, but the meaning behind Satan's religion remained the same. In the ancient world, the Baal religion stretched as far as Assyria.

Before long, Yahweh was not the only God. Lucifer introduced polytheism, the worship of many gods. The angel designed a deity pyramid. Men prayed to lesser gods for the issues of life. The lesser gods submitted to an assembly of higher ones. The fallen angels assumed the roles of the higher deities, while Lucifer held the position of supreme god. He charged the demons to assume the lesser roles. Demons mixed good with bad, blessing with cursing; they enjoyed their role as overlords. They ordered men to live within the rules of the idol. If men resisted, Lucifer gave permission to punish them. Through fear and awe, the people obeyed. Animated gods proved most attractive; it was easier for men to worship what they could see, feel, and experience. Baal evolved into a form of Pantheism. Lucifer found it easy to move men to reverence the cosmos and the elements of nature. Fruit, vegetables, and herbs had always been essential; men looked to spring to survive. It was the season of life when everything awoke from its slumber.

Through Baal, men worshiped the rebirth of spring and the alignment of stars. Nimrod became the reincarnation of the prime season. His spirit reemerged each springtime while his mother goddess, Semiramis, the queen of heaven, observed from above. Baal, the sun god, rejuvenated Nimrod with his rays of light. When winter dominated the sun, believers held a festival to coax it back. They called the gathering Saturnalia or the winter solstice.

Lucifer wanted to keep forms of Baal within religion. He did not want his system to fade, so he remixed and remade it. Generation after generation, culture to culture, Satan encouraged haughty men to tweak the gods. Horus became Tammuz, also Gilgamesh; Nimrod changed to Saturn and then Osiris—different names with subtle changes, all variations of Baal. Satan used these deity legends to loosely recount his greatness. In *The Epic of Gilgamesh*, the tale told of a demigod, along with his companion Enkidu, breaking through heaven by defeating Humbaba the Bull. Like Gilgamesh, Satan tried to take heaven. The story *The Enuma Elish* told of the young Babylonian god Marduk, victorious over the forces of chaos. Marduk became known as the creator of human beings. In the case of Lucifer, he allowed his angels to recreate men. In *The Descent of Inanna*, a god dies and returns from the dead. By ridding himself of the death curse, Satan gained the ability to return to heaven. Lucifer knew humanizing gods drew men closer because men related to gods that shared similar fates.

Sumerian cities began to appear along the Tigris and Euphrates Rivers—Ur, Kish, and Uruk, cities that became known as the cradle of human civilization. Sumerians knew of Nimrod; they credited him and Baal for their oldest city, Eridu. Sumer deities Engur, Nammu, Ki, and Enlil became the higher gods of water, air, earth, and mother heaven. Utu, the supreme sun god, and his sister Nanna, the moon god, kept men praying for their return. Lesser gods Gula, Ereshkigal, Enlil, and Inanna dealt with daily life. Each Sumer city was self-governing city-states. This displeased Lucifer; he wanted men under one rule. Using demons, Satan sparked city kings to battle one another, pitting one Sumer city against another. The threat moved cities to fortify their kingdoms. Lucifer desired an end to city kings because the people believed them to be gods. Their titles reflected the geographical area around the city they ruled. Mountainous regions viewed their king god of the sky. The fertile lands below called their lord the earth king, and the barren straits aligned their regent as the god of the underworld. Trust between cities continually eroded until new people overtook the region.

The Akkadians invaded Shinar. A more unified presence, they pushed the Sumerians to the southern lands. Lucifer stood behind the first Akkadian ruler, Sargon. As with Gilgamesh, Sargon became another incarnation of Nimrod. Satan stood behind the king, moving him to not totally discard the gods of Sumerians. Sargon did not want to keep the gods of a defeated people, so he mingled the Sumer deities within his own. He changed the names of Sumer gods and added traits to them. Along with seeing gods as elemental, Sargon added ritual purification, sorcery, and incantation into worship. Mirroring the ways of Baal, Lucifer pushed Sargon to ingrain the mysteries into the fabric of his empire. Demons used their deities to teach skills the angels taught before the flood. Sargon revered the sun god because the power of Lucifer shone over him. The angel refined Baal through the Akkadians, but this system was not yet what Lucifer envisioned.

A two-hundred-year drought destroyed the Akkadian Empire. The Sumerians and Gutians filtered back into the northern lands. Weak and unorganized, the Assyrians overtook them. Their central city, Ashur, named after the Assyrian god of war, was the people's favorite deity. A warring people, Ashur's wife Ishtar protected men in battle, and Nergal overlooked the plagues of war. Satan influenced the king of Assyria to accept a version of Baal. Molech became that version, a sun god that required human sacrifice. A large furnace for a belly, priests stoked it until the statue burned white hot. The ritual required babies thrown into the belly of the statue. The ceremony banged loud drums to drown out the wails of the parents and the shrieks of the children. On top of its head, Molech wore bull horns, and in the middle of its forehead, the god fashioned an all-seeing eye. Molech sat on his throne with outstretched arms, waiting to cradle his sacrifices. Lucifer's religious design became more natural, and more commonplace. Refined within each dynasty, the angel continued to influence men to insert pieces of Baal into their beliefs.

The Assyrian bureaucracy proved a more efficient system than small tribal communities. Governmental power was key for Lucifer

ANGEL'S INFLUENCE

because it was the arm of order. Satan wanted a controlling system that would amalgamate with his religion. Through the ages, he kept his Baal system alive. Conditioning minds with many false gods, men continued creating versions of old deities with an occasional serpent accouterment. A polytheistic culture took hold with Baal in the mix. The influx of gods scattered in every direction. In ignorance, multitudes followed doctrines associated with the old religion.

CHAPTER 7

A Thin Line of Righteousness

Filling the world with gods did not satisfy Lucifer; he craved subservience. Frustrated, he walked back and forth, searching for men to sway. Satan wanted those who rejected Baal. Within the seed of Adam lay a family line that followed Yahweh—a bright and glowing lineage, a thin gold thread weaving its way through dark cloth. Thinking about this line, one incident in particular Lucifer never forgot. It was a time before Noah when Yahweh openly challenged him. Back then Satan took pleasure in traveling to heaven. It pleased him to agonize Yahweh. Basking in his eminence, Lucifer knew every appearance reminded the host of his victories. After the banishment, the angels found his presence confounding. The rebellious cherub made the heavenly host uneasy. Each visit was apprehensive; angels attentively watched the reaction to his prideful arrogance. Vain, he lined up to present himself before the Father. Yahweh disdainfully asked, "Why are you here?"

"I have been roaming around the earth," he replied smugly. His hubris was static, soaked within his permeating reality.

Yahweh responded, "Well, have you considered my servant Job?"

In a distant posture, he said, "No, because you protect him. He only gives you homage because you protect him." Slowly, Lucifer's lips lifted. "Now if you let me torment him, I know he will curse you." Angels saw the belligerence in Lucifer's pose; all knew the angel wished to vie against Yahweh. Satan took on the challenge, taking

48

everything from Job except his life. Even at the point of death, Satan could not break him. Utilizing his jealous friends could not get Job to curse. When it came to choice, Job chose Yahweh.

Through the darkness of time Lucifer knew the Son kept watch over his righteous line. From Job to Noah, Abraham to Jacob, God protected them. Even when Pharaoh turned the Hebrews into slaves, God was there. All through the times of fear and resistance, God stayed near. Seeing this, Lucifer sought to find a weakness. Of the sons of Jacob, the angel found an ally. The tribe of Dan proved to be especially uninterested in God. Lucifer intrigued Dan and his children with secret knowledge. They were a perfect lineage to spread the awareness of idolatry. Satan knew Dan was the right choice once he saw his family crest. Bearing an eagle clutching a snake, the seal depicted the serpent as prey. In reality, Satan had the eagle in his clutches; he used Dan as a stumbling block. The influence of Dan turned the Hebrews into a wild, dark, and filthy lot. Miracle after miracle did not seem to faze them. Moses with the tablets could not save them. Interventions did not seem enough because idolatry crept into their souls. Faithless and whiny, the Hebrews fell backward. Yahweh proved to be a very different God than the gods of Egypt. Unlike seen gods, he was an unseen deity that did not fascinate the sight.

Yet within the chosen lay a portion that believed. Those that followed God separated themselves from those deceived by the tribe of Dan. Because of the faithful, Yahweh blessed the people in abundance. God showered them with promises. In times of uncertainty, he heard their cries. The children of Abraham found refuge in distress. Pagan kingdoms frightened them, but Yahweh rescued them in amazing ways. Still, deliverance never kept the people from veering away. In time, a pattern emerged; acknowledgment when troubled; forgotten in plenty. The Hebrews repeatedly witnessed the power of God yet continued to turn away.

Yahweh wanted to rule with the people, but the Hebrews found that unacceptable. The people demanded a king. Yahweh found them a king who fit their heart's desire—a king who loved God but loved himself more. Lucifer used jealousy to make King Saul unstable. Discovering that Samuel the prophet had anointed David as king, the rejection tipped his stability. Satan heightened Saul's insecurities, and the king of the people fell into madness. Saul became obsessed with killing his foe; his terror of David dictated his path. However, David loved Saul. He calmed him and fought for him, and never once did he resist him. A man after God's own heart, David replaced Saul as king. Under David, the kingdom grew; however, Lucifer tempted him to count the people. The consequences of his sin caused seventy thousand to die from disease. Out of love for David, God anointed his son Solomon with wisdom and appointed him builder of the temple. But the wives of Solomon beguiled him, and Yahweh stripped the kingdom from his son. For David's sake, God allowed Rehoboam, the son of Solomon, to keep the tribes of Judah and Benjamin. The rest of the tribes were ripped from the house of David. Yahweh gave them to Jeroboam of the house of Ephraim.

Desiring a clean break, the king of the north abandoned Yahweh. Jeroboam did evil in the sight of the Lord. His rule prompted a succession of rebellious monarchs. Each evil king led the people farther astray. Each godly king pulled the people back, but kings who desired to follow Yahweh became scarcer. Over time, the northern tribes fell into idolatry, and the southern tribes of Judah and Benjamin resisted temptation. The groves of Baal ever loomed over the people. The infiltration deepened with each ungodly king. The influence of idols dulled the senses. Godly kings tore down the groves and knocked down the temples of Baal. A succession of two or three wicked kings rebuilt them. Such back and forth made following Yahweh tedious; it instilled a longing to disobey. Less and less, the people desired Yahweh; the kings who observed him became rare. Idolatry had permeated so thoroughly that the people began to ignore Yahweh. They obeyed when demanded, but Yahweh did not reside in their hearts. Like the northern tribes, the southern people lusted after other gods. The meddling of Lucifer and his religion became a metastatic cancer.

Backsliding had become inevitable. The ten tribes eagerly embraced evil. The shift had been too far and too extreme; Jeroboam replaced the house of Levi with pagan priests. To their horror, the ten tribes changed their center of worship to Baal. This did not sit well with the inheritors of the priesthood. A segment of them returned to the southern tribes for the wrong reason. It was not for the sake of Yahweh that unhinged them; the Levitical priests could not stomach being replaced. Priestly authority gave them power over people. With them, some of each tribe wandered back to Judah and Benjamin. By the time the ten tribes fell, Judah and Benjamin retained a small representation of them. A seemingly terrible end, Yahweh allowed the northern tribes to be sifted. Once assimilated, the ten tribes lost their identity. Yahweh guided generations to carry out the blessing Jacob made to Joseph's sons. The offspring of the lost ten became a powerful country and a company of nations.

From the dispersal of the ten tribes sprang versions of the word of God. Many biblical systems emerged from the lost tribes. The distant interpretations revolved around one point: the Son of God. Like Lucifer, who diffused his religion, Yahweh spread his name. God subconsciously filtered inklings of truth within the ten tribes. Here a little, there a little, breadcrumbs of wisdom for men to find. Men yearned to understand, but interpretations proved elusive. Revivals opened minds; however, translation after translation, revision after revision became misleading. Cultures altered meanings; time changed words. Without notice, doctrines became paramount. Epiphanies formed and enlightened insights took shape; the analysis of men splintered the scriptures. Yahweh sanctioned the differences. He veiled understandings and blinded mysteries; believers dispersed into camps of theology. Doctrines of the lost tribes created rifts between each other. It also allowed wolves, dogs, and foxes to disguise themselves as men of God. It made it simple for Satan to insert deceivers among them.

The tribes of Judah and Benjamin met a different fate. Yahweh put them into the hands of the Babylonians. Unlike the ten, he gave them the gift of remembrance. No longer Hebrews but men of Judah, God allowed the Jews to keep their identity. Generations in captivity made them forgetful. God helped Nehemiah and Ezra regather shards of the law, and the people renewed their vow to God. Even with a promise, sin plagued those of Judah, Benjamin, and the tribal remnants. The people and their rabbi system became unrecognizable. The priests used their authority for self-gain. Their power left the helpless vulnerable because the rich ingratiated them. Self-worth and greed overwrote duty; leaders harmed the small and coveted the great. Yet eyes red with hatred did not see. Blindness clouded reason and evil diverted their commission. Blessed from the seed of Abraham, the Jews trod many shepherds with their feet. Pride and legacy became their mantra. The Jews held to their history, but they lost their peculiarity. The people once known as Hebrews no longer resembled Abraham.

Whether Jew or Gentile, the thin line of righteousness was difficult to find. Many were called; few were chosen. The Son knocked and listened for the calling of his name. Whichever way the door swung depended on the moment of decision. Each choice involved flickering microseconds, points when Yahweh withheld his omnipotence. Out of love, the Son allowed the gift; he left those moments of opinion solely for men. No matter how often Lucifer and his angels twisted and deceived, fault always rested on the determination of men.

CHAPTER 8

The Prophecy that Lucifer Feared

Of men, there was a man named Joseph, whose heritage was of David. Joseph came from the bloodline of Solomon, the kingly line of Judah. Of the line of kings, Jehoiachin had been cursed by God. The curse decreed that none of his offspring would sit on the throne. Due to this, scholars watching for the child of prophecy dismissed the descendants of Jehoiachin. Likewise, Lucifer bypassed Joseph due to his family tree. Although he met the legal standard, being a male of the accursed line disqualified him. However, Mary had a biological tie that met the prophetic criteria.

While in Babylonian captivity, King Jehoiachin married a widow named Hadcast. The daughter of Neri, Hadcast already had a son, Pedaiah. She gave Jehoiachin a son called Shealtiel. Although Shealtiel married, he died before begetting a son. With his death, God cut off the bloodline of King Jehoiachin. As in Jewish tradition, the half brother Pedaiah married Assir, his brother's widow. Their firstborn son, Zerubbabel, became heir to the king. Not from King Jehoiachin, but still of David, the title passed to Zerubbabel. Through him, the bloodline switched from Solomon to his older brother Nathan. The line of Neri, Zerubbabel, and Rhesa filtered down to Mary. The prophetic foretelling did not disclose the bloodline shift. Nor did any consider the prophecy to come through the genealogy of a woman. The shift threw off Lucifer and the scholars who continually searched genetic lines.

Being records never followed maternal bloodlines, Lucifer didn't catch the prophetic correlation. He followed the Jewish leaders who researched male lineages, waiting for them to discover their messiah. With only cryptic references, he watched the flow of time for clues that would expose the child. The old words called the child Emanuel, which meant God with us. *God is with us*, Lucifer thought. Satan mulled over the possibilities. Prior to angels mixing with women, the thought had never occurred. Offspring from angels gave credence to the blending of supernatural with the natural. *Could it be feasible that the child will be Yahweh? It would be no great feat for the Son*, Satan concluded. His focus remained centered on the lines of King David. Finding the child among the genealogies seemed daunting. Neither Joseph nor Mary piqued curiosity.

As was the custom, a man and woman betrothed for a year. It was a period of celibacy to ensure faithfulness. Joseph and Mary's fathers chiseled out the details of their engagement. Well into the betrothal, an angel came to Mary. "Hail, thou who art highly favored. The Lord is with thee: blessed art thou among women." Fear ran down her body; Mary hid herself in the corner of her room. Shocked that a man appeared within her private chamber, she worried how others would see it. Not realizing an angel stood before her, she quickly leaned forward, clutching her bedding. Pulling it down, Mary reared back to distance herself. Gabriel noticed her fear, "Fear not, Mary, for thou hast found favor with God." Afraid to speak, Mary listened intently to the words of the stranger. "Behold, thou shalt conceive in thy womb and bring forth a son. You shall call his name Jesus." The angel continued, "He shall be great and shall be called the Son of the Highest. He will come out of the line of David and retake the throne."

Confused, Mary thought he referred to a future firstborn between herself and Joseph. *Who is he?* she wondered. Fear turned into apprehension; if the stranger meant her harm, he would have done something. As she heard words like ordained and great purpose, her eyes widened. Realization hit her; this is an angel!

ANGEL'S INFLUENCE

As the messenger spoke, she kept pondering how the Lord would make this happen. The angel finished his proclamation, "And he shall reign over the house of Jacob forever, and of his kingdom, there shall be no end." Beyond logic, the angel spoke a revelation in a current sense.

Miffed, Mary said to the angel, "I am a virgin. How shall this be, seeing I know not a man?" The angel glowed with excitement. "The Holy Spirit of God shall come upon thee, and the power of the Highest shall overshadow thee: therefore also that holy thing which shall be born of thee shall be called the Son of God." While announcing the special tidings, Gabriel added more. "Your cousin Elizabeth conceived, though she was thought to be barren."

Mary lifted herself from the corner. "Elizabeth is with child?"

The angel looked at her. "For with God, nothing shall be impossible." The anxiety in her spirit subsided.

Mary accepted the words of the angel. In a submissive tone, "Behold the handmaid of the Lord. Be it unto me according to thy word." Her breath eased, and a cool comfort covered her being. Mary postured humility as the angel told her she was with child. Once the angel departed, the realization gripped her. It dawned on her that she was pregnant during the betrothal period. Others would label her as an unclean adulteress. Worse yet, the elders could judge her and stone her. Mary began shaking. She began crying while she paced the room. Remembering the angel telling her of Elizabeth, she decided to visit her cousin. Gathering her composure, Mary packed a few things. She thought, *There I could buy time to think.* Knowing none would accept such an outlandish tale, she set off to stay with Elizabeth. God knew Mary needed strength and reassurance. Through Elizabeth, she would find the solitude she required.

Seeing Mary from afar, Elizabeth felt the Spirit of God swell in her. As Mary approached, Elizabeth's baby leaped as they hugged. Beaming with joy and tears, Elizabeth cried, "Blessed art thou among women, and blessed is the child in thee!" Smiling, she asked, "And why has the mother of my Lord come to me? For as soon as I heard your salutation, the babe in my womb leaped for joy." She hugged Mary again, holding her tight. "And blessed is she that believes, for there shall be a fulfillment of those things which were told of her from the Lord." Mary broke down into a stream of tears. Her knees buckled; God gave her validation through the words of Elizabeth. Before she could tell her the reason for the visit, Elizabeth already knew. There were no more doubts; she believed.

Raising her hands to heaven, she said, "My soul does magnify the Lord." Mary righted herself. "And my spirit has rejoiced in God my Savior." Wiping her tears and calming her countenance, Mary smiled at Elizabeth. "God has regarded my low estate and made me his handmaiden: from henceforth all generations shall call me blessed." Excited, Elizabeth took Mary into her home. The women kept it a secret until Mary could not hide her condition. Both prayed and discussed the situation before them. Explaining a virgin pregnancy was inconceivable; who would accept that? But for the uncharacteristically action of Elizabeth and her unborn child, uncertainty turned to faith. Mary knew she had to tell Joseph.

In secret, Mary paid Joseph a visit. Her appearance surprised him, being they refrained from relations. He loved Mary and did not want to sully her. For Mary to risk such a visit had to be important. So he listened to how an angel appeared before her. Mary knew Joseph had the legal right to divorce her. Furthermore, he could have made her a public example. Stunned with disbelief, Joseph took in the explanation of his espoused, a difficult position for any man. "Are you telling me you're pregnant by God?" He saw her calmness, her peace that defied understanding. Slowly circling the room, Joseph pressed his fingers to his forehead. "Mary, I need some time to think." Mary saw the pained look; her future lay in his hands. Mary returned to Elizabeth to await Joseph's answer.

Later that night as he lay in bed, Joseph considered it all. A just man, he didn't want to harm Mary even if she had been unfaithful. Joseph hated the prospect of making her a public example. So he considered putting Mary away quietly. As he thought for hours about where to send Mary, Joseph fell into a deep sleep. Out of the dark corners of the room appeared an angel. The angel touched his brow and entered into his mind, "Joseph, thou son of David, fear not to take unto thee Mary thy wife, for that which is conceived in her is of the Holy Ghost." The words of Gabriel felt like a dream, "She shall bring forth a son, and thou shalt call his name Jesus; for he shall save his people from their sins." Just as the angel entered, he dissipated back into the shadows.

The next morning, Joseph woke, staring at the ceiling. He remembered the angel and the words he spoke. His mind was filled with questions. Unsure if it was real or entangled emotions, Joseph decided to follow the yearnings of the vision. He rose from his bed and went to Mary. He shared his dream with Mary. "Mary, to be honest with you, I am uncertain and confused. I want to believe, but this is so hard." She understood his withdrawal. The past months had filled her with faith. Mary was ready to accept the will of God. On his knees, he said, "Mary, I love you and want to marry you." With a slight pause, he touched her hair. "We are betrothed, and I see no need to continue waiting. I have decided to make you my wife." Concerned eyes sparked with joy. She cried. Joseph wiped her tears. "All will accept this as my child." He hugged her. Mary crumbled in his embrace. As a man, Joseph still did not totally comprehend it all. For now, he knew Mary was with child.

With an uncertain tone, he said, "I can't lay with you, Mary." She could hear the sadness in his voice.

"As a man, this hurts, but I will protect you and your child." She too had misgivings, but God gave her the evidence she needed. Resolving herself, Mary decided to believe for both of them. Her faith supported Joseph's insecurities. As God did for her, she would do for Joseph.

In a world trapped in reality, a virgin birth would be considered insane. However, Lucifer was a true believer. He had been watching for a virgin with child. By now, a prophetic master, Lucifer had become most proficient in sacred writings. Satan knew of the telling of a man who would be God. A God who would be the salvation of the world. A passive quality of a phrase that is code speak for *Yeshuah*. In Hebrew, the word is translated to "Yahweh to save." The translations, coded messages, snippets convinced Lucifer Yahweh was going to enter into the realm of men. The words *death blow* took on a whole new meaning. Prophecy gave him enough information to break the words of Yahweh and counter its revelations. Excited about this, Satan schemed to kill the Son of God. He had the pieces, but the puzzle still withheld missing parts.

CHAPTER 9

Enter the Messiah

In the second heaven, a great star exploded. The trajectory of light passed through the void and headed toward Earth. The record of old foretold of an unnatural star appearing in the sky. Greater than the others, the prophecy told of it pointing over the prince child. Aware that the immense light from this stellar body could be that light, Lucifer approximated its time of arrival. The implosion burst sporadically; the energy of light traveled in two waves. Lucifer projected the first light to show near the end of 4 BC and the second around early 1 BC. During this time, Rome, being so vast, was rotating their census by regions. Emperor Quirinius held a census for Syria and Judea in 4 BC. Being close to the time of the first light, Lucifer with his angels monitored Bethlehem. The angels and demons watched with interest to see if the child would come. When it became apparent the prophecy was not to be, Satan influenced men to conduct another census over Judea by the time of the next light.

In 2 BC, the senate bestowed the honor of Pater Patriae on their emperor, meaning "Father of the Fatherland." It was a most high honor for Caesar Augustus. Satan played on the pride of Augustus and moved him to immortalize himself. Excited, Caesar made a plan to highlight this esteemed title as a tribute to his greatness. A self-absorbed desire, the emperor wanted all his great achievements illustrated at his funeral. It was a legacy designed to be read upon his death. To do this, the emperor decreed a registration of the entire empire. The registration demanded all subjects in the kingdom register their allegiance, a unique and special census, not for taxation, but to quantify all resources financially and militarily. Ordered merely out of vanity, Augustus desired to create a *breviarium totius imperii*, a summary of all his accomplishments. At the time, Rome had yet to appoint a governor over the Jews. Once again, it was put upon Quirinius to take on the task. Being an autonomous client state under King Herod, Quirinius ordered the king to run the census over his people. Herod did not want to make waves with Rome, so he decreed every subject return to the place of their lineage. The scenario could not have been better; to order the people to their ancestral city delighted Lucifer. This would place another census during the event of the great light. A census derived from egoism, those of the house of David would have to return to Bethlehem.

Joseph and his young bride had to travel to Bethlehem. The distance from David's ancient home to Nazareth was about ninety miles. Not being a man of means, Joseph did not have the wealth to afford an animal for Mary to ride. Surmising the trip treacherous for a woman with child, he worried for his wife. Close to term, the decree filled him with tension because he knew the chances were probable Mary could give birth in the wilderness. Certain the walk would take more than eight days, the journey would prove arduous for her. The road had robbers, bandits, and not to mention wild animals. He decided to tag along with a group that was heading in the same direction. It was the best option, the best solution he could find for his wife. Those traveling with him observed Mary in anguish as she walked. Realizing that she would not make it, kindness overtook their hearts. The fellow travelers offered her one of their animals to ride upon. Exhausted but grateful, Joseph gingerly pulled his wife along.

The human part of Joseph still had doubts. Logically, he heard the words of the angel, but his weak flesh, along with uncertainty, haunted him. His internal churning increased as the baby grew; he felt more upset when he looked at the baby bump. Thoughts bantered on whether the child was from God or a lie. It was only human to avoid being scourged for infidelity. Despite doubting the unseen, Joseph had a tender heart and would protect the child. As the couple crossed into the boundary of Bethlehem, they felt a strange aura. Unknown to them, hordes of demons convened in the little town. The contractions became closer; clearly, Mary was suffering. Straightway, Joseph supported his wife and walked to the inn. "I see your problem, but we're all full," the innkeeper said. Panic escalated in Joseph; the influx of travelers filled the inn. Noting the fear in Joseph's eyes, the innkeeper said, "Look, it isn't much, but I have a stable along the hills. There you'll find a cave. It isn't much, but it is at least some shelter."

Desperate, Joseph replied, "Thank you, kind sir!" He carried his wife in the direction of the cave. "Hold on, Mary. We're almost there." The sounds of her crying were unbearable. With each contraction, Mary bellowed. At the base of the hill, he found the opening. As careful as he could, Joseph carried his wife into the cave. It was a shallow cavern, deep enough for animals to shelter from the elements. Smooth walls, the cave had a trough toward the back carved in stone. He unpacked the blankets, doing his best to make his wife comfortable. Joseph held her hand. With each contraction, her grip grew tighter and tighter. With each contraction, Joseph prayed louder and louder.

Demonic activity made the air in the city stagnant and dense. Hoards of angels moved throughout the inn and houses looking for signs of births. What seemed cruel, putting Joseph and Mary in a stable, in actuality was divine protection. The angels moved Joseph out of the city, away from Lucifer and the seekers. About this time, in a distant land, the men of Persia saw the magnificent display in the sky. They were scholars who studied the Hebrew writings. This spectacular star, a never-before-seen astrological sign, intrigued them. Excited, the magi combed through their text looking for any reference that correlated to the oddity.

In the book of Numbers, the men found scriptures telling of a coming Messiah. In the writings, they saw the description of an amazing star. It read, "A star will come out of Jacob, a scepter will rise out of Israel." High-brow men of knowledge, the thought of the sign of a ruler of the Jews overwhelmed them. Gleefully, they informed their king. They advised their lord of the astral evidence suggesting a king was to be born. As expected, their ruler listened to their findings and desired to give homage to the king of the Jews. It was advantageous to acknowledge a neighboring kingdom. As commanded, servants of the king loaded gifts of gold, frankincense, and myrrh, oils, perfumes, and medicines on carts. The instruction for the magi was clear; they were to honor the child in the name of the king of Persia. Setting off on their journey, they followed the bright star. Heading from the east, they trekked west toward the nucleus of the biblical accounts.

The miraculous star remained in the sky for weeks. Each evening, the magi waited for the star to appear over the horizon. As if alive, it led them, always staying before them. Each night, the celestial body illuminated like an angel. The men knew this was no normal phenomenon because the light moved against the earth's rotation. There was no logical explanation; the star did not stay fixated. It veered in an uncharacteristic way.

The light led them through the eight-hundred-mile trek from Persia to Jerusalem. Each night, the star faithfully appeared. It took the caravan forty days using the trade routes. Its light never dimmed until the wise men made it to the border of Jerusalem. Without warning, the brilliant star disappeared. The troop had traveled so far, charting this new event in the heavens. The luminous body now gone, it perplexed the magi. For forty days, the star led them on a journey, then it stopped. Unsure what to do next, the men assumed that the child must be a son of the king of Judea.

Anxiety filled the men, the magi desperately wanted to validate the writings of Daniel. Long ago, there was a magi named Daniel, a child of the Jews brought to them from the land of Judah. It was he who taught the magi the secrets of the Hebrew God. Faithfully, Daniel served the king of Babylon. Because he handed down his wisdom, the scholars wanted to believe. They wanted to find the child who was to become the King of the Jews. Strange to the land, the men knew nothing of Herod, called Herod the Great because he made many spectacular structures. A ruthless, barbaric ruler, small in stature, high in cruelty. Losing their beacon, the wise men decided to seek an audience with the king of Judea in Jerusalem.

ANGEL'S INFLUENCE

One of Herod's advisers said, "Your highness, there is a caravan of magi from a kingdom far away that desires an audience with you." When Herod heard this, it pleased him. The elder gestured to one of the servants to bring the magi to the door of the throne room. Herod's adviser continued, "They claim they have gifts from their king for the King of the Jews."

The words tickled Herod. A king full of self, his ego inflated at the announcement that a faraway kingdom came to him. "Send them in," Herod bellowed with pride. The wise men from Persia walked through the large doors. Bowing before Herod, the head of the magi rose and said, "Greetings, we come as representatives of the great Phraates IV, Arsaces, Son of Orodes II, King of Babylon."

Herod smiled and asked, "Welcome to my kingdom. Why have you come to me?"

The head magician responded, "We observed in the heavens the great star foretold in the scrolls of Daniel. Our king has given us passage to come and pay homage in his name." Befuddled, Herod sat stunned. The chief magi continued, "We of Persia are excited to witness the birth of the King of the Jews. Tell us, where might the child of destiny be as foretold in the prophetic writings?"

Now totally stupefied, Herod sat silent. After a static pause, he said, "Head Adviser!"

Fearfully, Herod's adviser moved to his master and bowed, "Yes, Your Majesty?"

Herod, glaring at the guests, said, "Tell me where is this Messiah to be born? Go to the chief priest and rabbis and inquire of them the scriptures concerning this star."

"Right away, your majesty." The magi of Herod with haste did the bidding of their master.

Resting his hand on his chin, Herod glared at the company from Babylon. He pondered what they spoke of since he held the title "King of the Jews." His thoughts turned, *Is it possible within his dominion lay a threat to his throne?*

While they waited, Satan persuaded Herod. Lucifer moved the king to consider his greatness. The magnificent structures he made, Masada, Herodium, and the enclosure around the Cave of the

Patriarchs. How he rebuilt the temple of the Jews and the artificial harbor at the port of Caesarea Maritima. His worthiness was undeniable, seen in all directions. The angel fueled his instability. Satan knew his insecurities controlled him. Emotionally shifty, Herod killed his wife Mariamne out of jealousy. Three of his sons died by his hand because of squabbles over succession. His strong compulsion for power made him irrational. Worldly and instinctive, he destroyed anyone who threatened his sovereignty. A perfect, egotistical pawn for Lucifer, he played on the paranoia of Herod. The king's eyes reddened as he considered the current threat. A bloodlust built in him. The silence in the throne room heated as the guest waited patiently for an answer. The wise men noticed a slow alteration in the character of the king. The more Herod looked at them, the more hostility filled him. Just before the king lost his senses, his wise men returned.

"My king, the scrolls tell of a baby that would be born in Bethlehem. The writings say that a great star would point the way," the adviser read from the scriptures. "Bethlehem, in the land of Judah. You are by no means the least among the leading cities of Judah, for from you will come a leader who will guide my people Israel."

The wheels in Herod's mind processed the words. His impulse was to kill these men because they did not come to worship him. However, doing that could bring the wrath of the Persian empire. Flipping like a switch, he spoke. "There you have it. The child is in Bethlehem."

Excited, the men from afar responded, "Thank you, Your Grace. Our travel has been long, and the star in the sky was our guide. Since it disappeared, we were in need of guidance. Clearly, your wisdom is unmatched."

The disposition of Herod changed from rage to benevolence. "Yes, go to Bethlehem and find the child you seek. When you find him, come back to me so I can go and worship him."

The magi of Babylon bowed to him. "Of course, Your Highness, we will send word once we discover the whereabouts of the child." The men of Persia left the presence of Herod. Quickly, he snapped his fingers. "Send spies to follow them, and when they find the child, instruct them to return quickly."

"As you wish, my Lord." Suddenly, nothing else in the kingdom mattered. Herod wanted to find the child of destiny. A man with a psychopathic, murderous heart, Herod desired to kill the infant.

The scholars from Persia created havoc throughout Jerusalem. People in corners, alleys, and homes contemplated the meanings of the prophecy. The subjects knew the hostility of Herod. Fear of the king ran through their veins. The men of Persia did not comprehend the scope of their predicament. They continued their mission and headed to Bethlehem. With no guidepost, the men started to inquire of the townspeople, quoting the scriptures as they traveled. "And you, O Bethlehem of Ephrath, least among the clans of Judah, from you shall come forth to rule Israel for me—one whose origins are from of old, from ancient times." They cherished the written prophecies; the magi wanted to affirm their knowledge. They were the priests and scholars, astute in languages, stars, literature both religious and secular. It was their wisdom of the world that their king depended on. Whether studies in the arts of divination, magic, dream interpretation, astronomy, secrets of the zodiac, their knowledge made them indispensable to their lord. Proof that the ancient words held truth would lift their status. Unknown to them, shadowy figures patiently followed them.

It had been months since the first appearance of the star. The angelic armies of good and evil were dispatched. Lucifer did not find the child. The angels of heaven moved him and protected him. The distance from Jerusalem was short; the wise men continued to ask about the birth. Many in the town reacted with confusion because they did not know of any such child. For weeks, the men quizzed residents, citing scriptures to them. Out of the probing, the magi heard tales from shepherds, tales scoffed off as visionary dreams from individuals that spent many nights alone in the fields. The spies watched. They witnessed them go from house to house. After a time, the men of Herod concluded there was no child. Returning to their king, they reported how the wise men scoured the town to find nothing. While the spies reported to their king, the magi came too far to stop. They sought out the shepherds.

Shepherds were men placed low on the social ladder. Victims of nonsocial, harsh stereotypes, they seemed nomadic to a civilized Israel. Many were deprived of civil rights. However, the Pharisees needed the shepherds to raise spotless lambs. Temple shepherds held a higher status than the rest. The wise men of Persia were directed to the fields where the shepherds lived. Finding them and sitting with them, the men remembered the night of the great star. Their tale began like any other night. The shepherds were abiding in the field, keeping watch over their flock on a beautiful, clear night when the keepers of the sheep saw the glory of the Lord shine about them. Light so blinding, night turned to day. Many shepherds dropped their staffs and bowed down. As they cowered, they heard a voice. The voice from an angel said to them, "Fear not: for, behold, I bring you good tidings of great joy, which shall be to all people. For unto you is born this day in the city of David a Savior, which is Christ the Lord."

They heard a multitude of the host praising God, saying, "Glory to God in the highest, and on earth peace, goodwill toward men." The shepherds told them that they found a child wrapped in swaddling clothes, lying in a manger. "Was the child the one?" Nodding yes, the shepherds said after the angels left, they discussed what had happened. The men decided to take their herd back to town and see what the townspeople had heard. Discovering the keeper of the inn had allowed a family to stay in his stable, the shepherds went to find a couple with a newborn. The baby was asleep in a trough filled with straw. The shepherds ended their account by telling anyone that would listen that the child was born. The residents heard the words, but being shepherds, they considered it a story of little value.

By now it had been days since the magi entered Bethlehem. They had heard the story of angels and a child; however, they were perplexed about how to proceed. The spies of Herod, having returned to monitor them, could not find them. They left again to let Herod know that the men had found nothing more than tales and stories. Satisfied, Herod decided to wait for their return. Seeing the magi again would prove profitable for Herod. He intended to make overtures of an alliance between himself and the king of Persia. But the return visit became uncertain, because the men of Persia grieved their

ANGEL'S INFLUENCE

failure. Frazzled the magi left the shepherds, disappointed, believing a king had been born, but they had missed him. In defeat the caravan made preparations to return to their homeland. As they set out to their surprise, the great star reappeared. It was not over Bethlehem, where they had searched, but farther west. Lucifer too saw the star, but not being in the right place, discounted it as an aftereffect of the first light.

Astonished and overwhelmed with excitement, the scholars couldn't contain themselves. What was most intriguing was the stability of the star. Looking at the light in the sky, the wise men noticed it didn't behave like the star that had led them. The first light moved and guided them. Now it sat in the sky, stationary. "Hurry, we must make haste before it disappears!" They wrangled their group and immediately set out. Through the night, they traveled. As morning loomed, the men marveled as the star stood stationary over a house. Joy filled them. "This is it! Come, brethren, let us go and see if there is a child inside."

Joseph answered the door. "Greetings. How can I help you?"

"Salutations! We are scholars, learned men of the order of the Babylonian counselor Belteshazzar, the one known in Hebrew as Daniel." Joseph did not know what to think. The magi continued, "Daniel, the great courtier who divulged the dreams of kings. We, wise men, have kept his words and his knowledge. Through the ages in our country, Babylon, the writings told of a great star that would reveal the King of the Jews."

In disbelief, Joseph looked and saw the Shekinah light over his home. Stuttering, he said, "You have come to see my son?"

Just then, the men heard the cry of a small child. Insecurely, Joseph replied, "Please come in."

The journey had been months. The wise men followed Joseph into the room where Mary sat with their son. Elated, the wise men dropped to their knees, posturing themselves before the child. They broke into praise. "Blessings and tidings from our king. The king of Babylon rejoices in the birth of the King of the Jews." The men lifted their eyes to heaven. "Truly, you are the King because the Star led us to you." They brought in the gold, frankincense, and myrrh, laying it at the child's feet. "Blessed is he of the Most High! We are witnesses! The words of our priest Daniel wrote for us to watch for the signs of the King."

As the praise finished, the star dissipated into the morning light. Joseph, who had tussled in his heart about his son, wept. First in Bethlehem, the shepherds, now men from afar. The riches they brought his son dazed him. Seeing the men bow to his son, uncertainty turned to assurance. Everything the dream had said concerning his wife and son was true. He praised God because the supernatural evidence cured his torment.

When the visitors made ready to leave, Joseph asked, "You have to leave so soon? Come, stay a little longer, and let me throw a feast in your honor."

Hugging him, they replied, "Nay, we have been on this journey for months. We must return to our king and share with him the great news that we found the child of prophecy." After they departed, they rested their caravan at a place outside the city. The men planned to rest, then revisit King Herod in the morning. Intent on keeping the promise, the scholars had no reason to hide their rejoicing. The old writings they had studied for generations proved true. As they rested, each of them had a separate dream. All were warned that Herod desired to kill the child. Sharing the dream one with another, the men realized the vision was from God. Decidedly, they traveled another route to avoid Herod and his spies. That same night, an angel came to Joseph in a dream and told him the child's life was in danger. Straightaway, he woke and followed the directions of the angel. He packed the gifts, provisions, his family, and left. He took his family to Egypt, out of the reach of Herod.

When it became clear the magi had deceived the king, Herod became unhinged. The spies quivered. They feared the rage could turn toward them. They missed the star; they failed because they didn't believe it. Tales of a great light, word of the star, cycled through rumors. Sightings reached Herod. At the time the king inquired, the caravan was still in his land. Not finding evidence of them, the spies said, "No, Lord, we cannot find any evidence of the wise men or their company."

Angrily, he turned to the spies. "If you had stayed with them, then we would have known if there was a child." All in the chamber cowered in fear. The king sat back slowly. "Those magi told me they saw the star some months ago." He gathered his thoughts. Considering the timeline from the wise men and his spies, Herod guessed the child to be a little older than a year. Lucifer, who had stood behind Herod, considered the timeline. He planted a thought inside the king. Herod called his henchmen. "Go and kill all children from the age of two and younger in Bethlehem." As he considered his words, he said, "I will not be mocked! Go and kill all the children. Find all children two years and under in all the coasts thereof and kill them too."

The loyal men bowed. "As you wish, my Lord." They left and carried out the bloody task.

It was lamented by the prophet Jeremiah: "In Rama was there a voice heard, lamentation, and weeping, and great mourning, Rachel weeping for her children, and would not be comforted, because they are not." Blood flowed through the country. The madman Herod missed the child. Joseph and his family moved out of the sphere of the slaughter.

In Egypt, God made a place of safety for the child and his parents. Joseph and Mary saw the power of God. Through the magi, they obtained wealth, enough to economically sustain them. Shepherds praised the child, and the Levitical priesthood knew the signs of the Messiah. They knew the child of prophecy was born. However, they could not find any child in the line that met their prophetic criteria. The Mosaic law spoke of a priest of the order of Melchizedek. Those of Levi believed God would show them the child of prophecy, and he would become their chief priest. The priests misread the words. The men of the Jews looked for a physical priest, not understanding the order of Melchizedek pertained to a future King of Righteousness. Born of the house of David, Yahweh came into the world. He became Adonai, meaning "my Lord," the title to a member of the Godhead. Lucifer failed in his efforts to kill the child. He knew Yahweh had entered the world because he heard the angels speak of Immanuel, the God that is with us.

CHAPTER 10

The World Sets the Stage

Five days before his death, Herod the Great named Archelaus king. On his deathbed, he ordered Israel's elite to be shut in Jerusalem's great hall, with his final order being to kill those in the hall upon his last breath. The paranoid king wanted to eliminate any opposition to the ascension of his son. The other siblings desired to rule but kept silent, remembering how their father had killed their brothers over it. So upon his father's death, Antipas challenged Archelaus for kingly rights. A great contention brewed between them, beginning to destabilize the region. Rome decided to intervene and split the kingdom. Archelaus ruled over Samaria, Judea, and Idumea, while Rome gave his brother Antipas Galilee. Of the two, Herod Archelaus proved to be an unbridled, vicious king, evil and more brutal than his brother Antipas, who was a politically distant monarch. Unlike Archelaus, Antipas desired a lavish lifestyle and wanted no part in Jewish squabbles. He surrounded himself with the Herodians, wealthy Jews who tolerated Roman authority. So when he divorced his wife Phaesalis of Nabatea to marry his half brother's wife, Herodias, the eccentric Jews looked the other way.

At this same time, Joseph and Mary still hid in Egypt. At the death of Herod, an angel appeared to Joseph in a dream, saying, "Arise. Take the young child and his mother, and go into the land of Israel. For they are dead who sought the young child's life." The family gathered their possessions and began traveling to Israel. Their first thought was to return to Bethlehem. As they entered their home-

ANGEL'S INFLUENCE

land, an angel warned of the cruelty of Archelaus, who ruled over Bethlehem. Fearful that Archelaus would continue to look for their son, Joseph turned to Nazareth, where an indifferent Antipas ruled. The decision fulfilled the prophecy that Jesus would be known as a Nazarene.

Joseph and Mary did what they could to keep their son safe. During their time in Egypt, his divine aura naturally flowed. Occasionally and innocently, hints of power seeped out. Both parents discouraged it, fearful it would raise suspicion. But now in Nazareth, a little older, Jesus understood the importance of control. Often, his mother kept him inside, helping her. Joseph daily took Jesus into his shop, teaching him carpentry. God the Father chose no better parents to shield his Son during his formative years. Knowing the task before them, they constantly prayed for guidance. Fear was always present; it drove them to keep the child secret. Jesus grew up good-natured. He kept the commandments and controlled his divine impulses. However, both Joseph and Mary knew that at some point the world would find him. But that was not theirs to decide; both kept their son close at hand. They trusted no one.

Jesus looked to God but had not yet connected with the Spirit of God. Like men, Jesus experienced the pulls of the flesh; his human self fought against his divine self. It was the time of innocence when children learned right from wrong. His divine knowledge developed as he learned to speak. Joseph, Mary, and the angels gave him the atmosphere to thrive. At any time, he had the authority to call on angels, command subjugation, and force human will. If he would have, breaking the curse would have been impossible. He voluntarily shed his divinity, shutting his power down. Jesus had to live, breathe, and walk as a man. Being human did not garner special access. Temptation came with the package, the task to live in sin yet be sinless.

When Jesus was twelve years old, the family traveled to Jerusalem for the Passover. About a day into the journey home, Joseph and Mary looked for their son among the relatives. Being the family caravan large in number, they realized they had left Jesus behind. Hurriedly, they returned to Jerusalem. For three days, Joseph and Mary looked

71

for their son. Hysterical, they hurried back to the temple, hoping the priest could somehow assist them. They had taken great pains to conceal him; both had worked so hard to protect him. Panic overtook Mary; she felt out of control. Entering the temple, she found Jesus sitting in the middle of teachers. The learned men sat amazed at the boy's words. They pelted the young man with questions and hung on his every word.

Mary said to her son, "Son, why have you treated us this way? Behold, your father and I have been anxiously looking for you."

Jesus saw her fear. "Why were you searching for me? Didn't you know I had to be in my Father's house?" Joseph and Mary knew Jesus would decide the time to reveal his identity. They knew angels hovered around them. They also knew darkness loomed in every corner and in every heart.

The Father charged the angels to watch. Commanded not to directly interfere in the dealings of men, the holy cherubs became spectators. Men were allowed to act of their own volition. In a minimal sense, the angels could alter circumstances, but their battlefront lay mainly in the spiritual realm. Like they did with Noah, they repelled activity that veered too close. They formed a wide hedge to veil the spiritual eyes that were searching for the child. Angels did their assignments; they sheltered Jesus from the minions that sought him. God allowed one exception; He gave them permission to keep him safe from harm. However, Lucifer, his angels, and his demons had no such parameters. Satan could influence and possess men. He knew the child's location geographically, but he could not find him. The angelic hedge gave it away, but it was too wide. God used his cherubs to take advantage of vague prophetic clues. They moved circumstances and allowed the kindness of others to shelter the child. Lucifer quickly realized killing the child would not be simple. To kill Yahweh, he would need the angels of heaven to forsake him. *If I could corrupt him, they would deem him unfit*, he thought. So Satan knew he had to do more than kill him; the Son had to sin.

At the same time, God was preparing his cousin John. His father, Zechariah, of the lineage of Aaron, did not believe. When the angel told Zechariah his unborn son was set aside, he doubted. For

ANGEL'S INFLUENCE

his weak faith, God muted his speech. As instructed by the angel, Elizabeth named her son John. Not a name in the family tree, many protested to Zechariah to resist his wife. To take a name outside the lineage prompted questions about whether the child be of true inheritance. Zechariah motioned for a tablet. The men implored him to write the correct name of his son. Zechariah looked at his wife. He knew what the angel had told him. He knew the loss of his speech was due to disbelief. Throughout the pregnancy, each attempt to communicate reminded him of his lack of faith. The angel, his wife, his speech became a testimony to his soul. The experiences of the past months opened his heart. It tore down his Levitical profundities. He turned his eyes to the tablet and wrote John. As soon as he resisted the pressure of his Levitical companions, the gift of speech returned to him. Words bottled up for eight months gushed out of Zechariah. He prophesied his son was the forerunner of the Messiah.

John was about five months older than Jesus. When Herod ordered the killing of male boys two years and younger, Elizabeth took him and fled into the wilderness. Herod's henchmen came to the temple to ask Zechariah where he had hidden his son. Failing to give an answer, they killed him where he stood. Living in the wilderness strengthened John. God sent an angel to look over the mother and child. Elizabeth, being an aged woman, had difficulty rearing her son. Living off locusts and wild honey, both found the solitude of the wilderness hard yet comforting. Isolation fostered fellowship; John turned his eyes to the Lord at an early age. In the manner of David, who daily meditated on the Lord, John dedicated himself to God. He grew strong, a brawny man who wore a garment made of camel's hair, held together by a goatskin belt. Very few lived in the wilderness, a place filled with deep ravines and rocky terrain, barren stretches with scant vegetation, making it an inhospitable place.

When God told him it was time, John came out of the wilderness. Filled with the Spirit, he emerged from the lower Jordan valley, preaching the coming arrival of the Messiah. John knew the Savior was alive because he had met him in the womb. With fire in his belly, he preached repentance, for the kingdom of God is at hand. Announcing the Light of the World has come, the One whose sandals he was not worthy to untie, John shouted and declared the coming kingdom, urging anyone who listened to repent and be baptized. Quickly, he became known as "the Baptist" because he baptized many in the name of the Lord.

It had been four hundred years since the Jews had witnessed miracles, four hundred years forgetting what the power of God felt like. Now a prophet was preparing the way for the greatest of miracles. Many desperate souls clamored for the words of the Baptist, but his baptism held no power. Herod feared him because John exposed him. The Pharisees and Sanhedrin scoffed at him, seeing him as nothing more than a wild man. He did not threaten their Jewish leadership. One thing piqued their interest: John's words concerning the Messiah. The Messiah of the Scriptures could change their influence over the people. Whispers swirled about whether the Messiah lay within their ranks. The leaders of the Jews wondered how the legal structure they had built would fit in with the man of prophecy. Lucifer had long ago corrupted the keepers of the law. The Levitical system was a den of vipers that used their influence to burden the people. John refused to placate them. The small and the great didn't matter; all have sinned and fallen short of the glory of God.

John was an easy man to find, baptizing daily at the place known as "Bethany beyond the Jordan." Many compared him to Elijah. Dunking believers under the water, he would say, "I baptize you with water, but there will come another who will baptize you with fire and the Holy Spirit." Each day, he emphasized the coming of the Man of God. One day, John saw Jesus coming down to the riverbank. He saw the emanating aura of the Spirit. "Behold the Lamb of God who takes away the sins of the world." Confused why the Son of God would come to him, John asked, "I need to be baptized by you, and do you come to me?"

Jesus replied, "Let it be so now, for thus it is fitting for us to fulfill all righteousness." John, hip-deep in water, fell to his knees. Jesus waded to his cousin. Both had run from persecution; both were hidden and protected from the evils of the day. John splashed his way back to his feet, placed his hand on the forehead of Jesus, and baptized him. When Jesus came out of the water, he went straight

ANGEL'S INFLUENCE

up. The heavens above him opened. John and all there saw the Spirit of God descend upon his head like a dove. The Spirit of the Father connected with Jesus. All heard a voice from heaven break through the stillness. "This is my beloved Son, in whom I am well pleased." A demon assigned to John heard the voice from heaven. Straightaway, it left and announced to Lucifer that he had found the child of prophecy now grown into a man.

That day, Jesus changed the meaning of baptism. John performed a physical action that held no binding authority, an activity that symbolized mending the divide between God and men. John knew neither would cross paths again. The events of the baptism of Jesus gave credence to his message. There was no denying the heavens opened. All witnessed the brilliant Spirit descend. Word spread of a man whom the Spirit of God had touched. Everyone in attendance heard John refer to Jesus as the Savior. The witnesses went out and told others John had identified the Messiah. The baptism marked the starting point of the ministry of Jesus. Word spread across the land. The news made its way to the leaders of the Jews and Herod.

CHAPTER 11

Temptations and Betrayal

John the Baptist became a thorn in the side of Herod Antipas, known as Herod the Tetrarch. John constantly condemned him over his incestuous marriage, noting that his niece Salome was the daughter of his new wife. The Jews called such a relationship "uncovering a brother's nakedness." John took every opportunity to expose the union. His wife, Herodias, hated the Baptist and wanted him dead. Eventually, Herod felt compelled to arrest John. He did this to placate his wife because John had been saying, "It is not lawful for you to have her." Although Herod found his teachings puzzling, he liked listening to him. He also knew many thought John to be Elijah brought back from the dead. His dilemma was clear: Antipas wanted to kill John for his wife but feared the people. Incarceration became the solution to his predicament since it limited the taunts and gave John protection from assassination. Herodias decided to plot a scheme to corner her passive husband. During his birthday celebration, Antipas became full of wine. Knowing he lusted after her beautiful daughter, Herodias asked Salome to dance at the party. An intoxicated Antipas, excited over her erotic dance, granted his niece a wish. As planned by her mother, she demanded the head of the Baptist. Bound by an oath in front of guests, a distressed Herod honored the request. His soldiers beheaded the prophet and brought his head to Salome on a platter.

Lucifer played on the insecurities of Herod. When Antipas heard of Jesus, he feared it was John the Baptist back to torment

ANGEL'S INFLUENCE

him. Above all else, he did not want to further rile the people. Faced with another prophet loved by many, Herod considered an indirect approach. Hoping his Jewish friends, the Herodians, could supply a solution, he asked for their help. The Herodians teamed up with the Pharisees to entrap Jesus in his words. Some Galilean leaders attempted to scare him. They sent word to him that Herod Antipas desired to kill him. Undaunted, Jesus replied, "Go tell that fox, 'Behold, I cast out devils, and I will continue to cure until the day I am perfected. Nevertheless, I must walk today, tomorrow, and the following day, for it cannot be that a prophet perish out of Jerusalem.'" The words jabbed the Jewish establishment. They knew Jewish authorities had a long history of killing prophets. His snarky reply pricked the corrupt bunch; Jesus fueled their ire. When word came back to Herod about how Jesus answered, he distanced himself. The prophet John had scarred his character. Herod did not want another righteous man to openly expose him.

Satan used many sources to tempt Jesus. Political and spiritual leaders followed him; the Herodians watched him; at every turn, Lucifer influenced men to test him. Yet none were able to outwit him. Lucifer decided to take Yahweh head-on. Led by the Spirit, Jesus learned the intent of Satan. He knew opening himself to Lucifer was risky. So Jesus began to pray and fast. Waiting for a moment of vulnerability, Satan noted how greatly weakened he had become. After fasting for forty days and nights, Lucifer presented himself before Christ. Knowing his fast had left him near starvation, he said, "If you are the Son of God, command that these stones become bread." With only the angels present, he implored him, "Turn it into bread. You created this stone. Surely you can turn it into something to eat."

Jesus answered, "It is written: 'Man shall not live by bread alone, but by every word that proceeds from the mouth of God.'"

In frustration, he lifted Jesus to the pinnacle of the Jewish temple. Looking down, he demanded, "Throw yourself down, fake god. Surely the angels will save you." Deep in his belly, he hoped Christ would heed his challenges; he wanted the angels to lose faith in him. Using the Scriptures, he said, "If you are the Son of God, throw yourself down. For it is written: 'He shall give his angels charge over you, and in their hands, they shall bear you up, lest you dash your foot against a stone.'" *Just heed my words*, Lucifer thought.

Jesus responded, "It is also written: 'You shall not tempt the Lord your God.'"

The words upset Lucifer because Yahweh implied he was his God. Thoroughly ticked, Satan carried him to a high mountain. Spanning his hand over all the kingdoms that were his, he said, "See all this? All these things I will give you if you will fall down and worship me!"

With the strength of the Spirit, Jesus firmly replied, "Away with you, Satan! For it is written: 'You shall worship the Lord your God, and Him only you shall serve.'"

Yet another deep cut, the words of Christ embarrassed the angel. Lucifer thought, *How dare he tell me I should worship him!* Knowing angels in heaven and on earth watched, Lucifer decided to leave. To resist the command would ignite an angelic conflict. Once Satan left, angels came and ministered to Jesus. The heavenly host saw how the Father heard his prayers. They saw Jesus strengthen because he submitted to the Father. Noting his hunger, the angels brought him food. As with the prophets of old, they refreshed him.

Hot with displeasure, Lucifer's hatred overflowed into men. Satan stoked the Pharisees and Sadducees to shadow Jesus, wanting them to use their authority to expose him. Moving legal and spiritual leaders to collaborate with the Herodians, Satan used everything at his disposal. With no justifiable cause, the priests gathered their resources, hoping to bind Jesus within the law. They got word that the disciples had crossed over the brook of Kidron. Summoning the follower Judas, the leaders knew the disciple was not what he seemed. As the keeper of the coin, he constantly slipped himself tribute. As the one who paid for expenses, Judas had no qualms about padding his pockets. With a self-serving heart, it was easy for the Pharisees to approach him. A man molded by the state, Judas was a perfect instrument and quickly became their informant. In return, the priests gave Judas the recognition he coveted. Their attention bolstered his importance, leading Judas to believe he could be the one to unite the Pharisees behind Christ. Their favor satisfied his pride, and

ANGEL'S INFLUENCE

in time, the priests coaxed Judas into divulging a means of meeting Jesus, expressing an interest to speak to him privately before publicly declaring allegiance. They carefully spun it, inquiring if he was the righteous branch they would follow. The men deceived Judas, letting him believe they wanted to support Jesus.

From speaking to Judas, the priests knew he loved him. They knew there was no grudge, no wedge between them. Understanding Judas believed Jesus to be a political figure, the priests set out to capitalize on their shared hatred for Rome. They hyped the idea of Jesus being the one to unite the people. Unknown to Judas, the chief priests and scribes sought how to take Jesus by craft and put him to death. They tricked Judas into believing they were like-minded. The possibilities excited Judas; he didn't see his actions as betrayal. He had witnessed the power of Christ countless times and knew no one could harm his Master. The Jewish leadership planted a thought, and Judas entertained it. It was not difficult to get him to this point; Satan had been prepping Judas for some time. Jesus knew what was swirling in the head of his disciple and also knew Lucifer conspired in the heart of Judas. Each side made their moves: one having authority but choosing to refrain, the other using all power at their disposal.

Earlier that day, Jesus and the disciples went to Bethany to pay Simon the Leper a visit. While there, a woman came into the house carrying an alabaster box of precious ointments. Rare and exotic, the extract inside came from an East Indian plant, a Himalayan aromatic of the ginseng family. Alabaster boxes, made of soft white onyx marble, came in intricate carvings and beautiful shapes. Walking in front of Jesus, she stopped and broke the seal of the box. Immediately, the scent of the oil permeated the room. Pleasant to the smell, all knew it was very expensive. Standing before Jesus, Mary anointed his feet and wiped them with her hair. Enraged, Judas could barely hold his composure, immediately expressing displeasure. "Why was this waste of ointment made?" The value of the ointment, equivalent to a year's wages, incensed Judas. He stammered, "That might have been sold for three hundred pence. We could have given that to the poor." His anger infected the others; they began to murmur against the woman.

Inwardly, Judas coveted the oil. Outwardly, his indignation stirred everyone in the room. Jesus replied, "Let her alone. Why trouble ye the woman? She hath wrought a good work upon me." Jesus looked at the woman and caressed her face. "The poor you have with you always, and whensoever you may do them good, but me, you will not have always." Looking at Judas, Jesus continued, "She hath done what she could. What she has done beforehand is to anoint my body to the burying. This is my burial ointment." Totally confused, Judas held his place, failing to comprehend. The others tried to process what Jesus meant. Knowing this, Jesus addressed them, "Verily I say unto you, wheresoever this gospel shall be preached throughout the whole world, this also that she hath done shall be spoken of for a memorial to her." The disciples absorbed the importance of the words. However, Judas remained silently smoldering. Satan moved his avarice consciousness; Judas became more disillusioned. His hope for a political Messiah stunted, hardness filled his soul. Bitter, Judas realized he needed to do more than coordinate a meeting. To push Jesus to use his power against the enemies of Israel, he had to force a conflict.

From that point, Judas continually contemplated betrayal. He knew the chief priests wanted to question Jesus before the high day. He also realized Passover fell tomorrow, and the people needed to present their sacrifices. From tomorrow noon until the sun ebbed below the horizon, the temple would sacrifice lambs. It was the time between the sunsets, the day blood would flow over the altar. Each family readied their lambs in preparation for Passover. It was an important holiday for the Jews because tomorrow, the people would submit their offering, take it home, and roast their lambs in anticipation of the Feast of Unleavened Bread. When Jesus announced they would eat later and head to the garden, Judas knew the seclusion was perfect. Slipping away, he went to the chief priests.

Hearing the news, the priests were grateful and promised Judas a monetary reward. Fearing that being gone too long would bring suspicion, Judas returned to the disciples. Upon his return, he found the apostles preparing a large room. Unknown to Judas, Jesus had instructed the disciples to follow a man carrying a pitcher. In faith,

ANGEL'S INFLUENCE

they went into the city and found the man. Following him, the man led them to a house. Entering the house, they asked to speak to the master of the house. Following the instruction of Jesus, they said to the man, "The Master says to you, 'Where is the guest chamber, where I shall eat the Passover with my disciples?'" The master of the house took the men to a large, fully furnished upper room. Seeing his fellow disciples busy, Judas easily blended back into the group. Like silk sliding down a chair, he went and procured items for the meal. The other disciples never noticed his absence. It was not uncommon for Judas to purchase essentials for the group.

As evening fell, Judas, along with the others, went to the room. The meal prepared, all necessities set, the twelve along with Jesus sat down at the table. As they were eating, Jesus said, "Verily I say unto you, one of you who eats with me shall betray me." Fear washed over Judas. How could he know? The disciples marveled at the thought. Astonished, each questioned themselves how such an act was possible. None foresaw the thoughts and motivation of Judas. When asked which one was the betrayer, he answered, "He who dips his hand in the dish with me." The answer was even more confusing since all had dipped a piece of bread or meat into the bowl. Jesus continued, "The Son of man indeed goes, as it is written of him. But woe to that man by whom the Son of man is betrayed! Good were it for that man if he had never been born."

Dipping bread from the same bowl was a common practice of hospitality and fellowship. With his words, Jesus turned the tradition into a device of betrayal, symbolic of intent; the betrayer was close and intimate. Peter beckoned John to ask who it was the Master spoke of. Out of the twelve, only John heard the identity of the traitor. He heard what Jesus said because he had laid his head on his bosom. So when Judas silently whispered to Jesus, "Is it I?" John heard Jesus whisper as he gave Judas a sop of bread, "Thou hast said." Perched above, Lucifer listened. Judas's eyes grew dark because Satan possessed him. For a short moment, the prince of this world and the Son of God glared at each other. Speaking directly to Lucifer, Jesus said, "What you do, do quickly." Inside, Lucifer smiled. Judas ate the sop and left. Being the keeper of the purse, the others never thought

81

anything of his departure. They figured Judas was asked to run and purchase something for the Master.

Peter looked at John. He could see his veins pop, yet he remained quiet. The uneasiness diminished as the meal continued, awkwardness turning to laughter. The group had been through so much; each saw a brother across the table. Jesus interrupted the merriment, gesturing for their attention. The men watched as he quietly took some bread, blessed it, broke off a piece, and gave each a part, saying, "Take, eat. This is my body." The words Jesus said when the woman poured oil on him still haunted them. All the men knew oil anointing happened at death; it was how mourners prepared a body. Now they listened to Jesus telling them to partake of his body. While they were attentively listening, Jesus picked up a cup, blessed the wine, and said, "This is my blood of the New Testament, which is shed for many for the remission of sins. Verily I say unto you, I will drink no more of the fruit of the vine until that day when I drink it new in the kingdom of God." More perplexed, the disciples wanted to ask Jesus what all this meant. Instead, they sat silent, sipping the wine as they looked at each other. What unsettled the men most was when the Master knelt down and washed their feet.

By now it was nightfall. Filling the night with song, the men followed Jesus out of the room. As they were walking, Jesus said, "All ye shall be offended because of me this night. For it is written, 'I will smite the shepherd, and the sheep shall be scattered.'" Stunned, the men grew anxious over the cryptic messages. Their Master had been saying unusual things all day. Jesus confused them more, "But after that I am risen, I will go before you into Galilee." Risen, blood, anointed burial—nothing was making sense to them.

Out of the silence of the night, Peter said, "Although all shall be offended, yet will not I."

Jesus replied, "Verily I say unto thee, that this day, even in this night, before the cock crow twice, thou shalt deny me thrice." The response stifled Peter; he stood dumbfounded.

Determined to declare loyalty, Peter said, "Master, I tell you now, if I should die with thee, I will not deny thee in any wise." The other disciples, hearing this, chimed in with their loyalties. Jesus

ANGEL'S INFLUENCE

began to walk towards the river. He said no more to Peter; the lack of response stabbed him. Crossing the river, the men went into the garden. It had been a confusingly strange day. Amazed to find a room during the busiest time, all assumed Judas had secured it. Normally, finding a room in the city during Passover was impossible; the disciples chalked it up to Judas. They assumed the Master had passed on the preparations to Judas, which is why none of them thought anything strange when Judas appeared later in the day. Now all were with Jesus except for one: Judas Iscariot.

Judas had come too far to turn back. Arriving at the house of Ananias, he asked what price he would receive for setting up a secret meeting. Both parties agreed upon thirty pieces of silver. The chief priests straightway paid Judas. Judas told them Jesus and the others would most likely spend the night in Gethsemane, a quiet garden that often provided a place for rest and prayer, a grove surrounded by olive trees. Judas knew Jesus cherished its beauty and seclusion.

Now in the garden, Jesus told the disciples, "Sit ye here, while I pray." All took rest, except for Peter, John, and James. The men followed Jesus a little further into the garden. He asked them, "My soul is exceedingly sorrowful unto death. Tarry ye here and watch." The three watched as Jesus walked a little further into the trees.

Barely out of sight, he fell to the ground, weeping and praying. Jesus pleaded with his Father that the hour might pass from him. Flesh shaking and full of despair, he asked his Father for strength. The prayer was intense, so heavy that Jesus began to perspire blood. He begged his Father, "O my Father, if it be possible, let this cup pass from me." He had come too far to stop, yet the weight was unbearable. He cried, "Abba, Father, all things are possible unto thee. Nevertheless, not what I will, but what thou wilt." His human self rebelled; Christ found himself in an internal struggle. An array of human emotions bore down on him; he kept repeating, "Not my will but your will be done." Lifting himself off his knees, he checked on his watchers and found them asleep. Shaking Peter, he said, "Simon, sleepest thou? Couldst not thou watch one hour?" By now, it was close to midnight. Awakening the men, Jesus charged them, "Watch ye and pray, lest ye enter into temptation. The spirit is truly ready, but the flesh is weak." He left them once again, praying the same words, "O Father, if this cup may not pass away from me, except I drink it, thy will be done." After a few minutes, he checked on the men and found them asleep once more. Heaviness overtook them; John, Peter, and James lacked endurance. Returning to pray, Jesus submitted himself to his Father until he knew Judas was near. Again, he found the men asleep. He did not wake them right away but said softly, "Sleep on now and take your rest. It is enough. The hour is come." When he knew the men with Judas were steps away, Jesus woke his companions. Walking back to the rest, he firmly roused them, "Behold, the Son of man is betrayed into the hands of sinners. Rise, let us go. Lo, he that betrayed me is at hand." Immediately, while he spoke, Judas appeared out of the darkness.

The elders gave Judas a select band of men with swords and staves, carrying lanterns and torches. They waited for the sign, a greeting kiss Judas would give. As their lights chased the night away, Judas walked up to Jesus, saying, "Master, Master," and kissed him. He peered into Judas's soul as he pulled back from the kiss. "Friend, wherefore art thou come?"

Looking at the company of men, Jesus asked, "Whom seek ye?" Christ already knew these were men influenced by Satan.

An answer came out of the group, "Jesus of Nazareth." Judas backed away.

With the authority that is his, Jesus declared, "I am he."

Immediately, the words confounded them. The power of the voice, the God saying "I am," spooked them. The divinity evident, the words made the company faint. Frightened, those who came to take Jesus hid themselves. For a microsecond, the godhead of Yahweh seeped out. They trembled.

Seeing what he had done, Jesus regained his composure and asked again, "Whom seek ye?"

Fearfully buckled on the ground, they said, "We seek Jesus of Nazareth."

Once more, Jesus responded, "I have told you that I am he." The men slowly regained their strength and stood on their feet.

ANGEL'S INFLUENCE

Looking at the group, Jesus said, "Are ye come out, as against a thief, with swords and staves to take me? I was daily with you in the temple teaching, and ye took me not, but the scriptures must be fulfilled." He gestured to his disciples, "If you seek me, let these go their way."

Out of the twelve, Peter carried a sword. He wore it to protect the group during their travels. Watching Judas kiss Jesus on the cheek, it dawned on Peter that the kiss was one of betrayal. Anger began to build; the thought of these men grabbing hold of his Master unhinged him. Peter drew his sword and swung wildly, cutting off the ear of Malchus, a servant of the high priest. Malchus grabbed his ear and reeled in pain. Immediately, Jesus held Peter's arm. "Put up thy sword into the sheath." Like a parent scolding a child, Jesus said, "All they that take the sword shall perish with the sword. Thinkest thou that I cannot now pray to my Father, and he shall presently give me more than twelve legions of angels?" He asked Peter, "But how then shall the scriptures of the prophets be fulfilled, that thus it must be? This cup which my Father hath given me, shall I not drink it?" The anger in Peter subsided. Confused and tense, he slowly returned the sword to its sheath. Jesus picked up the ear. Gingerly pulling Malchus's hands from his face, he placed the ear back where it had been cut and healed him.

With Jesus in custody, the men turned to grab the disciples. Scattering in all directions, the apostles dispersed throughout the garden. One apostle had but a linen cloth around his body. Pulling away from the captors, he left the cloth in their hands and ran through the garden naked. Knowing what had to be done, Jesus allowed the men to take him. Lucifer kept the men in a psychotic state, focusing them on the task at hand. Once they had secured him, Satan released their minds and allowed the men to regain their strength. The ones that chased the apostles returned empty-handed. Binding Jesus, the group walked out of the garden and into the night.

CHAPTER 12

The Trial and Conviction of a God

They marched Jesus to the home of an influential man named Ananias. Ananias had summoned his son-in-law the high priest Caiaphas along with certain elders and scribes. Knowing Judas was bringing Jesus, they gathered in anticipation. Reappearing from the depths of the garden, Peter followed the group. Keeping his distance, he was concerned for the welfare of his Master. Seeing men take Jesus to the home of the former high priest, he stood outside and warmed himself. It was early; darkness still prevailed. Peter noticed another disciple approaching. Panicked and in disbelief, he ran to greet him. It was John emerging from the darkness, whose presence calmed Peter. Returning the greeting, John came to speak to those who had taken Jesus. Excited to see another brethren, Peter walked with John and held the door for him. Once inside, he inquired about the reason they had taken Jesus. Ananias did not want to arouse the people, uncertain of how they would react to Jesus's arrest. Very few knew he had Christ in custody. To keep it quiet, Ananias gave John a vague answer, telling him Jesus was under questioning. As John exited, the doorkeeper asked Peter, "Art not thou also one of this man's disciples?"

Quickly, Peter snapped, "I am not." Fearfully, Peter moved away from the door and quickly returned to the coals to warm his hands among the servants and officers.

ANGEL'S INFLUENCE

Inside, Ananias presented several false witnesses, contrived witnesses who could not keep their story straight. Not allowing the failure to deter him, Ananias asked, "We are interested in your followers. Are they men that would influence the people?"

An elder chimed in, "What exactly is your doctrine?"

Jesus replied, "I spoke openly to the world. I always taught in the synagogue and in the temple, where the Jews always resort. Never in secret have I said anything." Jesus questioned, "Why ask me? Ask them which heard me. They know what I have said."

One of the officers, listening, struck Jesus with the palm of his hand, asking disdainfully, "Answerest thou the high priest so?" A subordinate priest took issue with his answer.

Calmly, Jesus raised his head and said, "If I have spoken evil, bear witness of the evil; but if well, why smitest thou me?"

Their attempts to find a credible witness failed. Many testified against him, saying, "We heard him say, 'I will destroy this temple made with hands, and within three days, I will build another made without hands.'" Poorly colluding, the scripted witnesses' testimonies conflicted.

Ananias asked Jesus, "Answerest thou nothing? What is it which these witness against thee?" Jesus said nothing. Again, the high priest asked him, "Art thou the Christ, the Son of the Blessed?" Bluntly, the question was asked repeatedly. "I adjure thee by the living God, that thou tell us whether thou be the Christ, the Son of God."

Jesus answered, "I am, and ye shall see the Son of man sitting on the right hand of power, and coming in the clouds of heaven."

Ananias rented his clothes and said, "What need we any further witnesses?" Looking at his peers, he said, "Ye have heard the blasphemy. What think ye?" All present condemned Jesus to be guilty of death. Some spat on him; they blindfolded him, covered his face in spit, and slapped him, saying, "Prophesy to us, who is going to strike you next?" The servants of the leaders hit him with open palms, mocking him, "Prophesy unto us, thou Christ. Who is he that smote thee?"

Peter, still standing with the servants, watched the door. One of the men around the coals noted Peter, "Art not thou also one of his disciples?" A maid coming up to the palace looked at Peter and said, "And thou also wast with Jesus of Nazareth."

Peter became rattled. Fear washed through his bones. "I am not," he said. Another servant, having been part of the arresting party, was certain it was Peter who cut off Malchus's ear.

A distant relation to Malchus, the man asked, "Did I not see thee in the garden with him?"

Peter relied on his Galilean dialect. He looked at the servants. "I know not, neither understand I what you are saying."

Light of day was creeping above the horizon. Peter walked away from them to the gateway. Again, a maid walked by him. She said to her fellow servants, "This is one of them." Peter, now frantic, shook his head.

Another servant said, "Surely thou art a Galilean. Your speech agrees thereto. Your dialect is that of a Galilean."

Peter began to curse and swear. "I know not this man of whom ye speak." Without warning, a cock crowed. A few seconds later, it crowed again. The color left Peter's face; he remembered what Jesus told him: Before the cock crows, you shall deny me three times. Peter grabbed his face and wept sorely.

The interrogation did not go anywhere. Ananias could not create a solid case against Jesus. As he stared at him, he recalled a discussion between Caiaphas and some Jews. In that discussion, Caiaphas surmised it was suitable for one man to die for the people. Unknown to Caiaphas, his words were prophetic. In truth, it was more expedient for him and his priests that Jesus should die. Jesus threatened the structure they had so painstakingly built. They wanted to be rid of him before the feast day; the problem was how to go about it. Ananias decided to leave it to Caiaphas, being he was the current high priest. Listening in, Satan was pleased to hear their intent to condemn Jesus and influenced the men to make their plan a reality. *Everything is going as designed*, he thought. Lucifer's scheme to kill Yahweh seemed inevitable.

However, according to trial decorum, the presumption of innocence until proven guilty applied. With no clear charges, Caiaphas could not openly examine Jesus. Up to this point, he had played the

ANGEL'S INFLUENCE

role of observer. Having to be hands-off did not interfere with discussing it before the Sanhedrin. It was decided that High Priest Caiaphas would formulate some official charges. Some of the Sadducees proposed assassination. The Pharisees rejected the suggestion since it could rile the people. All concluded a trial must happen with a clear indictment and sentence. To not do this could risk claims of corruption. The outcome of Ananias's questioning was relayed to Caiaphas. Those present read what transpired: As accounted, an elder asked him if he was the Christ; he responded with, "I am." When asked whether he was the Christ, the Son of God, he responded, "You have said it." Jesus further added, "But I say to all of you: In the future, you will see the Son of Man sitting at the right hand of the Mighty One and coming on the clouds of heaven." The report ended with the account of the priests tearing their robes, screaming he had broken the Mosaic law. The report finished with Christ, the accused, silent. When the leaders of the Sanhedrin heard it, they cried blasphemy.

By daylight, Jesus was presented to the court of the Sanhedrin, bound like a criminal. One of the elders asked, "Art thou the Christ?"

Jesus responded, "If I tell you, you will not believe. And if I also ask you, you will not answer me, nor let me go." All in the council sat silent. Jesus broke the silence. "Hereafter shall the Son of Man sit on the right hand of the power of God." Caiaphas had heard enough and straightway read the charges. With no objections, the court found Jesus guilty and sentenced him to death. However, fear of the people still loomed. The men did not want to be blamed for his judgment. Caiaphas could see only one option: present him before Pilate, the Roman prefect. For Rome to condemn Jesus, they needed a good charge. Rome did not care about Jewish politics. Only a charge that would directly threaten the empire would pique the interest of Rome. So it was decided to claim Jesus was plotting insurrection.

All agreed to deliver him to Pilate. The chief priest and elders decided to tell the procurator that Jesus declared himself "King of the Jews." Spinning the premise that Christ intended to take the region from Rome would suffice. Taking Jesus away, they made their way to Pilate. The sun soundly into the sky, the Jewish leadership pressed for an audience with the official of Rome. The men knew if Pilate condemned Jesus, the matter of the people would be of no consequence.

Notified by his servants that his judgment was needed, Pilate went out to the crowd. He looked at the leaders of the people and asked, "What accusation bring ye against this man?"

Like an eruption, many voices shouted out, "He is a malefactor, an evildoer. He perverted the nation and refused to give tribute to Caesar. He called himself Christ, a king."

Staring at the crowd, Pilate took Jesus into the hall of judgment. Now mid-morning, light presented itself in all directions. He looked upon Jesus. A long silence scratched the air. Pilate broke the silence. "Art thou the King of the Jews?"

Christ looked up to him, eyes of sincerity, piercing clearly through Pilate's soul. "Thou sayest it."

After another long pause, Pilate responded, "Hear thou not how many things they witness against thee?" Jesus remained silent. Pilate marveled at his silence. The quiet dominated Pilate. After a great pause and inquisitive pondering, Pilate returned to those who had brought Jesus to him. With decisiveness, he announced, "I find no fault in this man." The crowd, led by the chief priests, yelled how Jesus stirred up the people. Screams of how his teachings affected everyone from Galilee to Jerusalem. The response shocked and stunned Pilate.

Baffled, Pilate asked again, "What accusation bring ye against this man?" Voices in the crowd shouted, "If he were not a malefactor, we would not have delivered him to thee." They screamed over and over that, Jesus claimed to be the King of the Jews. Raising his hands to quiet them, he asked, "Take him and judge him according to your law."

The Jews shouted, "It is not lawful for us to put any man to death."

Looking at them as an inconvenience, Pilate turned and went into the judgment hall. He asked Jesus, "Art thou the King of the Jews?"

Jesus asked, "Sayest thou this thing of thyself, or did others tell it of me?"

ANGEL'S INFLUENCE

Pilate chuckled. "Am I a Jew?"

The men kept eye contact. "Thine own nation and the chief priests have delivered thee unto me."

Curious, Pilate asked, "What hast thou done?"

Jesus answered, "My kingdom is not of this world. If my kingdom were of this world, then would my servants fight, that I should not be delivered to the Jews? My kingdom is not from hence."

Pilate smirked. He bantered whether Jesus was sane or not. He asked, "Art thou a king?"

Jesus replied, "Thou sayest that I am a king. To this end was I born, and for this cause came I into the world, that I should bear witness unto the truth. Everyone that is of the truth hears my voice."

Astounded by the answer, Pilate asked, "What is truth?" He found no fault and felt it was a matter for the Jews.

The Jewish leaders stirred the crowd into a frenzy. Just a couple of days ago, the people revered Jesus. They laid palms before him as he rode a donkey into the city. Lucifer's demons possessed many in the crowd. The people seemed out of their minds. The crowd cried "Crucify! Crucify!"

A furor so great, they put aside their disdain for Rome and yelled, "Crucify him! Crucify him!"

When Pilate asked, "Should I crucify your king?" the chief priests answered, "We have no king but Caesar."

The angels who loved Jesus hovered in anxiety. The Father commanded them to restrain themselves. With pained faces, the host in heaven watched the Son endure a degrading, ungodly onslaught. No priest or leader had ever swayed loyalty like Jesus. The Jewish leaders waited outside the Praetorium. The Passover was drawing near, and none wanted to be defiled. The governor of Judea, Pilate, normally resided at the port in Caesarea. With rumors of rebellion in the air, he came to the city during the festival to observe the populace in Jerusalem closely and ferret out troublemakers. His presence became a perfect convenience for the chief priests and elders.

Pilate, not interested in prosecuting Jesus, asked the Jewish leaders a question, "Is this man a Galilean?" Desperate to be finished with this, he knew Galilee fell under Herod's jurisdiction. Hearing that Jesus began teaching there, the answer gave him an out.

The leaders responded, "Yes, he is a Galilean."

Pleased, Pilate, knowing Herod was in Jerusalem, responded, "He is a Galilean. He is one of Herod's subjects. You will find proper judgment through him." A shrewd politician, Pilate skillfully removed himself from the situation. He had more serious matters; rumors of rebellion were in the air. His goal was to maintain control, Pilate was not interested in fueling resistance. The last thing Pilate wanted was a trial that could further affect stability. Sending Jesus to Herod proved to be a diplomatic gesture. The two men disliked each other; the opportunity to smooth the relationship became an incidental bonus. The head of the Sanhedrin and the high priests glared at Pilate. There was nothing else they could say; his words were final. The men took Jesus to Herod.

Of the two palaces Herod had in the city, he was lodging in the palace to the west. When word came to Herod that men of Judah had brought Jesus to stand before him, he was exceedingly glad. Herod had heard of Jesus. He had heard of the miracles him and his disciples performed. Many stories swirled concerning Christ; Antipas desired a miracle. With glee in his heart, he could not believe Jesus stood before him. His heart paced; Herod could not hide his excitement. He questioned Jesus, "It has been told to me that you have blasphemed against God. It has also been told to me that you claim to be God." Jesus stood silent. Glaring, Herod asked, "Are you the King of the Jews?"

Immediately the priests and scribes cried, "He said it!"

Another voice shouted, "He said he would destroy the temple made with hands. Then in three days, he would build another temple without hands. He is not God. He doesn't have such power." Amazed, Herod listened to the shrill until it died down.

Herod looked at Jesus. "I heard you can do miracles. Can you do one now in front of us?" Jesus remained silent.

Deep down, Herod did not care what the others said. He allowed the audience for his own purposes. Yet more accusations bellowed from the onlookers. "This man claimed he would sit at the right hand of power. He speaks nonsense. He talks of coming in the clouds of heaven like a God. He said he is the Son of the blessed One."

One of the scribes said, "He told us he is the Son of God." One of the elders added, "Many heard him say this. He has clearly committed blasphemy before God and before us."

"Silence!" The crowd immediately stopped. Anger began to fill Herod. Jesus remained silent. It became clear no miracle was going to happen. Antipas spoke. "Well then, if this man wants to be a king, I will treat him as one." If Jesus was to give Herod nothing, then Herod decided he would demonstrate to Christ that he was nothing above his authority. Herod addressed the assembly. "Your claims do not justify judgment from me. This has been a waste of my time because blasphemy, I've been told, is considered an unpardonable sin. And yet you have brought him to me." Antipas reflected on the matter. "Since this man claims to be a king, I think it be fitting to make him one." Like Pilate, he saw an opportunity. With amusement, Herod called for the leader of his bodyguards.

The soldier gave homage, "My lord."

With an angered smirk, Antipas said, "Gather your men." Herod, being an overseer for Rome, it was common practice for him to be assigned seasoned men of war. Men who were not Roman soldiers but hired auxiliary troops. Their credentials steeped in fighting tactics, their specialty rebellion suppression. Men who guarded him, they protected the Tetrarch as well as followed his bidding. "Take him. Turn him into a king." With a slight chuckle, he said, "I want him to be adorned like a king. If he is a king, as they say, I want no one to doubt his sovereignty. He will be known as the king of nothing."

The soldier bowed. "As you wish, my lord." The chief soldier took Jesus to a room where his men of war had assembled. They mocked him, saying, "Hail, great king," and degraded him repeatedly by slapping Jesus. As they beat Christ, they played games. Soldier after soldier approached Jesus as one would a king, bowing and saying, "Hail, king. Hail, your highness. Hail, ruler," with impromptu language. Each strike stirred up violence, and each auxiliary troop vied to outdo the previous. Jesus stood silent, taking blow upon blow. The abuse intensified. They treated him like a fool and beat him with reeds. Christ became their pastime, the release of their stress. Chastising, demeaning chants were drowned out only by echoing slaps. After a time, the amusement tired. One of the soldiers found a worn-out robe of one of their officers. The color faded, yet it was gorgeous; they laid the robe over Christ's bruised body.

While his soldiers did his bidding, Herod sat and waited. He looked at the anger in the faces of the scribes and chief priests. He did not know what to make of the charges leveled against Jesus. He found him curiously strange. He never pleaded his innocence. What alarmed Herod even more was how Jesus seemed uninterested. It was not long ago that Herod had dealt with another who swayed power over the people. His dealing with John the Baptist was fresh in the minds of many—a situation that sent chills of rebellion over the people. Herod did not want to fuel them with another execution. The powder keg before him bore similarities. Herod had no interest in going through that again.

The chief soldier brought Jesus out and presented him. "Your majesty, hail the king of nothing." Before Herod stood a man swollen from head to toe. Bruises began to darken; no part of the body lacked discoloration. Herod could not hide his pleasure. Donning a smile of amusement, he said, "Look at this man. Now he bears the marks of a king." He looked at the audience. Not one word spilled out. Herod broke the silence with his judgment. "I have given this man what he deserves. He wanted to be a king, and I made him one." He looked at the accusers of Jesus. "I find nothing more to do with him. I will not pass judgment on him." In the end, Herod experienced some enjoyment. He washed himself of the matter in a playful yet advantageous way. Pilate sent him as a gesture; Herod returned the favor. Herod loved the banter with Pilate; he returned Jesus in a kingly fashion. Looking at the onlookers, Herod charged his officer. "Take him to Pilate. Give this man a king's escort. Make sure that Pilate knows and sees his arrival."

Pilate and Herod had a history of disdain for each other. The residence of the governor, or Praetorium, was located in the palace of Herod the Great, the father of Antipas. Pilate was a mean overseer of the people, known for his cruelty, following the path of Caesar Tiberius. To honor Tiberius, he erected golden shields with inscriptions commemorating him. The standards infuriated the Jews. In retaliation, they pleaded with the sons of Herod to act. This political, self-created maelstrom further wrenched decency between Pilate and Herod. The Tetrarch over the region did not appreciate the turmoil caused by Pilate's piety to Tiberius, nor did Herod like banners in his realm openly uplifting another over him. Protests did not persuade Pilate to take down the banners. Official letters sent to Rome from the sons of Herod and the Jewish leadership pressured Pilate to remove the shields. This action, among others, created a hateful rift between the two men. Now Pilate ingratiated Herod with a playful gesture. His acknowledgment to Herod gave him the gift of meeting Jesus. Herod one-upped the exchange, using Christ as a subject of entertainment between the two men.

When Pilate saw the procession and looked upon Jesus, his face lit up. Amused, he smirked at the spectacle. He stood at the step of the courtyard as the procession came near. The courtyard, paved with flat blocks of stone, layers of stone upon stone rose to a platform. On the platform sat a judicial seat where Pilate listened to trial proceedings. Behind the seat stood one of the walls of the old city. Pilate waited for the procession to make their way. The officer from Herod said, "Hail, Herod, king of Galilee, has sent you the King of the Jews." As the soldier placed his fist on his chest, he said, "He finds no fault in this king and has given back to you his highness."

Pilate could hardly contain his laughter. "Give Herod my regards. He truly has given this king proper homage, as I intend to do the same." With that, the men of Herod turned about and marched back to their master.

The accusers followed behind the procession. As Herod's soldiers marched away, the high priests and other leaders moved as close as possible to Pilate. Standing in the center of the courtyard, Pilate turned from Jesus and spoke to the chief priests and elders in a stern voice. "You rulers of the people, you have brought him to me as one that perverted the people." Indignant, his eyes fixated on them as he slowly walked up the stone, posturing himself on the judgment bench. "I examined him and found no fault in him." The crowd in the courtyard hung on every word. Pilate leaned forward with contempt. "Even after I touched on your accusations, I sent him to Herod, your king." Leaning back, he continued, "Surely the king over the land would do right by you." Slightly pausing, Pilate waved his hand toward Jesus. "Yet lo, here stands the man you accused, returned to my presence." Pilate convincingly put his hand on the bench. "Nothing worthy of death was done unto him. It is clear that Herod, the king over you, did not find fault in this man either." Frustrated with their cause, Pilate decided to chastise Jesus and then set him free.

There had been a Roman tradition, a magnanimous token of expression to the Jewish people. Each year at Passover, the representative of Rome released a convicted criminal back to the people. Pilate passed judgment. "Yearly, it has been the custom of Rome to set free someone at your feast, your Passover. Therefore, I will chastise this man for his transgressions to you. Once his punishment is over, I will set him free." With a wave to his captain of the guard, the soldier escorted Jesus into the hall.

Shock hit the hearts of the chief priests and the Sanhedrin. With a collective shout, they said, "Away with this man!"

Others shouted, "Release unto us Barabbas!" Pilate remained stoic. Stubbornness filled his bones; he was determined not to let the Jews have their way.

The guard pushed Jesus into an interrogation room. They called the whole band of soldiers to the Praetorium. Seeing an old robe on him, another said, "Oh, that will not do," and he ripped it off. The old robe covered a battered body. Disrobing pained Jesus; the heavy cloak compressed his bruises. The men dropped the beautiful purple robe, the proper color for a king. Striking Jesus with their hands, they chanted, "Hail, King of the Jews!" Laughter bellowed through the hall. The men, bound to a foreign land, despised its people. Contempt for the Jews and their ways tired them; the guards hated the atmosphere around them. Striking and laughing, the beating unleashed their pent-up anger. Each slap built on the next; Jesus

ANGEL'S INFLUENCE

heard their cursing and felt the moisture of their spit. The whole battalion took turns unleashing locked-up frustrations. Mocking, kneeling, hailing the king, they stripped his clothes.

A soldier held a whip, which they called the cat-o'-nine-tails. A specialty weapon, only trained soldiers in the art could use with precision. Masters of the whip pinpoint targets with the greatest accuracy. Nine thongs were separately strung from the whip handle. The cracker of each thong was tightly entwined with bone and metal. A weapon designed to do more than flog, it ripped flesh with each strike. Jewish lore dictated a flogging to be limited to thirty-nine times because anything over forty was considered a death sentence. However, the one holding the whip was not Jewish, and the men around Jesus no longer saw a human. Savagery trumped humanity; the men lost control. Tying him to the post, shouts of glee echoed with the sound of the first crack. Each flick, each crack tore more flesh. Over and over, cracks and jeers broke the silence. The soldiers encircled Jesus. Seeming like an eternity, the whistle of the whip and the crack of the strike. Christ buckled with each contact. The brutality persisted until furor waned; the soldiers untied Jesus from the post. Blood pooled on the floor. In the midst of it, a collapsed Jesus lay still.

Laughter exhausted, one soldier attempted to energize the thrill by placing a hastily braided strand of thorns upon his head. He pressed down firmly; blood gushed from points where the thorns pierced the skin. Two soldiers pulled Jesus up by the arm. Another man replaced the purple robe. Jesus jerked as the robe touched the open wounds. Cringing in pain, the wounds saturated the cloth and adhered to the skin. The robe turned from purple to red. Yet another guard stepped up and handed Jesus a reed, a scepter, and shouted, "Hail, King of the Jews!" Laughter erupted. Lining up, each saluted him in a demeaning way. Some took the scepter from Jesus and struck him on the head. When the mocking subsided, they ripped off the purple cloak. Tissue from the wounds pulled with the robe. Redressing his clothes, the soldiers put the robe back on and put the scepter back in his hand. The leader said to Jesus, "You are now ready to go back out and face judgment."

Pilate reappeared and retook his place on the judgment seat. Once he sat down, he declared, "See, I am bringing him out to you, that you may know that I find no fault in him." Barely able to stand, Jesus came out, riddled from head to toe. He wore a purple robe and held a scepter. Pilate was satisfied with the work. For an instant, Jesus became the center of a conceited contest on who adorned a king better, him or Herod. After seeing the level of abuse, Pilate felt assured the thrashing would satiate their hostility. He waved his hand to the crowd, "Behold the man!" Undeterred, the leaders stirred the crowd more.

The chief priest positioned men throughout the crowd to agitate them. Someone yelled, "Crucify him!" On cue, the words roared through the crowd. The reaction made Pilate's fear greater than before. He waved his soldiers to return Jesus to the hall.

Pilate followed and asked, "Whence art thou?" Jesus stayed silent. Pilate, fearful and arrogantly, said, "Speak thou not that I have power to crucify thee and have power to release thee?" Jesus answered, "Thou could have no power at all against me, except it were given thee from above. Therefore, he that delivered me hath the greater sin." The reaction baffled Pilate. *What is going on here?* he thought. He returned to the crowd, "Why, what evil hath he done? I have found no cause of death in him. I have chastened him." Pilate, cruel and unyielding, stiffened his stance even more. The situation began to take on a force of wills. Along with the shouting, he heard chanting, "Caesar is our king, and if you let this man go, you are no friend of Caesar's." Pilate hated the Jews.

The people of Judea have been nothing but trouble for Pilate. It had not been long since the Golden Shields incident. Threats of rebellion seemed constant. Jews were at enmity with Pilate over his lack of religious sensibilities. A man placed by Aelius Sejanus, he personally picked Pilate to govern the region. Sejanus hated the Jews and wanted to destroy them. True to Sejanus, Pilate had no qualms about insulting their way of life. Whether it was hanging golden images of Tiberius or minting pagan symbols on currency, he saw them as backward and nonredeemable. In the corridors of power, Sejanus represented Tiberius. Before Sejanus could achieve full authority, he needed to rid himself of Tiberius. However, Tiberius discovered the treachery of Sejanus and had him executed. Pilate knew all too well that since the execution, the emperor had been investigating and prosecuting any and all coconspirators. With that, Tiberius sent out a decree that any mistreatment of Jews would be met with harsh consequences. Pilate, being a Sejanus appointee, feared the light of scrutiny. The last thing he needed was negative reports from the Jews. His past dealings of baiting and tormenting came back to haunt him. Pilate needed to be known as Caesaris, a friend of Caesar. To lose the title meant to lose favor. Nor did being ostracized appeal to him. Above all else, Pilate desired to keep his position.

The Jewish leadership kept tabs on Roman power shifts. Shrewd and calculating, they knew with Sejanus gone, their influence over Pilate rose exponentially. Pilate was vulnerable, and he found himself the butt of sharper criticism. Jewish authority bordered on disrespect. Chief priests used his precarious position to demand a legal death sentence on Jesus. Not backing down, they flagged an indirect threat to Pilate. "If you release this man, you are no friend of Caesar. Everyone who makes himself out to be a king opposes Caesar." Their words cut Pilate. He deciphered the cryptic threat. His history of antisemitic policies witnessed against him. Under imperial censure, the Jewish leadership menaced him. A clear warning, their words implied the power they had. If Pilate did not relinquish his stance, then the Jews intended to ruin him.

There was no way out; Pilate had to pronounce a death sentence on an innocent man. Yet he deeply desired not to concede to the chief priests. Calling for Jesus and Barabbas, he paraded both men. Pilate pointed to Jesus. "Behold your king!" More cries bellowed from the crowd. Pilate asked, "Shall I crucify your king?"

The chief priests answered, "We have no king but Caesar."

"Now," he said, "I have the authority to pardon or condemn. Whom shall I set free?" He knew the chief priests were baiting him. His aversion to the Jews culminated. Pilate could feel the exhilaration of the moment, how he had disdain for these Jews.

With a collective roar, the crowd said, "Give us Barabbas!" Criminal or not, Pilate found his hands tied. He knew they would choose Barabbas. Facing a double insult, Pilate had to release a plotting, murderous rebel to Rome. A stirrer of sedition that deserved judgment. Quietly, Pilate sat on the judgment seat, realizing they delivered Jesus for envy. Jesus was innocent; they were jealous. Choking on words, Pilate could not pronounce the sentence. As he sat scanning the crowd, his wife sent him a message. In the message, his wife shared a dream. She warned her husband to have nothing to do with condemning this just man. She relayed the depth of the dream, and the turmoil she experienced. Pilate looked at Jesus.

With each moment, he saw more innocence, more purity. The crowd had not heard anything from Pilate for some time. They saw him in deep thought and toned down their noise. Pilate looked at the crowd. *Bent hearts, blind to logic*, he thought. His amazement put him in a state of disbelief. Pilate marveled at how the judicial leaders of Judea used their clout to kill one man. In a final plea to the crowd, he asked, "What shall I do then with Jesus, which is called Christ?"

They once again yelled, "Let him be crucified!"

He tried again, "Why, what evil hath he done?" The voices cried even louder. Seeing his reasoning heighten agitation, Pilate did the next best thing to following his wife's instructions, "Bring me a basin." With haste, a guard filled a basin with water. Pilate wanted no part in the killing of Jesus, "Thus you have chosen, and it shall be as you wish." As he washed his hands in the water, he continued, "You want Barabbas freed, then so be it." The crowd quieted down, listening to the decree from Pilate. Drying his hands, Pilate's eyes stopped directly at Caiaphas. "I am innocent of the blood of this just person: see ye to it."

Astonished, he heard the people answer back, "His blood be on us, and on our children." The scourging of Jesus was not enough; the people wanted blood.

Within eight hours, Jesus endured six trials. First, from Ananias, the high priest appointed by Quirinius. Then Caiaphas, the Roman replacement for Ananias, along with a trial before the Sanhedrin. Three Jewish trials resulted in three guilty outcomes. Each found Christ guilty of claiming to be the Son of God. Within that same day, three more trials occurred. Three trials were adjudicated by secular

ANGEL'S INFLUENCE

leaders. Herod saw nothing worthy of death, and Pilate proclaimed his innocence twice. The world of pagans saw no blemish in Christ. The leaders of the chosen failed to see their Messiah. Satan pitted all against Christ and finally got the desired effect. Jesus became a doomed criminal.

CHAPTER 13

To Live Is Defeat, to Die Victory

Caiaphas and Ananias got their wish; they and their cohorts achieved their goal. While Jews readied for Passover, unscrupulous men prepared their sacrifice. Through the night, they concocted charges, weighed options, and crafted intentions. The priests gathered, prepared, and isolated their lamb. Satan had done his work. Having no more use for Judas, Lucifer departed from him. When Judas came to his senses, the gravity of the situation took hold of his soul. He never expected such an outcome; looking down, he saw blood on his hands. Distraught and beside himself, Judas stormed into the temple. "I have sinned in that I have betrayed innocent blood."

Posturing indifference, the chief priests shooed him. "What is that to us? See to that yourself." Their words impaled him. Insane with grief, he threw the silver at their feet. The coins slid across the temple floor; Judas wanted no part of the blood money. With stiff backs and puffed chests, the priests stood motionless. Seeing the lack of moisture in their eyes, their disinterest unmasked his importance. The rapport Judas thought he had was an illusion. Swiftly, he turned and walked out of the temple. Breaking down, his legs collapsed with each step. The realization hit him; he was nothing more than a useful tool who had betrayed his Master. Filled with remorse, he went to a field he had prearranged for purchase. In the solitude of the field, Judas hung himself. Being a place few traveled, his body dangled until decay took hold. When the body dropped, the impact split Judas open. His entrails oozed everywhere. The blood of Judas saturated the ground he intended to buy.

Looking at the silver on the floor, the chief priests picked it up. Holding it in their hands, they said, "It is against the law to put this into the treasury since it is blood money." Knowing Judas had secured a field, they decided to complete the purchase. The council made it a potter's field, a burial place for criminals and foreigners. Others renamed it the Field of Blood because traitor's blood tainted it. The words of Jesus rang true. He taught that to gain the world profited nothing if it meant losing one's soul. In the case of the priests, the words bore witness; they exchanged their souls for power. The merchandising of the day was incomplete because Jesus had yet to die.

Those who loved Jesus found themselves soul-searching. Weighty questions captured them; they wondered if obedience to the Master secured a similar fate. They remembered Christ telling them, "If anyone wishes to come after me, he must deny himself, take up his cross, and follow me. For whoever wishes to save his life will lose it, but whoever loses his life for my sake will find it." It was a time of reflection; the apostles felt numb, lost, and scattered.

At the same time, Pilate placed a cross on the back of Jesus. Crucifixion, the trademark of Rome, was reserved only for those condemned by Romans. Their destination was a hill shaped similarly to a skull, called the Place of a Skull. In Hebrew, the hill was known as Golgotha. However, Jesus had already taken an unruly beating from Herod and Pilate. An unbearable weight became too much for a frail Christ, who collapsed under the cross. Seizing a traveler, the soldiers compelled him to carry it. A journeyer from the countryside, Simon the Cyrenian, who came to Jerusalem for the feast, picked up the cross and dragged it behind a stumbling Jesus. The crowd lined the streets, and many people followed him and the Cyrenian. Professional wailers lamented. Hearing them, he lifted his head slightly and with much effort, Jesus turned to them, "Daughters of Jerusalem, weep not for me. Weep for yourselves and for your children." He shuffled a little further and with a labored breath, said, "In the days are coming in which they shall say, 'Blessed are the barren, the wombs that never bore and the breasts which never nursed.'" The words shocked the women; they thought it a strange thing for a dying man to speak. Their crying immediately stopped, and the spectators quieted their noise. Jesus spoke again, "Then they shall begin to say to the mountains, 'Fall on us' and to the hills, 'Cover us.' For if they do these things in a green tree, what shall be done in the dry?" All who heard the words found them confusing; none could comprehend the meaning behind them. Jesus foretold a future world, a time when it would be a blessing to be childless. His inference to the crowd was that if innocent blood could be shed in times of plenty, how would it be during times of despair?

Along with Jesus, two other men carried crosses through the streets. All three walked the long path, the road winding to Calvary. The executioners placed Jesus between the others. Stripping the condemned, the soldiers laid them down. One by one, they drove iron nails into the joints of the hands and feet. Each strike of the hammer echoed through the air, shrieks offset the echoes. The soldiers hoisted the crosses into previously dug holes, deep enough to hold the posts. Their bodies jarred when the crosses dropped. Blocks jutted out from the cross points, aligned at the shoulders, the blocks forced the criminals to lift themselves by their feet. If their bodies dropped, pressure from the blocks caused slow suffocation. Each tried to endure the weight of their body against the distress of the stake in their feet. Unlike the two around him, Jesus's nerve endings were already heightened from torture. Customarily, the Romans offered sponges soaked with wine and myrrh, a natural sedative, but Jesus refused the sponge. Not wanting dull senses, Christ had to experience every moment with a clear mind. By now, the sun burned down. It was about the sixth hour, and over the city, clouds formed. The elements hid the sun, and a looming darkness covered the light. People became uneasy; the darkness brought on a frightening aura.

Four soldiers at the base of the crosses rifled through the garments, moaning as their backdrop. They callously divided the possessions of the condemned, tearing Jesus's clothing into four parts, each taking a share, until they came to his coat. It was a high-quality seamless coat, woven from the top throughout. Not wanting to ruin it, the soldiers decided to cast lots for it. Watching the soldiers were Mary, the mother of Jesus; her sister; and Mary Magdalene. Standing at the base of the cross with them was John, the disciple of Jesus. Jesus said to his mother, "Woman, behold thy son." He looked at John, "Behold thy mother." Jesus lifted his eyes to heaven, "Father, forgive them, for they know not what they do." All stood and watched.

Along with the people, the Jewish rulers observed the spectacle. Subordinates of the chief priests derided Jesus, saying, "He saved others. Now let him save himself. If he be the Christ, the chosen of God, then show us and save yourself."

The Roman soldiers picked up on the chiding and chimed in. "If thou be the king of the Jews, save yourself." One soldier put a sponge filled with vinegar on the end of a stick and lifted it to the mouth of each man. When he came to Jesus, the soldier pulled it away each time he put it near Jesus, like a cat playing with a mouse, he parroted the rulers, "Save yourself."

Above Jesus, Pilate ordered the men to nail a sign. It read in Greek, Latin, and Hebrew, "*Jesus of Nazareth, the King of the Jews.*" Pilate wanted to prick the Jewish leadership; he loathed the position they put him in. Protesting the sign, the chief priest demanded it be changed to read, "He said he was King of the Jews." Knowing they had no position to complain, Pilate smugly replied, "What I have written, I have written." To further irritate them, Pilate had it done in all languages, ensuring all witnessing the crucifixion would not miss the inscription.

Two thieves hung with Jesus, one to the right and one to the left. Seeing men wagging their heads, repeating over and over, "Ah thou that destroyed the temple and build it up in three days. Save yourself and come down from the cross." The condemned men, miserable in their state, parroted the banter, "He saved others. Himself he cannot save." Layers upon layers of incessant mocking, over and over Jesus heard, "Let Christ, the King of Israel, descend now from the cross that we may believe." The verbal barrage made a dismal impact. A final temptation, the irritating chiding came from all sides. Lucifer tried to anger Jesus; he wanted to dupe him into saving himself.

One of the thieves, filled with bitterness, said again, "If thou be the Christ, save yourself and us." The words incensed the other.

Using his last bit of energy, he said, "Dost not thou fear God, seeing thou art in the same condemnation?"

Taking a labored breath, he said, "We are justified. We are receiving the due reward for our deeds, but this man hath done nothing amiss." With a momentary weep, he said to Jesus, "Lord, remember me when thou comest into thy kingdom." His words deeply moved Christ. Out of the human debris, he heard a repentant soul. The glimmer of light cooled his soul; it comforted him. Jesus said to the man, "Verily I say unto thee, today shalt thou be with me in paradise." The tormentors were an exercise in temptation. Satan teased Jesus; he knew at any time Christ could shed his flesh and come down. It was a pleasurable pastime for Satan, seeing the downfall of Yahweh.

The sun had reached its apex, and the temple was finishing their sacrifices. Jesus cried with a loud voice, "*Elo'i Elo'i la'ma sabach'thani?*" Words of brokenness, it was the pain of separation. In desperation, he cried, "My God, my God, why hast thou forsaken me?" God the Father could not bear to see his Son suffer. The unnatural darkness, and the elements veiled the ugly task. From noon until three, Jesus felt the darkness, the abyss that comes with sin. The Father severed his Spirit from him. Such separation proved more unbearable than any strike, pierce, or blow. Both Gods wrenched. It tore Jesus asunder while it broke the Father's heart. Angels wept. Those in the crowd who heard the cries asked themselves if Jesus was calling for Elias.

The separation had to be done; otherwise, all would have been for naught. The day was growing short, and the Feast of Unleavened Bread was at hand. Jesus said, "I thirst." One of the soldiers at the base quickly grabbed a sponge filled with vinegar. Pressing it between a hyssop branch, he lifted it to his lips.

As the branch neared, someone in the crowd shouted, "Let alone. Let us see whether Elias will come to take him down." A crowd filled with demons, they continually riled the hearts of the people.

Jesus cried out, "Father, into thy hands I commend my spirit." With his mouth, he squeezed a little vinegar out of the sponge. As the branch lowered, Jesus said, "It is finished." No sooner than he had cried, he died. The minions of Lucifer drove the nail, but it was Satan who influenced the death of a God.

Fully into the ninth hour, God the Father severed the parocheth. A thick curtain that separated the Holy of Holies, he ripped it from top to bottom. The Father did not want any man to claim credit for destroying it. At the moment of the death of his Son, an earthquake shook the region. An intense shaking that moved rocks and opened graves. Out of those graves, saints thought dead walked into the city. All who saw quivered. As word traveled through the crowd, the chief priests and elders wondered in disbelief. A servant from the temple hurried to them. He announced that the veil had been torn. In the midst of the chaos stood a centurion. Noting the darkness and hostile reverberation, he scrutinized Jesus. Wondering what kind of man induced such ire, the officer witnessed the light break through the darkness. He felt the earth weep. Hearing screams and cries of fear, the officer knew nothing was coincidental. Without warning, the centurion glorified God. His soldiers stopped. Fear surrounded the centurion, and suddenly, his men heard him say, "Certainly, this was a righteous man."

Knowing the high day was upon them, the Jewish leaders approached Pilate. They requested him to break the legs of the men. It was unacceptable to leave bodies hanging through the feast. Doing this sped up the death process because, once broken, they would suffocate. Pilate granted their request and ordered the soldiers to break the legs. The soldiers shattered the legs of the thieves. When they got to Christ, he seemed dead. To make sure, one of them ran a spear through his side. The spear pierced Jesus's lungs and ruptured his heart. The puncture missed Christ's bones. Blood mingled with water trickled down his side.

The evil one took pleasure in the depravity. As soon as Satan knew Yahweh had died, he released the minds of the people. Dazed, the people began to come out of their darkness; they regained control of themselves. Craze changed to sorrow, and riotousness turned to lamenting. The people realized what they had done. The Jewish leaders stood astonished at the emotional shift. The crowd began

D.S. BOYCE

weeping and beating their chests. An unbelievable rush overcame the people. Slowly, one by one, they dispersed until no one stood at the cross. By this time, Jesus's mother Mary, Mary Magdalene, and John distanced themselves. They joined others who stood afar. Jesus's half-siblings James, Joses, and Salome stood with them. Far on a hill, many who loved Jesus mourned.

CHAPTER 14

The Burial and Return

Curious how fast things change. Yesterday, Jesus dined with his disciples; now he was gone. It's unimaginable the speed of betrayal or how quickly adoration could turn to grief. After the death, Joseph sought a private audience with Pilate. A man from Arimathea, he was a wealthy trader and a member of the Sanhedrin. Like Nicodemus, another secret follower, both silently witnessed the unjust treachery perpetrated against Christ. Boldly standing before the prefect, he begged Pilate for the body. It was a risky request, being that Jesus died through the cunning of his peers. Pilate had no interest in how long men hung nor if it defiled Jewish law. But this day proved different because the Jews had cornered him. Riding on his arrogance, the chief priest demanded the bodies not hang through the high day. Summoning his centurion, Pilate asked, "Has any of the condemned died?"

The centurion checked. After a short time, the officer returned, "My lord, all hanging have expired. At your request, the bodies are being taken down."

Pilate marveled at how quickly they had passed. "What have you done with the condemned man with the sign?"

The centurion replied, "My lord, the one with the sign is still hanging. The men have yet to take him down."

Quickly, Joseph bowed. "My lord, that is the one I seek."

Pilate did not fight the request; the recent strain between him and the Jews drained him. "Centurion! Give this man the body." Grateful, Joseph thanked Pilate for honoring his request.

Nearby, Nicodemus waited. Of all the members of the Sanhedrin, he alone knew Joseph's intentions. He brought with him a mixture of myrrh and aloes to help wrap the body. Carrying a hundred pounds of ointments, the men hurried.

By now, the sun had touched the horizon. With the help of servants, the men took the body. Nearby, Joseph owned an elaborate sepulcher. Located in a beautiful garden, it had been prepared for Joseph himself. It was a new, unused tomb hewn in stone. Hastily, they wrapped the body in long strips of fine linen doused in spices. Anointing Jesus, they laid him in the grave. The servants rolled the stone over the entrance just moments before the sun dipped below the horizon. Exhausted but content, they finished the burial by the end of Passover. Hurriedly, Joseph and Nicodemus went their separate ways, both had to ready themselves for the Feast of Unleavened Bread. Mary Magdalene and Mary sat close by, watching the men. Knowing the body was improperly prepared, the women planned to return. It was decided to ready myrrh and purchase other spices after the holy day.

At the end of the first day of Unleavened Bread, the chief priests and Pharisees approached Pilate. Concerned with rumors, they said, "We remember that that deceiver said, while he was yet alive, 'After three days I will rise again.' Command therefore that the sepulcher be made sure until the third day, lest his disciples come by night and steal him. Then they can say unto the people, 'He is risen from the dead,' so the last deception shall be worse than the first."

Pilate, tired of Jewish business, said, "You have a watch. Go your way, make it as sure as you can." Securing guards from the governor, the Jewish leaders left. Spies of the Sanhedrin had watched Joseph claim the body. The priests knew where he had laid Jesus. The Jews, accompanied by Roman soldiers, went to the tomb. Seeing the stone in front of the entrance, they ordered the guards to nail iron stakes into it. Long pins were wedged into the groove, a hollowed niche where the stone rolled. With the stone lodged by the stakes, the Jews stationed two guards in front of it. Confident the tomb was secured, the Jewish leaders left the garden. Pilate loaned four soldiers to the priests, two-man shifts to keep watch for three days. It was evening time; Christ had been in the grave for a day.

It was the beginning of the second day since the death of Christ. A day between the high days, gave Mary Magdalene, Mary, Salome, and John a day to gather spices and wrappings. When it came to burials, responsibility fell on the immediate family. The unexpected demise of her son caught Mary ill-prepared. With haste, the women went into the marketplace, acquiring the necessary items for a proper dressing. Gathering materials, they spent the rest of the day grinding and steeping spices. By the time sufficient oils had been readied, the sun touched the horizon. Frustrated that time had elapsed, the women found themselves unable to go to the tomb. The weekly Sabbath had begun, a holy day when all rested from labor and spent time with God. The women could not rest; all they could think about was Jesus in the tomb.

Pent-up anxiety filled them. No sooner than the sun dipped, Mary Magdalene and Mary, the mother of Jesus, collected the wraps, burial ointments, and oils. Now dark, being the Jewish day fell from sundown to sundown, the two women walked to the tomb. It was just past midnight when they made it to the garden. Although night ruled the sky, it was considered early morning. As they walked, they questioned how to roll the stone. It had been three days, two holy days with a day in between, since Christ died. Carrying torches, the light tapped every figure in the garden. Shadows danced between the tombs, without warning, the earth began to shake. So great was the shaking, the women fell to the ground. Unknown to them, an angel of the Lord descended from heaven and rolled back the stone.

Scrambling to their feet, they struggled to pick up the items they had brought with them. Darkness blanketed them, and in fear, they hastily moved through the graves. Approaching the site, the two women stopped. To their astonishment, the stone in front of the tomb was open. A heavy thick disk wedged in a track; the pins hammered into the stone had been sheared off. The Jewish leaders secured the stone, but now it was open. Amazed and afraid, the women recoiled, holding each other. Above the stone, a silhouette sat over the grave. Looking at them, the figure lit up; it was an angel sitting on top of the stone. Bright as lightning, clothes white as snow, the angel dropped down between the guards. The soldiers had collapsed at the sight of the messenger. Laying on the ground, they appeared to be like dead men. The angel said to the women, "Fear not ye, for I know that ye seek Jesus, which was crucified. He is not here, for he is risen, as he said. Come, see the place where the Lord lay." Terrified, every bone in their body shook. Slowly, they entered the opening, never taking their eyes off the angel.

Inside, they looked at the slab where the body had lain. It was empty except for the presence of a young man. Confused, the women looked at him. He sat on the right side of the slab, clothed in a long white garment, his brilliance scared them. The man said to them, "Be not frightened. Ye seek Jesus of Nazareth, who was crucified. He is risen; he is not here. Behold the place where they laid him." The young man gestured to the linen next to him. It lay undisturbed as if a body had been in it. The young man charged them. "But go your way. Go quickly and tell his disciples that he is risen from the dead. Tell his disciples and Peter that he goes before you into Galilee. There shall ye see him, as he said unto you. Lo, I have told you."

Still shaking, the women backed out of the tomb, never turning away from the man. Exiting the sepulcher, their eyes bulged. Completely traumatized and in disbelief, the women wondered who could have stolen the body. As they queried, two men stood by them in shining garments. Thoroughly terrified, they fell to their knees. Lying speechless, Mary and Mary Magdalene prostrated themselves. The two men gently looked upon them and asked again, "Why seek ye the living among the dead?" Shaking uncontrollably, they could not comprehend the words, knowing they had witnessed Jesus die. The men continued, "He is not here, but is risen! Remember how he spake unto you when he was in Galilee?" Still crumbled before them, the women tried to recall, but fear jumbled their thoughts. Knowing their confusion, the men reminded them, "Remember him saying the Son of man must be delivered into the hands of sinful men. Remember he said he must be crucified and the third day rise

ANGEL'S INFLUENCE

again?" The soothing words opened their minds; their memories of the Master returned to them.

After the death of Jesus, the apostles feared for their lives. They gathered in a secret place; however, Peter was not with them. Filled with shame and loathing, Peter could not forgive himself for denying Christ. Some of the group found Peter and coaxed him to join them. Through the wee hours, they spoke about recent events and what to do next. The disciples knew the women had gone to the tomb. Filled with deep sadness, the men thought their efforts were in vain. Unbeknownst to them, the women had ran from the garden. As the two ran, they saw Joanna walking with some others. Excited and out of breath, Mary Magdalene and Mary shared all that had happened. Shaken and afraid to speak to any man, Mary, Joanna, Mary the mother of Jesus, and others ran to the disciples. By the time they reached the place where the men stayed, they were trembling, tired, and winded. Breathing heavily, the women rushed to the door. The loud slam startled the disciples. Rambling and stuttering, they told an amazing tale of how the grave was empty. Mary Magdalene ran up to Peter and John. "They have taken away the Lord out of the sepulcher, and we know not where they have laid him." Listening to the words, the men thought the women irrational.

However, Peter and John took the words to heart and ran from the room. Both men reached the tomb before the change of the Roman watch. Stepping around the current guards unconscious on the ground, John stooped down and looked into the tomb. He saw the linen clothes intact; the wrappings laid out. Peter walked past John into the sepulcher. Inspecting the wrap, he wondered, *How could anyone have taken the Lord's body and left the clothes undisturbed?* Next to the linen, the napkin used to cover the face had been neatly folded and set aside. John walked into the grave. He inspected the linen that had wrapped Jesus. Confused, Peter walked away in disbelief. While Peter tried to make sense of it, John believed. It was a great mystery; both saw the grave and burial linens but no body.

Mary Magdalene returned to the grave, not having the strength to keep up with Peter and John; she followed them from a distance. Standing outside, she wept as Peter and John quietly walked past

113

her. Mary slowly pivoted to the men, hoping they would say something. Crying and sniffing, she stooped down and looked into the tomb. To her surprise, she saw two angels sitting inside. Turning back towards John and Peter, she watched as both slowly disappeared into the garden. Perplexed as to why neither spoke of the men, she turned to speak to them. Both dressed in white, one man sat at the head of the linen and the other at the foot. Staring at Mary, they asked, "Woman, why weep thou?"

Mary replied, "Because they have taken away my Lord, and I know not where they have laid him."

She felt a presence behind her. Turning around, she saw a man standing outside the tomb. Mary thought he was a gardener tending to his work. The man asked, "Woman, why weep thou? Whom seek you?"

Politely, Mary said, "Sir, if you have carried him away, tell me where you have laid him, and I will go get him."

Turning back to the opening, Mary did not realize it was Jesus who spoke. Lovingly, he said, "Mary."

Immediately, her eyes widened; Mary knew that voice. Turning back to the man, her eyes welled up. Tears streaming, voice breaking, she said, "Rabboni?" She immediately lunged toward Jesus to embrace him.

Putting his hand up, Jesus said, "Touch me not, for I am not yet ascended to my Father. But go to my brethren and say unto them, I ascend unto my Father and your Father, and to my God and your God." As soon as Mary heard the words, she ran back to the disciples. By this time, John and Peter had confirmed the accounts of the women. All heard the condition of the tomb and that the body was missing. The disciples began to mourn. Jesus was gone, and they knew not who took him. While they grieved, Mary opened the door. "I have seen the Master! He is alive!" Puzzled, the disciples perked up and began to quiz her. They wondered if the men Mary saw were the ones who took Jesus. She told them of the man she thought a gardener but turned out to be the Master. Skeptical, the disciples could not bring themselves to believe.

ANGEL'S INFLUENCE

Right after Mary ran from the tomb, Jesus ascended. His ascension made him the intercessor, the One that filled the gap. Angels watched in anticipation, waiting to see the Son of God. In an unexpected moment, Christ showed himself in front of the throne. The angels looked at the Son; all saw the holes in his hands. Yahweh demonstrated his resolve; he went into Satan's realm and overcame him. Returning wrapped in a golden girdle over a white cloak, the Son gave homage to his Father. Hair white like wool and brighter than snow, the Son's eyes pierced the angels. His feet burned like brass; the energy rose from his feet to his head. The intensity disturbed the air; the angels kneeled before the Son. It was the everlasting fire, the display of glory both Father and Son shared. Bowing to his Father, he said, "I accomplished the task." The Ancient of Days smiled. With the ascent to heaven, Yahweh broke the curse. But Jesus knew he could not leave the disciples in their current state. His death caused such trembling; the hearts of the apostles fell into despair. For his teachings to move forward, the men he cultivated had to open their eyes. The Son venerated his Father. As suddenly as he appeared, Christ returned to earth.

Back on earth, the disciples assumed Mary was grief-stricken. However, the women believed Mary and followed her back to the garden. As they walked through the garden, Jesus met them, saying, "All hail."

Recognizing him immediately, the women fell at his feet. Kissing his feet and worshiping him, their dejection turned to jubilation. Jesus said, "Be not afraid. Go tell my brethren that they go into Galilee, and there shall they see me." Mary Magdalene, Joanna, Jesus's mother, and the others rose from the ground. The women forgot about the two men at the tomb. The recent events no longer mattered because they saw the Master. A third time, the women returned to the disciples. Rejoicing and singing, they entered the room and told the disciples what the Lord had said. The men could not bring themselves to believe because Jesus had not appeared to them. By now, the light was close to overtaking the night; the relief watch approached the tomb. Seeing the state of the tomb and the unconscious guards, fear ran over them. Shaking the guards out of their stupor, the soldiers knew the consequences of losing the corpse.

Concern filled them, assuming the guards had fallen asleep. Roman soldiers understood that if they failed at their post, the penalty was death. With the tomb empty and the watch overpowered, the four guards returned to the city. Knowing Pilate had given the chief priests authority over them, they straightway reported to the Jewish leaders. Angered that the tomb had been unsealed, the priests assembled the elders. They realized that they had lost the body. The Sanhedrin gathered to discuss a course of action. Thinking the followers of Jesus intended to lift the prophet as the Messiah, they had to get ahead of them. The Jewish leaders decided to pay the guards for their silence. The priests and elders promised the four soldiers protection from Rome and their governor. They vowed to persuade Pilate if punishment ever presented itself. The promise covered the relief watch and the guards that were found unconscious. The soldiers accepted the money since the alternative was death.

Before the guards returned, the priests asked them to reseal the tomb. Honoring their wish, the men returned to Pilate as if nothing had happened. The guards never spoke of it, confident the chief priests and elders would discount it. The Jews decided to fabricate that the guarded tomb was never disturbed. In a contrived cover-up, the priests controlled the narrative. They spread the word far and wide that the tomb remained secured. They cited the sworn testimony of the guards and let the people believe the body was still there. The leaders decided to persecute anyone who claimed otherwise.

Prior to Mary declaring she saw Jesus, Cleopas and his wife left. The couple had spent time with the disciples and heard what had happened to the tomb. They left, thinking someone had stolen the body of Jesus. Living in the countryside, the couple journeyed home to a little town called Emmaus. As they traveled, they talked about the recent days. Saddened by the death of their Master, they tried to make sense of it. As they walked, a nearby traveler appeared and heard the conversation. Coming beside them, he asked, "What manner of communication are these that you have with one another as you walk and are sad?"

Cleopas and his wife told him of their loss. Cleopas said, "Are you a stranger in Jerusalem? Have you not known the things which have come to pass in recent days?"

The man asked, "What things?"

Cleopas replied, "Concerning Jesus of Nazareth, who was a prophet mighty in deed and word before God and all the people."

His voice cracked. "How the chief priests and our rulers delivered him to be condemned to death and crucified him." He paused to keep his composure.

"We trusted that it had been he which should have redeemed Israel. Besides all this, today is the third day since these things were done."

There was a small distance of silence before Cleopas spoke again, "Yes, and certain women of our company made us astonished, telling us they had seen a vision of angels, which said he was alive. Certain of us went to the grave and found it as they had said: empty."

The stranger replied, "O fools, and slow of heart to believe all that the prophets have spoken. Ought not the Christ to have suffered these things and then to enter into his glory?" The words astonished the couple; they found it odd that a stranger who didn't seem to know had chastised them.

Interested, they listened as they drew near their village. Knowing the stranger was not from Emmaus, Cleopas asked him to abide with them. They offered their home to the stranger, saying, "Stay with us, for it is toward evening, and the day is far spent." The stranger obliged. As they ate, the man took bread, blessed it, broke it, and gave it to Cleopas and his wife.

As soon as they received it, their eyes were opened. Realizing the stranger was their Master, Jesus vanished from their sight. They looked at each other and said, "Did not our heart burn within us while he talked with us by the way, and while he opened the scriptures to us?" Fatigue left them. They rose and hurried back to Jerusalem. Walking through the night, they found the eleven still gathered, with many supporters staying with the disciples. As soon as Cleopas and Mary came through the door, they shouted, "The Lord has risen indeed! He appeared to Simon." The couple shared their experience on the path and how Jesus had broken bread with them. Inconceivability overwhelmed the disciples; despite multiple testimonies, the men could not bring themselves to believe.

Since the dispersion in the garden and the crucifixion, fear still had hold on them. Afraid, they huddled together with doors shut, waiting for the chance to leave the city. Hearing the accounts of the women and now Cleopas and his wife sparked more confusion. Some thought trickery was at play; maybe their friends had been deceived by others. Others could not get past the finality of death.

While they spoke, Jesus appeared through the closed doors. Before anyone could process it, he said, "Peace be with you." Terror ripped through the room. The group could not believe their eyes. They thought they were seeing a spirit. Jesus said to them, "Why are you troubled? Why do thoughts arise in your hearts?" He lifted up his hands. "Behold my hands and my feet. It is I myself. Come, handle me, and see for yourself. A spirit does not have flesh and bones as you see I have." The men gathered around Jesus. All present looked at his hands and feet. They saw the damage that only the stake could make. Roaring praise filled the room. Elation overtook them. However, inside some minds lingered the reality of death. While they wondered, Jesus asked, "Have ye here any meat?" They gave him a piece of broiled fish and a honeycomb. Jesus took it and ate. After tasting a little, he reminded them, "These are the words which I spake unto you. While I was yet with you, that all things must be fulfilled. These things which were written in the law of Moses and by the prophets, in psalms concerning me. Thus, it is written, and thus it behooved Christ to suffer. I, the Christ, had to rise from the dead on the third day. That repentance and remission of sins should be preached in his name among all nations, beginning at Jerusalem." He looked at them. "And ye are witnesses of these things." Dead silence filled the room. Walking through them, he continued, "I send the promise of my Father upon you. But for now, tarry in the city of Jerusalem until ye be imbued with power from on high." Thomas, absent, did not see the appearance of the Lord.

Later on, Didymus, also known as Thomas, returned. Jesus had left by the time he made his way back to the others. When hearing the joy and excitement, Thomas felt annoyed. He did not see any evidence to merit joy from his fellow apostles. Their joy countered his grief; his sorrow clashed with them. When they reported they had seen the Lord, it irritated Thomas. Disbelief fueled him; he felt insulted at their merriment. Thomas said to them, "Except I shall see in his hands the print of the nails, and put my finger into the print of the nails, and thrust my hand into his side, I will not believe."

For the next eight days, Thomas listened to the new line of discussion. He sat quietly, internally scoffing at the encounters many shared. As before, the doors to the room were shut. Like the first time, Jesus appeared in the middle of the room. Christ greeted them, "Peace be with you." The chatter in the room stopped. All faced the Lord. Stunned, Thomas looked at Christ. His sight betrayed him; he turned to the doors. Jesus weaved through the men until he faced Thomas. Looking at him, he said, "Reach hither thy finger, and behold my hands, and reach hither thy hand, and thrust it into my side; and be not faithless, but believing." Thomas was beside himself because his grief was so deep. It was a level of lamenting he thought the others could not reach. Touching the marks of the nails and feeling the edge of the puncture, he knew this had to be his Master. Doubt melted away. Thomas began to weep. Collapsing to his knees, he stuttered, "My Lord and my God."

Jesus said to him, "Thomas, because thou hast seen me, thou hast believed: blessed are they that have not seen, and yet have believed." From that point, Jesus remained with his disciples. He clarified his message and taught them the deep meanings of that message.

From that moment, the disciples no longer hid in fear. Openly, Jesus unfolded all the words and parables he had told them. No mystery was hidden; Christ prepared them. As instructed, the disciples traveled to Galilee. Shortly thereafter, some of them fished in the Sea of Tiberias. Peter, Thomas, Nathanael, John, James, and two others fished all day. The men caught nothing from their boat. The sun peeked over a clear blue horizon. Looking toward the shore, they saw a man standing there. It was Jesus, but they did not recognize him. Jesus called out to them, "Children, have you any fish?"

They answered, "No."

Jesus called back, "Cast the net on the right side of the boat, and you will find some." Still not knowing who it was, they cast their net on the right side. To their astonishment, the net filled with fish. Strands of the net stretched from the weight of the catch. Fearing it would break, they held the load on the side of the boat. Rowing to shore, they realized it was the Lord.

John said to Peter, "It is the Lord!" Upon hearing this, Peter put on his coat. Straightaway, he dove into the water and swam as fast as he could to Jesus. Being a hundred yards offshore, the others rowed the small vessel behind Peter. With the weighty catch still on the side, the men dragged the net to land. Peter had already sat down by a fire of coals.

Jesus had fish and bread, smoking, ready to eat. Jesus said, "Bring some of the fish which ye have caught." The haul was overwhelming, with 152 in total. Peter and the others found it a miracle, being the net had not split. Jesus said, "Come and dine." All sat and ate, each content to be with the Lord.

While they fellowshipped, the morning cast a sweet breeze off the water. Blue sky and white clouds made the moment special in their hearts. As they ate, Jesus asked Peter a question, "Simon son of Jonas, do you love me more than these?" Truly a bold question, all wondered how Peter would respond. It was always a contention among the brethren, who loved Jesus more and whom Christ favored most. All perked up.

Not wanting to offend the others, Peter answered, "Yes, Lord, thou know that I love thee." Peter knew he had displayed weakness. During the trial, Peter put self-preservation over love for the Master. Jesus knew he loved him, but he needed Peter to be strong and unyielding.

Jesus said, "Feed my lambs." The men continued to eat. A few minutes later, Jesus asked Peter once more, "Simon son of Jonas, love thou me?"

Again, Peter responded, "Yes, Lord, thou know that I love thee."

Jesus said, "Feed my sheep." Words seemingly redundant had a cryptic message. Jesus wanted Peter to bring new converts into the fold; he had to nourish the lambs into sheep. The Lord desired Peter

ANGEL'S INFLUENCE

to feed the gospel and shepherd the Jews. A third time, Jesus asked, "Simon, son of Jonas, love thou me?"

Peter, now grieved that the Lord had asked him three times, replied in a serious tone, "Lord, thou know all things, thou know that I love thee."

Jesus knew that swirling inside the recesses of Peter's mind was shame. The first time Jesus asked, Peter flippantly answered. It was an answer meant more to jibe at the other men. The second time, Peter realized Jesus wanted more; however, when asked a third time, his shame welled up inside.

Everyone around the campfire sat quietly. Some were looking at Peter, while others directed their eyes to the fire. None of them knew how to avoid the awkwardness. Speaking directly to Peter, he said, "Verily, verily, I say unto thee, when thou wast young, thou girded thyself and walked whither thou wouldst, but when thou shalt be old, thou shalt stretch forth thy hands, and another shall gird thee, and carry thee whither thou wouldst not." The words struck Peter; his heart melted. Peter had grown; he remembered how his faith had flourished and his zeal for Christ had strengthened. He would need that zeal to face the Jews. Jesus explained his mission and how it would end in his death. Peter looked down; the words rang through him. With compassion, Jesus said to Peter, "Follow me." The other disciples wondered what Christ had in store for them.

Envy surfaced within Peter. He looked at John. Peter never forgot how John approached the chief priests without fear while he cringed in denial. Hearing that he was to be martyred and what was to become of him, he asked, "Lord, and what shall this man do?" Peter wanted to know what was to happen to John.

Jesus rebuked Peter, "If I will that he tarry till I come, what is that to thee? Follow thou me."

Misunderstanding, the others perceived that Jesus meant John would never die. Each disciple accepted this, and Jesus added no more. John would outlive the rest; he was set aside to write the things of the future. The men started asking their fate. Each wanted to know what path Christ had set for them.

By now, word had spread that Jesus lived. Believers traveled from all over to Galilee. Five hundred followers journeyed up the mountain to see Christ. As promised, Jesus appeared before the crowd. Many fell and worshiped. Jesus taught them, saying, "All power is given unto me in heaven and on earth. Go ye therefore, and teach all nations, baptizing them in the name of the Father and of me. Teaching them to observe all things whatsoever I have commanded you, and, lo, I am with you always, even unto the end of the world." The miracles, returning from death, and the acts of Jesus anchored faith and solidified his teachings. Everything Jesus said and did became important. He prepared his children, showing them signs and wonders. A demonstration for testimony's sake, all shared the good news that Jesus is the Savior of the world.

CHAPTER 15

The God that Comforts

Time with the disciples neared its end; soon, Jesus would leave them. Prior to his departure, he spent time with his half brother James. James witnessed the power of Jesus; he knew the truth of his brother's deity. Compelling the rest to join them, Jesus and the disciples traveled to Bethany. They settled on the eastern side of the Mount of Olives. Just outside the city of Jerusalem, Jesus said, "Peace be unto you: as my Father hath sent me, even so send I you." After he spoke these words, the Lord breathed upon the disciples. A sudden rush of power coursed through their veins. The Spirit of the Father funneled out of Christ and into each of them. Jesus felt the rise within them. "Receive ye the Holy Spirit." Spirit-empowered from on high, the power shimmered down on the men like ice flakes falling in light. Particles in the shape of flickering tongues landed on each of the disciples. God gave them the gift of speech. Tongues of living fire; blue fire essence.

Surrounding the light, seraphim, cherubim, and ophanim observed the fire pass over the stones. The fiery river, mingled with ice, ran down from heaven to earth. Encircling the spiraling flames, innumerable angels moved along the stones, listening to prayers and waiting to fulfill them. Seated at the apex of the fire flow was the Ancient of Days. With hair white as wool, he was pure illumination, an indescribable emanation. His power, only accessible through his Son, ignited the disciples. The men shared in the essence of the Father and became siblings with Christ. It was a power the disciples repeatedly saw Jesus tap into; believing made the connection possible. Jesus called the Spirit that opened their eyes the Comforter. Like prophets of old who conversed with angels, the men saw heaven open before them. Jesus gave them a stern warning. "Whose soever sins you lay aside, they are remitted unto them; and whose soever sins ye retain, they are retained." All listened. To access the power, the men had to put away sin. Sin blocked the Spirit; each, in their own way, processed the gift.

Recalling how Jesus subjected himself, all recognized how he daily yielded to his Father. Each took in the depth of the parables, the lessons, and every word Jesus shared. Prepared for their calling, the disciples bowed and worshiped their Master. The Lord lifted up his hands and blessed them. After the blessing, he departed. The disciples watched the Son of God lift into heaven. Joy filled their bones, and every fiber, and sinew ignited. Watching Christ ascend, they remained there long after they lost sight of him. The fire at the camp long extinguished, they stayed, worshiping and praising God. From that day forward, the men boldly went into the temple. It had been fifty days since Jesus rose from the dead. For fifty days, he walked with them. They called the day Pentecost, the day Christ left and gave them the Spirit known as the Comforter.

In heaven, the strongest of the angels began to proclaim with a loud voice, "Who is worthy to open the book and to loosen the seals thereof?"

Seraphim began chanting, "Holy, holy, holy, Lord God Almighty, which was, and is, and is to come." Lightning flashed and thunder sounded; within the rumbles and streams of light, a figure appeared. It was the Son of God returning to the throne. His appearance was as bright as fine gems: jasper, sardius, emerald—reds, blues, greens— tethered by a line of gold. The crystal below the throne amplified his brilliance. The angels wept for joy, and an elder cried, "Weep not. Behold, the Lion of the tribe of Judah, the Root of David, has prevailed. He is the one who is worthy to open the book and break the seals." An unspeakable number of angels hovered around the throne.

About one hundred billion hosts shouted, "Worthy is the Lamb that was slain to receive power and riches, wisdom and strength,

ANGEL'S INFLUENCE

honor and glory, all the blessings that are rightly his to claim." All creation rejoiced.

Heaven listened to the creatures on land and sea chant, "Blessing, honor, glory, power be to him that sits on the throne and to his Son, the Lamb, which saved us forever and forever." Yahweh, the Son of God, took the book. His victory gave him the authority to hold it. The seals around the book laid out a timeline. It was a very special book that gave Christ the authority to unleash the future.

Bowing down, the twenty-four elders received a good report. The Father said, "Sit at my right hand." Crackling around the two-seated throne, lightning and thunder. With each strike, colors splashed off the translucent crystal. The Son took his seat. The illumination of Father and Son dispersed a spectrum in all directions. From the throne, both Father and Son burned hot like brass. An amber-colored fire mixed into the colors; it sparkled throughout the lightning. All in heaven witnessed the light of glory. Attached beneath the throne was a wheel of eyes. Filled with innumerable eyes, the circle reached from heaven to earth. Eyes that saw all things in the second and third heavens, they faced in all directions. Through them, the aggregate of visions tied the throne to everything. Stationed by the altar and in front of the throne was a creature. The supernatural being linked the eyes to the angels. At the direction of Yahweh, the creature energized the host. Having the qualities of an ox, lion, eagle, and man, it mirrored the character of Jesus who became a man, served lowly like an ox, demonstrated strength like the lion, and rose like an eagle. It was an incarnation, a visible manifestation of its Master.

In front of the throne stood seven angels, seven observers of the believers of God. Christ held the angels in his right hand; they were his stars, his servants over his people. The followers who walked with Jesus began to separate from one another. With each split, Yahweh assigned an angel to keep watch. Eventually, the children of God were divided into seven churches. For each church, an angel; the believers branched into an elaborate menorah. They became a candlestick that represented seven variations of faith in Christ. All followed Jesus but differed in interpretations. The collective became known as Christians. The watchers assigned to them warned and

nourished their charges. It was a creative, intricate structure, a menorah filled with innumerable lights. The lights inside were the souls of
men filled with the Spirit of God. Centered in the candlestick stood
Jesus, the Savior of the world. No matter the principalities, powers,
might, and dominions, the future of the world lay in the hands of
Yahweh. One hand held the stars, and the other secured the book.
The Son of God won the right to control the angels and decide the
fate of Lucifer.

CHAPTER 16

Infiltration of the Thin Line

Satan watched the angels unroll the stone. He knew Yahweh had left the tomb to present Himself in heaven. When the Son returned to Earth, Lucifer assumed he had been rejected. Believing that killing Christ condemned him, Lucifer was stunned when Christ rose again. Straightaway, he shot to the fringes of heaven, waiting in anxious anticipation to see what would happen next.

In heaven, the atmospheric air was filled heavily with static electrons. With each moment, the energy increased, consolidating at the throne. Within the streams of light, Lucifer witnessed the Son appear. Everything froze. All stood still in the light. After the light lowered its radiance, the Father and Son embraced the affection unnerving Lucifer. Pulling back, God the Father addressed Jesus, "Precious Son. You, being made better than the angels, are more excellent than them." Immediately, Satan understood the spirit of the words. The words barbed him; they pointed to him. The Father asked, "Can any angel claim you to be his Son? Can any of them say, 'I will be your father, and you will be my Son'?" Groaning, Lucifer turned red with envy. Beside himself and startled, he stared as the Father continued, "You, my Son, being the first begotten, the firstborn of the sinless, have won the admiration of all angels." All hosts, well versed in the history of rebellion, understood the expression. Looking through the angels, the Father said, "Who made the angels spirits? O' winds, who made you ministers of fire?" With a nod of pride, he continued, "Therefore, worship my Son."

Power surged from the Father. Lucifer barely saw past the pulses. Touching the Son, the Father energized him. An immense dynamism passed through the Son and to the seven angels who stood ready. All accepted their place because the angelic host believed. The Father finalized his speech. "I give you authority, my Son. From this day and forever, this scepter of righteousness and this kingdom are yours." He handed Jesus a golden scepter. "You are the same yesterday, today, and forever. You will never fail." Rotating slowly, he inspected the angels. "To which of the angels said at any time, 'Sit at my right hand until I make all enemies your footstool?'" The Son took his place on the throne.

As Yahweh touched the chair, Lucifer jolted; his whole being quivered. Peering his fiery eyes at Lucifer, the words from the Father cut him. "We created in our image. That image is now the heirs of salvation. This promise is not for you because your design was not considered." Lucifer realized the ramifications of his actions. The Father decreed, "What you have taken, the evil you have caused, all of it is now on your head. Your actions brought instability to heaven and brought doubt on my Son." With searing words, the Father passed judgment. "That corruption you created is now placed on you. This mark cursed man to death. It shall likewise curse you." Hot displeasure etched his face, "You, Lucifer, are from this point forward banned from our sight. With this curse, the doors of heaven will be shut to you." With a deep breath, he said, "Begone!" The red dragon, who knocked a third of the stars, the Leviathan that made war in heaven, fell back to Earth.

All in heaven witnessed the darkness of death land on Lucifer. Without warning, a crack echoed through the air. Jesus broke a seal on the book. A flash of light encircled Yahweh. All in heaven heard another sharp sound, a sound that rumbled through the air. The face of the lion of the creature shouted in heaven, "Come and see."

Once the light diminished, Yahweh was no longer at the throne. In the middle of the clouds of heaven stood a white horseman. Sitting upon the white horse, the Son of God held a bow, a long-range weapon designed to levy damage from a distance. Christ had pulled the arrow and shot it to Earth. Lucifer saw the bright light expand at the point of impact. Lining the heavens, a thin vapor strung from heaven to Earth. Satan followed the line. On Earth, the misty line frayed in many directions, attaching to those that followed Jesus. The Spirit of God invaded the Earth. Hundreds of lights flickered; the disciples were no longer the only ones with the Comforter. Following the thin strand, he understood the purpose of the arrow. It was the thin line of the Father's Spirit. Once inaccessible, now obtainable, the line tied the two realms together. Yahweh dispatched the seven angels.

Jesus broke another seal. With a crack, Lucifer reeled in hostility. Suddenly, a barrier encompassed him. In pain, he shouted, "I have been cast out." The mark locked Lucifer permanently from heaven. Consternation filled Satan. He shouted to heaven, "Was not I in that certain place with you?" Disgusted that men held greater potential, he said, "What is man?" The pain of separation drove the angel mad. "Why care for them? Or even for your Son that you gave such attention?" Raising his face, he screamed, "Why did you set him lower than me, lower than angels, then crown him with glory and honor?" Satan's eyes filled with hurt; they reflected his pain. "Now you have set all in his hands and subjected everything under his feet—you left me nothing!" With the strike of an arrow, men could become sons of God. Drawing his sword, he proclaimed, "Curse or not, I will be god." Seeing the connection infuriated him. His hatred burned; the hostility transformed Lucifer. He raised his head. "I'm going to destroy you! Those you protect, I will make them regret hearing your name!"

In heaven, the face like an ox yelled, "Come and see." Lifting himself on a fiery steed, Satan declared war. With the second break of the seal, Lucifer became the red horseman.

A third crack echoed through heaven. With the crack of the seal, a black horse appeared. The rider held balances in his hand. The face of the beast, with the appearance of a man, cried, "Come and see." The horseman held a scale to weigh the infirmities of men.

The beast shouted, "A measure of wheat for a penny, and three measures of barley for a penny, and thou hurt not the oil and the wine." Power over equilibrium, the black horseman weighed the consequences of conflict.

Satan committed himself to snuff out the light. Using his minions, he created wars and rumors of wars. Kings and worldly powers focused on Christians and enlightened Jews. *I am the father of lights*, Satan thought. *I will plague them, starve them, kill them*. His calibration affected economics; the black horseman regulated the consequences of Lucifer's campaigns. Beginning with the same Jews that crucified Jesus, Satan moved them to exterminate any that believed. The leaders of the Jews recruited a highly respected man. Both Roman and Jew, they tasked Saul to hunt down believers of Christ. Often, spies provided tips and hit lists for the Jewish establishment. Using these leads, Saul brought many before the Sanhedrin.

Crack! The sound reverberated through the cosmos. Within the darkness appeared a pale rider. A seal that complemented the third. The face of the eagle said, "Come and see." A sickly, yellowish-green horse, riddled with disease and war, famine followed wherever the horseman went. Its thin ribs pierced outwardly; the pale horse could barely stand. Sitting on the grizzly bay mare, a rider who had a name. This rider's name was death, for many would die. Hell and the grave followed the rough rider. His purpose was swift like the eagle, his talons deep and sharp. The workers of Satan morphed into tools for the black and pale riders. They stole livelihoods, crushed welfare, and killed without conscience. The most prolific of them, Saul, who coldly held the coats while they stoned Stephen. He was a devout Jew who callously and systematically ferreted out God's people. A peer of the Jewish leadership, his zeal for tradition and the law was unmatched. If left unconstrained, Saul would have demolished the church before it got started.

An unwitting pawn of Satan, Jesus wanted Saul to become his man. Chosen at a crossroads in Damascus, Saul became the messenger of God to the Gentiles. In his blindness, he heard Jesus speak, "Why do you persecute me?" Devastated that he had killed believers of the true God, Saul hid himself for three years. Through his fractured state, he experienced a revelation: a surreal vision of the One who spoke to him at the crossroads. In an out-of-body experi-

ANGEL'S INFLUENCE

ence, Saul found himself caught up in the third heaven. Sobbing, he pleaded for understanding. "Why did you choose me? What possibly could I do for you?" God opened his mysteries to Saul. Yahweh knew the depths of his wrenching; it made Saul a perfect vessel. The zeal in Saul became a zest for God. His name brought terror to believers. In a symbolic gesture of forfeiture, Saul changed his name to Paul. Jesus calmed his turmoil; Paul returned, strengthened to face the ones he had persecuted.

He first visited Peter. A Jew well-versed in the law, Paul was Peter's best choice to gain access to the apostles. For fifteen days, they communed; Paul shared all his revelations from God. Peter united Paul with James, Cephas, and John. Barnabas witnessed his sincerity, accompanying him on many missions. By now, many had heard that the one who once destroyed now believed. Some embraced him; others did not. Some applauded; others subverted. The presence of Paul conflicted with power struggles and deviant plans already in play. Satan never allowed Paul to free himself from his past, and God gave him a mountain of patience. A complete transformation, his life became his penance. For fourteen years, he sacrificed his strength. Five times whipped, thrice beaten with rods, once stoned and left for dead. Paul endured three shipwrecks, each time floating on debris day and night. Perils from beasts and danger from robbers, even countrymen assumed friendly threatened him. Wearisome, often preaching while hungry and thirsty, Paul whittled away to an unrecognizable state. Some thought him weak because he looked weak. Few knew the countless times he fasted, naked and cold. His personal demons drove him; Paul could not let go of his past.

A Hebrew of Hebrews, his pedigree: circumcision. God blessed Paul with a gift: a thorn in the side, a permanent scar loaded with insurmountable grief. Paul had killed so many, an impossible restitution that bloodied him. Accepting his infirmities, Paul took on established bureaucracies and suspect believers. A messenger of the devil continuously reminded him of his thorn. Satan refused to let others forget his murderous campaigns. God used Satan to buffer him. Three times he begged God to remove it, but each time he heard, "My grace is sufficient." The thorn kept him dependent on

God. Despite the interference of Lucifer, Paul counted it all for glory and gave himself to Christ.

In Jerusalem, the Jews accused Paul of stirring up the multitude and defiling the temple. Using his Roman citizenship, Paul requested a Roman trial. This change of venue spared his life because the Jews intended to kill him. It provided an opportunity to set up a church in the Roman Provinces. Predominantly Gentile, the church had an element of Jews. Conflict arose over the debate of law and grace. Sin could not mingle with grace, nor law impute righteousness. Paul reminded the church cleaving to legalities and worldly pleasures made men slaves to sin. Jealous Gentiles and envious Jews could not obtain grace. Believing exclusiveness through forefathers did not guarantee the gift. Wishing for a favored history did not qualify them. Paul brought them together through the teaching that Christ died for all. The truth of his messages gained support. These supporters helped him in areas that had not heard the good news.

In Ephesus, Paul placed Apollos, a Jewish Christian, over a church. Mythical legends of Gnostic teachings crept into the congregation. Timothy, along with Tychicus, traveled to help Apollos clarify scripture. Gnostic teachers had undermined the church, teaching the principle of elevated knowledge. Encouraging the pursuit of individual potential, Gnostic members in the church inspired lessons of innate happiness. They promoted the light of self over the light of Christ, peddling self-introspection through self-exploration. Gnostic ideas of awareness misled believers. The church began to puff up and became heavy in legality. The law of the commandments became tools of judgment. The church was in peril of becoming loveless. Hearing Paul and others preach the love of Christ, the church received instruction. From it, many hosted church meetings, sharing the testimonials of the labors of Paul.

Traveling to Corinth, Paul befriended a man named Titius Justus. He stayed with him and built a church. For eighteen months, both men preached, converting the chief priest Sosthenes and his servant Stephanas. A melting pot of cultures, the city housed Jews, Greeks, and Italians. Parishioners from Corinth held prejudices against transients. Originally from Athens, Stephanas found the church slow to embrace him. Stephanas and other transplants followed Paul, but the church remained divided on whom to support. Many elevated Alexandrian Apollos, some listened to Peter, and a few lifted Cephas. Charity did not come easily because many expected a return for their donations. The divisions led to some claiming esoteric knowledge. Crispus and Gaius wrote to Paul, updating him on the struggles at Corinth. Rather than lean on their failures, mistakes, and immaturity, Paul preached love and forgiveness. The words of charity paid off. Titus brought news that the Corinthians yearned for the benefit of Paul. Understanding the rifts, Paul considered whether, in pretense or truth, those of Corinth heard the gospel.

Finding himself in the town of Lystra, Paul commanded a lame man to stand. Witnesses shouted in their language, "The gods have come down to us in human form." Believing Barnabas and Paul were gods, the people listened. Turning a great number of Jews and Greeks, believers became known as the church in Galatia. However, within the city, Jews poisoned minds and stirred unrest. Radical Jews spread fear and terror; they agitated the city against Paul. Stoning him, they dragged Paul to the outskirts of Galatia. Relieved that Paul survived, Barnabas took him to a safe place. Once able to travel, Paul journeyed to Derbe, Lystra, and Iconium. At every turn, Jews challenged him, citing the law, not the path to salvation, the Jews discounted Paul's teaching of grace. The Jews did not like the Galatians justifying themselves through any means other than the law. Paul countered with, "For freedom, Christ set us free. Stand firm then, and don't submit again to a yoke of slavery." The Galatians loved Paul. The church became a testimony, a light in the midst of Jewish legality. Countering hardened Jews proved difficult, but some Jews contributed to the truth. Some helped in the gospel, others administratively. Concerning Jewish legal matters, Zenas, a faithful lawyer, gave Paul a wealth of counsel.

Continuing through Asia Minor, Paul came upon a city by a small river. A main route of trade, merchants frequently traveled along the roads that converged in Philippi. A place of commerce, the city housed a mixed population of Greeks, Romans, and Jews. The church began when Paul led a household to Christ. His teachings intrigued the citizens because Paul preached neither Jew nor Greek, neither bond nor free, neither male nor female, but all one in Christ. Converts represented all segments of the social strata. The crossing of lines did not sit well with the aristocracy. Epaphroditus, a trusted friend, informed Paul of the brewing dissension. Centered in the turmoil was a feud between two sisters, Euodia and Syntyche. Both members, the sisters risked eroding faith in the church. Using the friction as an opportunity, Paul sent letters teaching the meaning of fellowship. Encouraging the sisters to unite, he compared them to an example of Christ. Luke journeyed to Philippi and settled the church. Under his leadership, Philippi flourished. In appreciation, the people continually blessed Paul. No matter where Paul traveled, the church supported him.

Faithful laborers set up a church in the city of Colossae. Aristarchus, Marcus, Archippus, and Epaphras became the foundation of the church. Central to the worship of medicinal arts and Cynic philosophies, the human worship affected believers. They explored the search for serenity and happiness, desiring to discover human newness. Sounding close to the new man in Christ, the teachings of Paul intrigued them. When Paul taught to be absent from the body is to be present with the Lord, Cynics took great interest. Into spiritual health and physical fitness, Cynic believers tried to mix their ideas with the words of Paul. Also, within the church, Jewish exorcists asserted their power to call out demons in the name of Christ. They called themselves the Sons of Sceva. Although not founded by Paul, his first encounter with Colossae came from an incarcerated slave named Onesimus. Paul led Onesimus to Christ, then sent him back to his master Philemon. In the hand of the slave was a personal letter from Paul. Philemon read the letter and embraced Onesimus. In a demonstration of forgiveness, the Colossian church witnessed love. Both master and servant became strong supporters of the church and brothers to Paul.

Fellow servants stood with Paul. Facing imprisonment and harm proved unbearable for some. One companion, Demas, deserted Paul. When word came that Demas had journeyed to Thessalonica, Paul followed. Beginning a church there, members took the end-time prophecy literally. Believing the return of Jesus imminent, they became idle, receiving donations from others. Thessalonica devalued their productivity; the church became a burdensome stone to fellow believers. Hearing Paul preach charity, they formed a pretext to create a parasitic lifestyle. Misinterpreting community service to mean aid, they became lazy. In a letter, Paul clarified the importance of works and the difference between the actions of the spirit and the flesh. Charging the church to remember their example did not change some. Shamefully, a few chose to drop their labors to be evangelists. These believers did not care to preach Jesus, but to claim residuals that came with the title.

All through his travels, Paul wrote letters. His faithful stenographer, Tertius, tirelessly penned his words. Each writing addressed real obstacles vying for control. Jews wanted a hierarchy over Gentiles. Opposite the Jews, a segment of Christians demonized the Old Testament. Labeled Cathars, they argued that evidence of the Spirit exhibited itself through speaking in an angelic language. Then there were the Ophites, who introduced Gnostic ideas. All factions disparaged the gospel and reinterpreted scriptures. Satan sent tares among the wheat. They were Belial masquerading as light, turning energetic believers lukewarm. Hot one minute and cold the next, God spat the lukewarm out of his mouth. The Lord refused to mention them because they needed only themselves. To turn believers, these groups frequently accused Paul of fleecing the churches. Paul never forgot how Phygellus and Hermogenes successfully turned the western part of Asia Minor away.

Lucifer continually pushed contrary ideologies. He sent teachers to alter meanings; they successfully melded into the churches. The differences created variations of faith; Christians began to fight over doctrine. Groups pigeonholed scriptures to fit because established denominations required it. Groups catered to theology by solidifying doctrine in institutions of higher learning. The carnal could not comprehend how so many interpretations came out of one gospel. This situation spun non-denominational groups attempting to distance themselves from doctrine. Churches of love steered away from sensitive topics. The children of God became ignorant and unlearned.

From heaven, the Son watched the churches. Within those who professed Jesus, he witnessed a faithful few. Pleased with them, he said to his Father, "Father, I am pleased with what my servant Paul has accomplished in my name."

The Father smiled. "Son, you are the first and the last. If you desire to bless those you love, then so be it."

Jesus decided to write the most faithful names within his kingdom. Vowing to etch their names in the great white stone as a remembrance of the few who wholeheartedly buried themselves in baptism. Christ proudly exclaimed, "Are they not special, Father? Those that confess me without fear, I will give them hidden manna. Like I did my servant Paul, I will open my mysteries to them." Christ confessed them to his Father. Their faithfulness brought access to doors of escape and doors of protection. Yahweh knew his children had little strength, so he hedged them. They were his first fruits, the elect that shunned sin.

CHAPTER 17

Iniquity Made the World Wax Cold

The people within the candlestick grew in number. They expanded from Asia Minor into the European continent. Filled with fire, believers evangelized many in the name of Jesus. The energy of the Spirit carried itself far from Jerusalem. No longer limited to one region, the belief system expanded over a large part of the Roman Empire. They called themselves Christians, and their religion became known as Christianity. Satan lost control of the thin line of believers. The expansion upended Lucifer, and even with all at his fingertips, he could not stop it. Having authority over kings, magistrates, and Jews proved ineffective because he underestimated the power of the light. The Spirit of God pushed through the dark world Lucifer created. The fire became a beacon, and many coveted it.

The spreading of the light infected Satan; the invasion suffocated him. Outwardly hostile, inwardly insecure, the uncertainty of it flooded his thoughts. A feeling of ire filled Lucifer because he could no longer control his future. His countenance plummeted; the abyss loomed over him. Internally, Satan turned blacker than the thickest muck in a cauldron. Dysfunction moved his baser impulses because the outcome was not what he had envisioned. Hidden below the discontent and aversion lay the true agitation—Satan felt anxiety. Psychic tension became his companion. The heaviness of the curse mark was a constant reminder of his recklessness. A label of doom, an unavoidable fate, hurled Satan into a state of uneasiness and distress. He could not stop the apprehension. Judgment awaited; fear replenished anxiousness. On borrowed time, Lucifer questioned his existence and carefully contemplated his purpose.

How could God declare everything good if he created evil? he thought. *God created me, yet God proclaimed my deeds, my desires ungodly. How could that be?* Satan questioned. Contemplating the gift of choice, Lucifer shuffled through his memories. From his position as covering cherub to his defeat at the cross, Satan considered every moment, every move he made. Out of the angels, he alone opted to pick alternatives to the status quo. The Father gave the gift to the angels, and the Son gave it to men. However, the gift produced self-limiting outcomes. Satan queried, "If choice had boundaries, could it repair anything or undo everything? Furthermore, if choice dictated good and evil, then what dictated right and wrong?" After all, God decreed everything good, and no matter the choice, it had to be, in some sense, good. Likewise, if creation emanated from God, then Satan, being part of that origin, had to be good. Considering his beauty, his construction, his unmatched ancestry, his uniqueness made him a phenomenon, an enigma. Lucifer recalled how distinct God made him. His design unmatched, his majesty unparalleled, Satan pulled himself out of his dejection. Rearranging his thoughts, Lucifer exclaimed, "Indeed, I am the pure one." Satan concluded the standards of good and evil were misconstrued. What was thought evil was not necessarily erroneous, and good was not always right because everything created was meant for good. Everything he accomplished he credited as good for the growth of men. *Without his influence, the Son would have kept the world simplistic and innocent,* he thought. Satan understood his purpose. He was meant to interpret good and evil to men. His thoughts conclusive, Lucifer appointed himself the narrator of right and wrong.

His initial inhibition fragmented; he severed his bond with the Father. The hope of sitting on the throne no longer constrained him. Looking over everything, he shouted, "Follow me, and I will give you heaven on earth." Pumped with fiery indignation, Satan implemented two strategies. First, he decided to misdirect light. Within

ANGEL'S INFLUENCE

mankind, Lucifer searched for men with the right mindset. He needed leaders with the proper processes to mix truth and lies on a world scale. A select elite groomed by Satan would develop his definition of right and wrong. Through Satan, they would amass wealth, authority, and power. They would become his circle, his men to do his bidding. These elites would recruit candidates and advance the ambitions of Satan from generation to generation. They would be the angel's unseen force that would levy the torments of men at the seat of Christians. Just like Alexander the coppersmith who ensnared Paul, the thought of Christians falling into the throes of self-preservation delighted him. Satan wanted men to lose faith. Once doubt shifted faith, Christians would have nowhere to lift their heads or strengthen their knees.

The second thing Lucifer needed was a mechanism to counter Christianity. Satan decided to mold and craft a church of his own. Called Christian but modeled after ancient Babylon, the church would overlord kings, shed blood, and control times and statutes. Satan would fill her cup with darkness; her doctrine would be Christian with a mysterious Kabbalah renaissance. Lucifer's religion of old would be its foundation; his church would shine light on one side and dark on the other. Dualistic in nature, men would see its mercy, but the inward workings of the religion would be cruel and severe. It would become a powerful religion with daughter churches planted all over the world. Backed by the influence of Lucifer, it would gain wealth and lift an army of clergy. Its grand frameworks and magnificent chapels would be beautifully crafted to beguile the sight. Using Rome as its strength, Satan intended to build a church like none other, one that would spread its tentacles everywhere.

Lucifer commenced to reconstruct light. Arrogant men proved plentiful; Satan found no shortage of the intellectually enlightened. Gathering his elite, he plotted multileveled schemes in their hearts. Adding to his inner circle, he added spiritual teachers filled with delusional deception. One influencing the secular and the other the spiritual, both comprised of power-hungry men. Behind both systems, an army of angels and demons waited, ready to assist. Through his elite and church, Lucifer would deceive, and they would become the faces of Lucifer's Ashlar stone. Within the depths of humanity, he found his subjects. Through the swaying of Caesars, he assembled his church. Both stood ready, poised to be unleashed upon the world. Without warning, the sound of a crack reverberated from heaven to earth.

CHAPTER 18

Fifth Seal of Martyrdom

With a crack, the world grew grim. Satan stood behind the Caesars. He influenced them to see Christians as nothing more than objects. Nero lined his evening walks with burning bodies on trees. Stitching Christians inside animal pelts developed into a most entertaining sport. Leaving the head, hands, and feet visible, the host unleashed ravenous dogs on them. Guests shrieked in laughter as believers crawled away like four-legged beasts. The Caesars quickly discovered killing Christians was politically advantageous. The practice established an expedient outlet to pacify Jews and pagans. Even with satanic motivation, rulers could not disrupt the followers of Christ. Irritated that cruel treatment did not shatter Christian faith, Lucifer thought, if the shepherds died, the sheep would fall. Satan inflamed men to hate teachers of Yahweh. He moved them to incite violence against anyone who preached the gospel.

Delirium filled the air; disturbances of consciousness broke out everywhere. Evil men erupted at the sound of the word of God. Satan compelled rulers and crowds to kill ministers of Christ. Paul died by beheading, and the Greater James by the sword. Philip, Matthias, Andrew, and Simon befell crucifixion, with Peter crucified upside down. Spears pierced Thomas, and Matthew faced impaling, then beheading. A crowd stoned James the Lesser, and the ministry of Jude ended with a volley of arrows. Men skinned Bartholomew, also known as Nathanael, alive. Within a short span of time, death befell key leaders. Confident the loss would dishearten followers, Lucifer took delight in the bloodshed. To his dismay, killing them did not crush the religion. Rome could not force Christians to abandon their God for Rome's "pax deorum" or a "peace of the gods" system. The failure of rulers to eradicate God's people frustrated Lucifer. Frustration filled him. He needed something more persuasive, more powerful than kings and Caesars. Satan decided to put his influence behind his church. Until now, small and insignificant, it lay in the shadows of Rome. As the power of the Caesars waned, the false church rose.

The fifth seal began a time of patience. Quickly breaking after the fourth, it was an age that wore out the saints. Satan developed an innocuous plan. A masterpiece of artifice devised to combine Christianity with his sect. Declaring a series of judicial commandments, the head vicar sent the mandates throughout the empire. Immediately, dissenters refused to acknowledge the proclamations. Lucifer had little patience for rejection. Those who refused the decrees of his church died. To cover spilled blood, Satan memorialized martyrs. Blessed with special abilities and divine powers, his church modeled them into icons of worship. Rewriting lore kept people ignorant. Turning atrocities into holy sacrifices made for easy control mechanisms. Lucifer hated men of God who tried to educate. As leaders died, others stood for the gospel. John Wycliffe died for demanding commoners access to Bibles. William Tyndale was targeted for translating scriptures into English. Jan Hus, John Calvin, Ulrich Zwingli, Cranmer, Latimer, and Ridley perished at the stake for obstinacy. Crazy and ironic, the establishment that killed them honored them.

The false church became a church that catered to everybody. The Anabaptists, Waldensians, Novatians, Lollards, and Paulicians opposed its meddling. Nonconformists sparked rebellion over infant baptism. Satan hated baptism. He despised any thought of a covenant sealed by blood. A ritual signified by water, it tied Yahweh with believers. Lucifer wanted to compromise it and destroy the earnestness of the induction. It reminded him of a pathway closed to him. The rite between heaven and believers drove him insane. He wanted to sever the writings that tied believers to God. Lucifer muddied truth; he used his church to halt scripture translations. In defiance, learned Christians verbally passed down the words of Christ and baptism. The forced theological, political, and jurisdictional demands upended the gospel. The upheaval began to affect cultures within the empire.

To further cloud the truth, Satan impelled leaders to do icon worship. Some Christians thought image worship was heretical and idolatrous. Determined not to see God in any likeness, many snubbed the order. In response, the church decreed the filioque clause. Latin for "from the Son," it dictated the Holy Spirit can reside in symbols. Implicating that the head of the Roman church spoke the will of the Son shocked Christians. Two doctrines vehemently opposed men sharing the character of God. One group certified the Spirit came from God alone. The other believed it flowed from both Father and Son. Neither accepted the pretense of the superiority of the filioque clause. Christians wanted no part in following anyone who demanded leadership by divine right. The church threatened excommunication to any that rejected its authority. Excommunication meant no jurisdiction support, border protection, or spiritual conflict resolution. In the eyes of the false church, noncomplying Christians were no more than heretics.

Christianity grew into a counterculture. Believers became highly suspicious of governments that entangled themselves with the false church. Cryptic codes, secret gestures, and symbols of communication emerged as believers hid their intentions. Unable to monitor actions, Satan moved his minister to send patriarchs to govern. Declaring himself "first among equals," the pontiff designated a system of equals with the church head as overseer. Charged with upholding the policies, patriarchs became an extension of the church. Many patriarchs sided with those under them. Satan didn't consider the compelling power of the people. Doctrines became problematic because they hindered the success of assimilation.

Arianism denied Jesus was equal to God but of the same substance as God. They refused to respect the church head as a deity on par with Jesus. Acacian believers bickered about whether Christ had a divine nature or human and divine quality. They dismissed men who claimed to be equal to Jesus. Baptism and divinity were not the only sensitive topics. Celibacy, fasting, anointing, and the procession of the Holy Spirit became impossible to adjudicate. Christians denied alterations to what they believed. Latin churches respected Roman law and scholastic theology. Greek congregations craved theology through philosophy and putting concepts into worship. Neither side wanted to abandon ceremonial languages. Then there lay the constant threat of Muslim encroachment. Christians chided the church, faulting them for their inability to protect those they claimed persuasion over.

Satan invented a healthy hatred between Christians and Muslims. A division that began between Isaac and Ishmael, a history laden with scorn. Muslim raiders desecrated holy sites. Christians cried for a call to arms. In response, organized knights backed by the church and bands of commoners gathered into two armies. The laymen's army called themselves the "People's Crusade." Ignoring the main force, the "People's Crusade" rushed headlong into Muslim territories. Ill-prepared and underarmed, Muslim forces easily crushed them. The other army, dressed in red with the symbol of the cross, took a more strategic approach. Organized and efficient, the army of the church massacred all that resembled the enemy. In the wake of their destruction, knights murdered Jews. The slaughter strained Jewish-Christian relations. Called "Crusaders," each knight under the charter pledged an oath to the leadership of the church. They promised to claim all regained lands as divine conquests. A cunning acquisition, the overreach left a bitter taste. The carnage inflamed Muslims. Satan put in their hearts Jihad. They wanted to cleanse the world of Christians.

The crusades gave the church incredible power. Craftily, Satan used war-hardened men to exterminate disloyal factions. With extermination came lucrative spoils. Lavish living at the foot of bloody corpses did not prick hearts because those killed resisted assimilation. Word spread that the church hierarchy created an official office. Called the "Office of Inquisition," it systematically eradicated dissension. In Spain, thirty-two thousand died from the Inquisition. Inquisitors tortured fifteen thousand Knights Templar who refused

ANGEL'S INFLUENCE

to remain Crusaders. Fringe groups like the Cathars felt the long arm of the church. Judicatories traveled from town to town searching for heretics. Confessed apostates received whippings and or forced pilgrimages. However, to get a lenient judgment, confessions had to include the names of others. Testifying under duress, tortured souls named neighbors, friends, and even loved ones as heretics. To not give a name meant certain death. Criminals had no rights, and no allowance to face accusers. There was no counsel to dispute statements. The condemned had no way to clear their names. With the guidebook *Conduct of the Inquisition into Heretical Depravity* as a reference, Inquisitors used wide abuses of power. Acquiring possessions inspired their overreach. Targeting wealthy citizens, interrogators pilfered a portion before sending the rest to the church. Guilt or innocence didn't matter. Many died because of possessions.

Open hostility fell against the hunters of the church. To avert blame, the church placed responsibility on converted Jews. Demons riled people against Jews. Possessed crowds pushed censure; soon, Jewish Christians took responsibility for plague, abducting innocent boys, and poisonings. The Inquisitors and the church welcomed the diversion. Well-established families stoked aversion by claiming Christian Jews secretly practiced Judaism. Greedy kings joined the chaos. They arrested Jews, stealing a portion of their wealth before confining them into ghettos. Regions welcomed Inquisitors to interrogate Jews. Hundreds were burned at the stake.

In Spain, the excessive cruelty reached the pews of the church. In response, the head bishop sent a representative to form a legal council. To halt random bloodshed, the inquisitor general devised a legal tribunal. Formal trials elicited confessions; the public procedures turned into insincere shams. The facade of fairness pleased Lucifer. The power-hungry Inquisitors went too far and veered towards clergymen. Satan stopped any that menaced those loyal to his church.

Executions came to be known as *"Auto da Fe"* or Act of Faith. A holy title to Inquisitors who vowed to faithfully vet heretics. Stripping indicted prisoners down to undergarments, executioners strapped cords around hands and feet. Cords that cut to the bone, intentionally uncomfortable to gin confessions. With a nod, limbs stretched tightly above and below. Cords wrenched appendages with each volley of questions. Interrogators switched from pulling to twisting, tighter and tighter, farther and farther arms tugged, with each click muscles tore and shoulders left sockets. Doctors stood ready to reset joints. Non-confessors recovered in jail. Once healthy, the defendants appeared again before the court. Interrogators wrapped a heavy chain around already bruised and battered arms. Pulling them to the sides, offenders turned slowly around a beam behind a seat. A slow turn cracked limbs while squeezing torsos. Once again, doctors stood poised to reset joints as interrogators repeatedly inflicted pain. Gracious courts allowed confessed prisoners to heal before being released into society. Labeled heretics, they spent the rest of their lives as cripples. For those who held on to innocence, fire at the stake became their lot.

Atrocities heightened into an art. Demented interrogators became vindictive to those unable to compensate them. Susceptible to evil, Inquisitors recruited fellow citizens to participate in torture. Incited by fear, inhabitants ripped stomachs open and packed corn into victims. Releasing hungry pigs, the crowd watched as animals devoured their intestines. Other impoverished were held in baskets and smeared with honey. Tied down for hours against their will, the honey attracted ants, wasps, and bees. Unable to stay calm, tormented subjects repeatedly endured stings. Dragging by horses, skinned alive, and boiled in water, Inquisitors used any available means to punish the poor. Nothing compared to the suffering inflicted by the breaking wheel. Tied to a wheel, Inquisitors ordered limbs of victims hammered to a pulp. Exposed and fleshly, they left them to die from exposure, blood loss, or by birds of prey. Cruel and grueling, each torture served as examples.

Christians lived day by day, not expecting to live. Heavily yoked with seemingly no safe haven, many hid from Inquisitors. People everywhere resented the "Office of Inquisition" and the church that made it. Death had filled its cup. Satan knew he had to rearrange the soiled reputation of his church. Moving the Holy See to revamp its tainted image, he renamed the office to the "Supreme Sacred Congregation of the Roman and Universal Inquisition." A renewed extension combated Protestant heresy. The campaign switched from martyring to burning literature labeled *Librorum Prohibitorum.* Writings, mostly Protestant, ignited the streets; the policy followed Christians to the new world. It became clear to Lucifer the stain over his church did not cleanse easily. The unpopularity of the Inquisition forced another policy change. The church renamed the office a third time. Renamed the "Congregation for the Doctrine of the Faith," it shifted from executing heretics to defending the church from heresy. Wisely justifying past deeds, it promulgated and defended the past policies of the false church.

Through the office of the "Congregation for the Doctrine of Faith," the church painted itself as heroes of the faith. Religious extremists became perfect targets to build a positive reputation. Hiding Jews from Aryan murderers, protecting like-minded churches from invading ideologies, shuttling wanted pastors for standing up to evil, such efforts slowly healed the past. The change eventually persuaded Protestants to absolve the history of the false church. Quickly, it became the world monitor of good and evil. Posturing opposition to persecution, the church became the primary force for outlawing Christian extirpation. Multiple layers of hypocrisy rebuilt its image. All corners of the free world began to accept the presence of the church.

Those in heaven watch Lucifer and his church. All witnessed the conflict initiated by the seals. Cracked and broken, it triggered a period of physical and spiritual war against humanity. The blood of martyrs filled the altar. Saturated with souls, vapors rose under it. A perpetual bellow, the cries within the smoke demanded justice. "Wait, my beloved, wait for me," Yahweh whispered. The whisper followed a promise: "I will return for you and make right what has been done." The weeping turned in the air. Sweeping up the gradine insufferable cries. The pain of his people swelled up inside Yahweh. His empathy overwhelmed him; he stood before the host. "My people who know my name will shine like the luminaries in heaven. I will open the gates of heaven to them." Looking at the mist carrying souls, the Son turned to his Father and said, "Father, it cuts me to listen to the woes." The Father stood up and stepped down to the altar.

He ran his hand through the slow swirling vapor. Soaking up the pain, he felt the sorrow. Turning to him, the Father said, "It is difficult. Be patient, my Son. For now, it must be. We must allow those that seek their lives to have their way." Lifting his hand out of the bitter incense, the Father pressed his chest. Looking to the heavenly host, he said, "Fear not for the servants of Jacob and of Israel will be saved from afar. Stay strong for those of faith." Walking back to his seat, he reassured his Son. The comfort moved the Son to address the angels. "I promise there will be an account for the suffering and deviant acts of Lucifer."

Looking at his Father, the Son said, "I will not forget those that assisted in the plundering of these souls. Those that love me will I bring before me and none shall be afraid." Hearing the words, the angels rejoiced! They did not know what else would come, but they waited in anticipation for the opening of the book.

CHAPTER 19

The Reality of Dark and Light

Even the weak can be motivated. Men feared more than death; they feared entrapment. In a physical world, freedom was translated into possessions. Dangling amenities before feeble souls aroused all kinds of human behavior, characterizing them as instinctive creatures. Just like inquisitors, kings, and priests who craved riches, Satan arranged his world as a place of pleasure—a domain where tangibles measured worth and men valued acquisition. Rewarding them for obedience, Lucifer watched his chosen men supervise wars, raise conflicts, and fuel crises. Subjugating minds required stimulation. The men of the inner circle became power brokers over economies, armies, and cultures. The aim was the distortion of reality; Satan wanted to attack the minds of men.

Implementing theosophical ideas into mainstream tenets of good and evil, the men in the shadows filled discourse with inaccuracies. Misinformation flooded every source, and common folk found it hard to decipher. The proprietors of indiscernible information called themselves the Universal Brotherhood, a mysterious cult tracing its roots back to Lucifer. Many spiritualists coveted the mystical rituals privy to the sect. Gifted with angelic knowledge, the chosen executed the divine plan code-named Darma. To protect his ten kings, Satan created outer elements to insulate them. Using lesser groups as barriers, indistinct smaller circles buffeted the real charter of the brotherhood. Free Masons, Skull and Bones, Thule Society, Bilderberg, and Illuminati caught the interest of conspirators. From them, more outer rings like Rosicrucian and Golden Dawn contributed to further hiding interior agendas. A stratified layer of diversified parts craftily veiled the dealings of the Universal Brotherhood.

Woe unto them that call evil good and good evil. Meticulously, the brotherhood rewove the concept of right and wrong. Century after century, they slowly twisted darkness for light. Deification teachings of good magic versus bad, positive vibes versus negative waves, mental empowerment over God—all were part of the intricate deception. A driven projection to rewire how the world sees truth from lies. Reprocessing the definition of integrity, actions once believed right became wrong. Norms turned chaotic. Satan pulled on darkness while the illuminated Lucifer tugged on the light. Light and dark became superficially different. The world networked a humanistic construct where men decided good and evil, both notions trekking back to Lucifer. The brotherhood commandeered teachings, anchoring tidbits of fact with fabrication. Rewriting the past, and transforming heroes into villains, media puppets became mechanisms of control. All facets shared a similar reality—Lucifer's version of truth.

The world became a system of the exoteric and esoteric. The esoteric inner circle ran the exoteric masses. The repetitive formula always began with a thesis, and antithesis, and ended with a synthesis. Like literature, the thesis defined the subject to be affected. The brotherhood manufactured problems to push the general population to react. As Lucifer's elite initiated problems, the world's antithesis or reactions demanded solutions. It was the final stage, the answer or synthesis to the crisis that mattered. A well-hewn conflict resolution recipe required a matching narrative. Media puppets dutifully spun agenda-supporting stories. The winning narrative redefined light and dark. For Lucifer, the only important perception was the Ordo ab Chao or the reality of the dialectic. The elite named their method Hegelian dialectics. The technique fed truths in stages, shuffling them within untruths to perplex the people. Half-truths reinvented thought, and new ideas restructured reality.

Coacula, code for breaking down and building back, became the desired method to remold mindsets. Satan wanted to concoct an end to God by aspiring men to be part of the apotheosis. New age philosophies cropped up everywhere, claiming Christian doctrines were archaic lies. Numbing spiritual movements labeled Christianity as hypocrisy. It pleased Lucifer to see Christians bickering about insignificant things; the wedges caused more rejection. The people of God became their own worst enemies. Diluted minds set the bar high on expected perfection, anything less justified Christians as hypocrites. An unimaginable standard, the flaws of believers made it easier to entrap minds into disobedience. Tearing down and rebuilding perceptions proved most important to fulfill the Hermetic model. The men of the inner circle used the model successfully. They managed to isolate believers, labeling them strange and unconventional.

Part of the new age revival included a push for mentalism. A new and thrilling alternative to Christianity, it focused on the idea that thoughts shaped reality. Believing the universe akin to a mental projection, searchers of awareness sought to unlock brain potential. Spiritualists desired to find harmony between the seen and unseen. Both wanted to achieve their personal Age of Aquarius. As part of the dogma of the reset, people dreamed of unreachable abilities. Beginning with the idea that change comes from within, Lucifer strung marionettes to believe their actions were their own. Grassroots causes sprang up everywhere, movements that jeopardized congruity. Life turned into a paradox of an intolerant society tolerating intolerance. The brotherhood continually broke harmony to eliminate threats of instability. Relieved and grateful for the heroes of stability, the world fell into a state of mental manipulation.

The pattern of breakdown and rebuild gradually set a rhythm. A cyclic loop that kept the world in a state of imbalance of vibration. The elite never allowed rest; everything moved, and everybody had to vibrate. The instability reinforced negativity, men continually longed for peace. Understanding this, the architects of society designed scenarios of cause and effect. A redundant pattern, the rules of cause and effect led to the belief in chance. Lucifer swiped away erudition of a God that controlled destiny. Cause and effect created unpredictability since it came without warning. Ignorantly, professionals and ministers adopted chance in their lessons. Luck became part of the norm. The war over the mind progressed well, and it pleased Satan.

Then there was the gender conflict. The philosophy is that masculine and feminine features manifest on all planes of consciousness. The concept began long ago with Buddhists merging masculine energy Shiva with feminine energy Shakti to find fullness. Masculine and feminine importance highlighted occult ideas. Bolstering mystics used sexuality as purification. Gender partnership became synonymous with remedies to bias. Suddenly, honor was not only a male trait; the ideology changed fixated roles. Acceptance of gender functions revived spiritualism, hypnotism, tarot reading, and even gypsy fortune telling. Chanting took on deeper expressions; minds began to accept nonconventional gender assignments. Men and women dreamed of being each other. Gender equality turned from rights to soul-searching journeys. Media sources inundated viewers with gender issues. Another narrative of disorder, Lucifer wanted to dull moral resistance to sex reassignment therapies. His elite financially backed medical research to solve their manufactured gender dysphoria crisis.

Science and technology became key control mechanisms; however, advancements developed into intrusive and distrustful entities. Knowing the insecurities of men, the media flaunted technological achievements. Christians rallied against barcodes because many believed it a path to the end times mark. But barcodes streamlined company distribution. Chips appeared in banking and credit cards, making monetary transactions simpler. Men loved the convenience, even Christians enjoyed the perks of barcodes and microchips. The corporate world fell in love with applications and phone scans. Thieves and intrusive actors gave way to wireless security systems. Technology monitored behavior, solved crimes, and listened to conversations. Unlocking the genetic code created new cures, and ended genetic deformities, and life-threatening mutations. Visionaries considered cloning and the possibilities of cryogenics. The excitement over AI (artificial intelligence) pushed for disease-free futuristic physiques. Thinkers envisioned having self-sustaining bodies run by AI imprints of the psyche. Deoxyribonucleic acid, or DNA, became a

ANGEL'S INFLUENCE

genetic fingerprint. DNA forensics identified eye and hair color, gender, and ethnicity. Microchip insertion opened narratives for a higher quality of lifestyle. What Christians called the mark had the ability to open doors, start machinery, and secure personal and economic information. To be chipped meant freedom, a convenience that came with a swipe. With all its good, technology had a dark side. The new science provided a means to track dissenters and believers of Yahweh.

Those who worshiped technology unknowingly became slaves. Algorithms and AI systems took over ideas that affected daily lives. More and more, men thought living for God was not living. The system had no place for Christians; believers fell into distress as they watched their prosperity and families suffer. A world full of idolatry, witchcraft, and hatred encircled them. The media welcomed ambitions, wrath, strife, and sedition over peace, love, or forgiveness. Heartless envying, murders, and acts of drunkenness became commonplace; Satan welcomed revelings of all sorts. Christians lived in a foreign land where both the simple and wise dwelt in confusion. A masterful desensitization performed on a world scale, men became deaf to the Word of God.

CHAPTER 20

Lucifer's Prophetic Reality

Knowing of a predicted catastrophe, Lucifer desired a sign. Meticulously, he used unreasonable and wicked men to effect change, but he wanted a sign to implement his final phase. The centerpiece of his plan was a man that would be the catalytic instrument to bring about his kingdom. Within his elite, he cultivated a man, an unobtrusive figure groomed to be possessed by him. But before the rise of his vessel, Satan watched for an indicator. Within the prophetic language, the Apostle John referred to a woman with stars over her head and the moon at her feet. Believing the cryptic warnings of coming disaster, Satan watched the stars. He embraced the sky; he believed there was an omen meant only for him. A signal of dire portent, he believed the stars would reveal the time to implement his godless order.

One night, the constellation known as Virgo appeared. The outline of a woman, her feet hovered over the moon. Above Virgo, a circlet adorned her head. Stars in the constellation Leo crowned the woman. The rare alignment invigorated Lucifer. "This is it! The woman of the words," he shouted. What made the astrological sighting most rare, was a great light illuminated in her body. It appeared the woman travailed with child. Satan had no doubt his man of sin was to be that child. A messiah with him inside living among the people. Being Lucifer the light bearer, it seemed fitting to animate his incandescent glow through a man. Satan watched the astrological pairing through the night.

As morning closed, the sun peeked over the horizon. The rays clothed Virgo before it hid her from sight. Seeing this quickened his spirit. Satan thought, how fitting the sun adorned her. Throughout history, men worshiped him through the sun. Certain the sign was meant for him, Satan fell into a deeper state of delusion. The countdown to calamity was apparent; Satan readied his angels and primed his men to strike. He planned to take advantage of the seal destined to bring the earthquake. At their lowest point, men will seek a messiah, he surmised. With the sign in the stars, Satan entered into the man, his Antichrist.

His chosen man grew up worshiping the dragon. The same dragon with seven heads and ten horns, known in heaven as Lucifer. The angels of God marveled at this beast. They saw how the cherub turned into an abomination. Donning crowns on each head, through time he amassed kingdoms. Kingdom after kingdom, each cycle amalgamated governments. The restructuring continued until Lucifer formed a system filled with capable, manipulable states. From the dragon protruded ten horns. Each horn represented a man groomed to control. All powerful in their own right, they were ten kings who freely gave Lucifer their strength. They were men who had no kingdom but lived like kings. Men made by the aggregating strings of the influence of Lucifer. Through them, he unified economies, media, and political landscapes.

The angels from heaven noted that a dragon's head drooped low. Dangling lifeless, shriveled, and bruised, it amassed an immense blow. It was the head that received a deadly wound at the cross. The heavenly host pitied Lucifer. The dead head always present, a grim reminder of his curse and his loss. For all his actions, the angels knew the cherub flailed in vain. Lucifer, the red dragon, the red horseman showed all vestiges of his ancientness. There from the beginning, luring angels from heaven, he waited in anticipation to kill the Christ child. Constantly steering the world in a fashion to gain an advantage. In his defiance, Satan believed the end would find him victorious. Confident in his efforts, he assured himself, because he saw the sign.

Many times, Archangel Michael has pitted his army against the forces of Satan. Unseen battles have always raged around mankind. In response to the aggression of Lucifer, the Son sent four strong angels. These angels extended their hands, holding back the winds filled with calamity; the gale was held fast. A silhouette, obscured by the sun, ascended to the boundaries of Earth. It was an angel holding the seal of the living God. Peering down, he cried with a loud voice, "Hurt not the earth, sea, or trees until we have sealed the first servants of our God on their foreheads." The four angels that held the winds listened to the angel. The seal gave it the authority to speak the will of their Master. Immediately, lights flickered all over the planet. An illumination of the Spirit ignited in the center of foreheads, invisible to the naked eye but visible in the spiritual realm, identifying the most devoted of God's people. The seal did more than recognize them; it selected those worthy to escape the beast and his system. The lights shone brightly, breaking through the blight of lost souls.

Satan could see his prey; he saw them and wanted them. The light, meant to be a beacon, became a target. Lucifer grinned. "I can see them!" The ones he accused day and night were ripe for the taking.

The angels cried, "Woe to the inhabitants of the earth and the sea, for the devil has come down unto you, having great wrath, because he knows he has a short time before his final judgment." Those believers found not worthy of protection became the remnant. At the breaking of the seal, they were destined to become part of the second harvest. In the coming chaos, the remnants will find themselves at the mercy of Lucifer and his system. God allowed it because there was guile found in them. This will be the trial of faith; it will be a time never perceived as possible. At the rumbling of the quake, all will fall into a state of abandonment—an unthinkable test, a time of great sorrow. Many will suffer separation; the connection with God will seem gone. Yahweh will hear them, but he will not respond. For a season, Satan will have his way. All scriptures had to be fulfilled, and all seals had to be opened. He who endures to the end will be saved.

CHAPTER 21

The Seal That Set the Trumpets to Sound

In the end times, wars and rumors of wars dulled the senses. Across the planet, seismic activity erupted in many places. Accounts of both became so common that hearing them stirred little concern. Signs of the prophetic words testified against the human race. Yahweh held the book. With each crack of the kingly signets, he moved closer to opening it. Lucifer hated that Yahweh held it because the book meant Christ controlled time. The seals of war were his; the book of trumpets was his. Yahweh had the power, and Satan abhorred that he did. All who read the scriptures knew of a specific day, a moment in time when the earth would reel like a drunkard. On that day, Satan plotted to implement his insidious plan. In the height of panic, no one would notice the disappearance of Christians. His men of power prepared to gather and annihilate the children of God.

However, the real prize he sought was God's elect. These followers loved equally, forgave always, and never faltered in the face of adversity. Their walk was fierce, their prayers heavy; they lived with Jesus in mind. They were shining beacons, the first fruits of God. Satan had the reprobates. He was not interested in the spiritually dead or lukewarm ones. Influencing weak, prideful believers ignorant of scripture proved easy. Lucifer used them to throw stumbling blocks at the feet of the elect. Nominal Christians, lacking the same degree of devotion, became their greatest enemies.

As time marched on, Lucifer pushed governments to harden their stance on worship. Word of Christian brutality in faraway places trickled through chat channels and social blogs. Congregations prayed, and others sent monetary aid to support struggles of faith. In the free world, battles centered around policies that curtailed speech and expression. Negative positions wanted Christians seen but not heard. For now, freedom of worship existed in democratic societies. However, a cloud loomed. Many felt uneasiness mentioning the name of Jesus. Christians were labeled extremists, Bible beaters with zero tolerance. The narrative swayed alternative lifestyles to think Christians hated them. Misconceptions layered hatred upon hatred. Officials sent spies into churches to seek proof of hate speech. Writings were censured, Christian logos banned, anything that acknowledged Christ was frowned upon. God's churches became known as a collection of false cults. Spiritualists felt Christian ideas held back their utopia.

Social change influenced religion. Believing in Christ, once expected, turned unconventional. Governments proceeded to treat Christians as fanatics. For many years, they had categorized them. Workers of the brotherhood tirelessly assembled lists from tithes, church membership, and charity donations. No longer mainstream, churches closed, others were vandalized, leaving those in pews uncertain. Christians caved to labels of hypocrisy, pressing ministers to alter their messages. This bending of truth had a twofold effect. Churches grew, but it was Laodicean-style houses that flourished. Secondly, preachers avoided upsetting topics. Feel-good spiritual centers are what Lucifer wanted. Of those churches that advertised "come as you are," Christianity became nothing more than social clubs. Limited growth didn't help the people because scriptures never defined the time of the seal. Believers sighed in relief, believing God would spare them from the end-time tribulation. Lukewarmness felt cozy, as comfortable as a warm beautiful day.

One bright morning, the blue sky painted a picturesque scene. The aroma of fresh air cloaked the trouble that lay on the horizon. In heaven, Yahweh pressed against the seal. At the breaking of the sixth seal, the lithosphere began to vibrate. An insignificant rum-

ANGEL'S INFLUENCE

ble accompanied a low hum. Normally stiff, the layer of the mantle exhibited signs of bowing. Pressure from the outer core pushed on the hardened crust. Fine fissures of heated ore appeared all over. The nearly solid mantle could not withstand the force beneath it. Without warning, the ground exploded across the globe. Liquid gushed from the earth; it was a massive earthquake. Violently, everything shook. Trees rocked and lost their fruit. Roads buckled, holes opened, houses tumbled, and waters moved. It seemed strange to see a beautiful sky above while the earth cracked and broke below.

Within hours, the calm skies changed. Knowing who believed in Christ and where they were, the dragon unleashed his army. Like a flood, it moved over the land. Under the guise of humanitarian troops, desperate men welcomed their aid. Within their scope, the military helped citizens, but a select number went against the woman, the believers in Christ. Those caught were sent to die in specially designed prisons. Christians were easy to find because they looked for help. The chaos made finding them simple. Others fought for their freedom. Believing in rights and fairness, they never conceived of the evil before them. Godly men resisted and paid with their lives. They chose to take up their sword against the powers that hunted them. No one helped Christians. Out of fear of retribution, friends and family ostracized them. Men betrayed them, believing it was the will of God.

Aftershocks rumbled for days. The aftermath of the earthquake proved overwhelming. Cleanup and emergency crews stretched themselves to the breaking point. Many jurisdictions, incapable of answering calls for help, saved who they could. Lucifer continued seeking Christians. Warned by angels, the elect of Christ fled. Angels, disguised as strangers, assisted their escape. In faith, they moved, not knowing where the Spirit was to take them. A relentless pursuit followed. The earthquake disrupted cameras and tracking devices. For all Lucifer's technology, his surveillance and facial recognition systems could not find God's elect. In anger, Satan stoked the hearts of the pursuers. He drove his armies to push harder. The military used every gadget at their disposal. As they closed in on the children of God, the earth listened to the command from heaven. Heat from the atmosphere created a heavy mist. The fog blocked visual sightings. Smaller eruptions carved trenches along pathways. Large equipment became useless because the armies could no longer navigate. Dust in the air blinded helicopters and planes, a frustrating interference because nothing was going to stand between Satan and his quarry. Suddenly, without warning, the mighty hand of God reached down and ripped open a crevice. The ground swallowed men and their war machines. All who wished them harm dropped into the depths of the earth. As God promised, the earth helped the woman.

Overshadowed by the greater issue, the chase for believers quietly unfolded. Through the chaos, Lucifer lost sight of the elect. With the speed of an eagle, angels guided them into the wilderness, a predestined place of safety where God intended to nourish them. Spread across the planet, here a little, there a little, wherever a worthy child of God lived, God protected them. Three and a half years of protection were promised by God, slightly longer than the sounding of the trumpets. Of the world population, only 144,000 Christians were sealed with the Spirit on their foreheads. The worthy ones escaped the effects of the quake and the demonic system. Along with the disappearance of Christians, the destroyed army was listed among the missing. No one questioned the losses because the numbers were staggering. Failing to catch the prize, Lucifer turned to those left. He took hold of the remnant of Christ.

In heaven, the Ancient of Days watched the cruelty. Next to him, the Son stood lamenting the effects of the seal. Both watched their will for mankind unfold. Like those under the altar, the Son held his place. "Just a little longer," he told the blood of the crying. But before his return, the world had to atone. Yahweh knew Lucifer had his puppet ready. All in heaven witnessed the marionette rise out of humanity. It was the little horn that the kings of the brotherhood worshiped. The symbolic horn, the man of sin. Situated next to him, a two-horned ram, a spiritual leader of the false church. The prophet rose with equal importance because the world cried for God. He supported the man known as the little horn. As scripted, when a desperate world begged for salvation, the prophet would announce the messiah, and men would believe. Yahweh called him Antichrist, Satan's

ANGEL'S INFLUENCE

man of sin. A copycat manifestation the world welcomed because he will save them in a most dire time. Both horns created a smooth collaboration. The Messiah and his prophet passed themselves off as sent by God. In reality, they were spokesmen for the dragon.

CHAPTER 22

The Rising of the Beast

Yahweh cracked the seventh seal. With its breaking, heaven froze. For a period, nothing moved; all stood still. Without warning, seven angels broke the silence. All seven appeared suddenly in the presence of the Lord, trumpets in their hands, ready to sound at the opening of the book. Before opening it, Yahweh said, "My Spirit shall not always strive with man." With a solemn exhale, he opened the book. Immediately, the link between the Spirit and men severed. Simultaneously, the cries under the altar rose to a deafening pitch. An angel walked to the altar, standing between the seven and the altar, it picked up a censer. Filling it with fire, the angel spun the thurible over its head. Smoke streaked in a circular motion. With a great thrust, the angel hurled it to Earth. The hot censer hissed as it tumbled. Within the hiss, garbled voices mumbled and whispered. Crackling loudly through the void of space, thunder and lightning accompanied it. Fire flashed as it crashed into the ozone barrier. The atmospheric breach set off storms all over the planet. The censer hit the planet with a resonating boom. The impact set off a seismic sound wave, triggering another earthquake. Blood mingled with fire saturated the ground. With the first fruits sealed and the blood of the saints poured, the four angels who held the winds dropped their hands. The whirlwind once held back was now unleashed. It was the beginning of the three woes.

The first angel blew his trumpet. The whirlwinds repeatedly lifted moisture. With each updraft, heat from the censer dispersed and solidified. Precipitation fused, and ice particles sealed the coals. Stones were cold on the outside and hot on the inside crystallized. The hail took on a fiery hue. Storm clouds pushed them back and forth; the atmospheric heat amplified the air. Winds began to rotate; the storms turned into supercells. Swirling winds moved like hands, molding and compressing the coals. Without warning, a downdraft of a supernatural scale slung them to earth. The cool outer shells did not have time to melt. The hot-cold mix traveled across continents, torching everything in its path. One-third of the earth burned. Of that, a third of the trees and green grass disappeared. The tectonic collision awakened more volcanic activity. Mountains shifted, and islands moved. One particular island chain had a peculiar formation jutting off it. Precariously hovering over the sea, the protruding rock had the mass of a mountain.

The second angel sounded its trumpet. Intense shaking shifted the island. Lava spewed fire and ash all over the mountain. The upheaval propelled the jutted rock into the sea. Out of nowhere, waves swelled from its entry point. Beneath the waters, the displaced rock mass caused a submarine landslide. Changes in the sea floor accelerated ripples; the kinetic energy created a tsunami. Across the ocean, the wave rolled, from east to west, south to north, the waters moved. In the deep, it seemed insignificant; however, in shallower waters, the wave became apparent. Coastal dwellers noticed the tide pull, all witnessed the massive crest breaking before them. A super tsunami hit everything in its path. The giant swell destroyed one-third of the ships in the world. Churning and shifting, receding waters carried debris and people away. Survivors suffered head injuries and/or broken bones. Large amounts of building materials and sewage turned the ground toxic. Uprooted plants and downed trees exposed a fragile ecosystem. The coasts had become wastelands. Saltwater washed away fertile soil, and huge sand deposits reshaped beaches. Sea urchin and abalone communities disappeared. The decay contaminated everything. Disease spread, and exposure exacerbated the situation. Those left alive found themselves without basic needs. The devastation took on a psychological toll. Stress and anxiety made people crazy.

The upwelling of the deep disturbed the nutrient balance. Heat from the burning mountain oxidized the surrounding waters. Red algae flourished, and the ocean looked like blood. Thick and dense, the blooms blocked the rays of the sun. Aquatic life experienced oxygen deprivation. Algae clogged the gills of fish, and shellfish could not breathe. Harmful gases created a red tide on an enormous scale. The released gases smelled like rotten eggs. Starving for oxygen, one-third of the sea creatures died. Foam, scum, and mats of algae washed along the shorelines, bringing fish and other lifeless creatures to the coastlines.

At the sound of the third trumpet, a great star plunged toward Earth. Men knew of the asteroid because technological advances had identified its orbit. They called it a near-Earth object; the space rock had traveled many times through the solar system. During its current cycle, it hit a gravitational keyhole. The drag moved the star closer to other stellar bodies. Heat from the sun affected the six-mile rock, causing it to begin spinning. The asteroid pulled away from its normal trajectory. Unnoticed in the chaos, the large meteor grew closer to Earth. Hitting the ozone, the concussive noise scared men. Looking to the heavens, the world saw a large star that seemed to hang in the sky. An enormous sight, all grew faint as it penetrated the atmosphere. Friction from the mesosphere ignited its gases. Brilliantly afire, the asteroid glowed like the sun. An accompanying sonic boom made the superbolide split in two. As the two halves traversed across the sky, windows shattered, and infrastructures crumbled. The shockwave downed scores of trees across the region. High in iron, the thermal ablation made the meteor glow a reddish-yellow. They called it Wormwood, a falling star. One half hit land and the other water, obliterating many towns and villages. Vast craters scarred the land, and tremendous earthquakes shook the continent. Within hours, the mainland turned into a scorched hellscape. People underground survived while incalculable numbers became sick. Within hours of impact, one-third of the rivers and aquifers turned bitter. Freshwater became undrinkable.

With the sound of the fourth trumpet, a change occurred in the heavens. Airborne debris from the meteor and volcanic ash blocked sunlight. Burnt powdery residue, like obsidian sackcloth of hair, hung in the air. The mighty wind unrolled soot like a scroll across the sky. Ash, fires, and finer debris created a long-term impact on winter. The moon became two-dimensional; its silhouette barely shone through the thickness. The film took on a sepia toning; the moon looked bloody. The sun hid for a third of the day, and the moon disappeared for a third of the night. Part of the day and night became pitch black. The cloud cover obscured the luminous points; the universe disappeared for a third of the night. Men panicked because they could not see the stars. Many feared more heavenly bodies would hit Earth.

Quickly, temperatures dropped. The blocked sun stopped vegetation growth. Acid rain made soil acidic, and a fine layer of clay pellets covered everything. Invasive species prevailed. The world faced massive starvation. Rich and poor, small and great hid from the face of God. People fell, and others died as they called out to the heavens. Voices everywhere cried to the mountains. "Fall on us and hide us from the face of him who sits on the throne. From the wrath of the Lamb." The world imploded. Crevasses pressed surface areas; fissures vomited sulfur.

An angel flew in the midst of heaven. The angel shouted with a loud voice, "Woe, woe, woe to the inhabitants of the Earth by reason of the other voices of the trumpet of the three angels, which are yet to sound!" Humanity begged for a savior.

Lucifer watched the wailing of men, salivating at the suffering, knowing the world was ready for him. Out of the chaos rose his man, the one Lucifer possessed. Having Satan within, the man called Antichrist took on his characteristics. He stood as fearless as a lion and faced the misfortunes that plagued Earth. Holding his head high, he stomped heavily like a bear; the man of the dragon crushed stubborn resistors. With fallen angels at his side, the Antichrist wooed the nations. His tongue was smooth, his charm elusive, and his decision-making swift like a leopard. He had the face of a man but the spirit of a beast. With the power of Lucifer, the Antichrist accomplished many things. With a ferocious demeanor and unyielding will, he emanated a mysterious power. The dragon-flesh combination entitled the Antichrist to share a name of notability—an ancient title known by few but revealed in the old writings.

From the birth of civilization, the words told of a name men feared—a king of an empire that created the way of paganism. Known as the Assyrian, through history, his name passed into obscurity. However, Satan revived the old king within his Antichrist. Both shared a lineage that trekked back to where the mysteries began. The Assyrian and the Antichrist, one in spirit—the first a messenger of Lucifer, the second the messiah of Satan. The dragon used them both, but concealing a deadly wound made possession of the Antichrist different. It made him a man alive yet dead. The world marveled at him. His beastly charm was irresistible, his persuasion indisputable; he pulled the world back into the light. All wondered after the Antichrist, the second Assyrian, and the system he built.

It takes great talent and skill to conceal one's talent and skill. The man of sin shared power with another—a false prophet who prophesied great things. Capable of miracles and divine visions, he predicted earthquakes and the falling star. Quickly, he got the world's attention. His doctrine propounded all good because all things came from the Lord. An old fundamental vision of Assyrian origin, it led weary souls into darkness. His teachings motivating, his lessons convoluted, under the guise of virtue men did unimaginable things. The world needed a release from the mental strain of the trumpets. Surmising activities that relieve pain as good, many turned to drunkenness, rioting, and wantonness. Recent events pushed women to illicitly move from bed to bed. Those who held little knowledge wedged themselves in tributes and customs. The prophet became a light because he helped the helpless. Gratitude rang out, but neither the Antichrist nor the prophet owned them because men did not possess their mark.

Houses of worship became havens for ravens and all sorts of dirty birds. Landing on congregations, the filth lodged in their horns. Old beliefs adopted new ideas. Religions merged because of the teachings of the holy man. The false prophet claimed authority over angels, but secretly Lucifer within the Antichrist ordered them to obey. Both men, flamboyant as sounding brass, were crafty

ANGEL'S INFLUENCE

like tinkling cymbals. The prophet proved outwardly charitable and inwardly cunning. The Antichrist solved the problems that plagued men. Through demonic influence, both became the answer to a physically and spiritually spent world.

CHAPTER 23

The Trumpets That Drop the World to Their Knees

A part of the world fell into a desperate state. The continent hit by the asteroid lay in devastation, with many dying from tainted water. The region known in the old tongue as Gog suffered greatly. Panic ensued, and the people lamented. The leaders of Gog had to act quickly; they needed to find water for their people. Yahweh intentionally moved the bitter star toward Gog because, for generations, their hearts had stood against the descendants of Israel. These descendants were not Jews but part of the lineage of the lost Hebrews. Their country, affluent, was a product of the blessing to Manasseh, the younger son of Joseph. God took the subjugated from the first Assyrian captivity and made a nation. Manasseh, a country never before seen in history, was a place of plenty and abundantly gifted. Yahweh knew the men of Gog would never move against a land free of walls, bars, or gates. The people of Manasseh scared them because they were of great strength. Gog always coveted their wealth and opulence; now they needed their lakes and waterways. The Son had to force Gog to attack. Yahweh seized them by the jaw with a grappling hook and pulled Gog to act against the lost tribes of Israel. Summoning allies, Gog built an impressive army. A coalition known as Magog, with Gog as their leader, planned to enter at the weakest point. The army decided to breach the northern parts of the country.

The surrounding countries, once friends, became enablers. It was a time of many deceivers. Manasseh had been infiltrated with despotic traitors and surrounded by salivating conquerors. Notwithstanding the poor response for aid, the people lobbed arrows back at Gog. The invading army swept through the land because they entered at a sparsely protected point. The conflict pleased Lucifer. He found pleasure in seeing men harm each other. To Satan, nothing was more gratifying than watching the desperate annihilate the unsuspecting.

Yahweh, too, observed the invading force. With interest, he watched the army reach a huge valley nestled between mountains. Within the mountain range lay two supervolcanoes. Awakened from the upheaval of the sixth seal, both still retained their magma chambers. Vesiculating gases rose within the conduit of the greater alp. Its ducts expanded, and clumps of gas slowly stretched its containment capacity. Narrow confines not designed to hold pressure began to bulge. Surface rocks cracked just as the army marched through the valley. Suddenly, without warning, the super volcano erupted. An eruptive column shot into the air. An amazing flare spewed up and outward, ejecting fire at an unbelievable velocity. The power of the earth unleashed its fury upon the raiders. Immense boulders rained down. With a massive expulsion, the ground awakened. Stone upon stone crushed flesh. Hot magma covered men; the warring faction could not resist the mountain. The explosion of the greater mountain triggered the lesser volcano. Within minutes, a salvation of biblical proportions played out over the northern parts of Manasseh. God stopped Gog and Magog.

The countryside soaked red in blood. Once the activity of the mountains ceased, Manasseh began to clean up what remained of Gog. Recovering the dead became overwhelming because the carnage was massive. Bodies piled upon bodies, a toll so deep flags marked the dead. The cleanup became an overbearing task. For months, they stacked bodies and flagged corpses. The stench became poignant; the government of Manasseh cried to their allies for help. Others assisted; time passed; flesh turned to bone. Hired contractors loaded bodies onto vessels and planes. It took seven months to bury the dead. Resources spent and labor costly, a valley east of the Dead Sea became a mass burial ground. It was an uninhabitable place full of salt and sulfur. The people continued to clear the mangled machinery and usable equipment. Retooling what they could, much of the debris became fuel sources. A terrible event turned into a blessing for those in need of heat and energy. The army of Gog produced seven years of combustible matter—an unquestionable outcome because it was done by divine command. The angels in heaven considered the destruction.

Yahweh, knowing their hearts, addressed the host. "I pulled the men of Gog to attack the land of plenty. Likewise, I turned back the army of Gog and Magog." The angels watched the power of God explode the mountains. Nothing was natural about the hailstone, fire, and brimstone. The Son judged Gog, a people who rejected him. Gog and Magog populated a part of the world that followed other gods and persecuted those who loved him. Yahweh created their desperation; he led them to their demise. The Son heard the astonishment and addressed the host, "Gog hated my people. They came ready to take a spoil and found nothing but ravenous birds and beasts." Looking down to earth, he continued, "I will rename their burial place Hamon-gog, for the bodies of Gog filled it." *Hamon-gog*, meaning multitude of Gog, rested along the sea hot with sulfur.

The fifth angel blew its trumpet. With the blowing of the trumpet, Yahweh summoned a messenger. Giving the angel a key, he gestured for it to go. Leaving the throne, the great cherub descended to Earth, carrying the key to the bottomless pit. Deep into the bowels of the planet, it traveled, passing through air and into the deepest trenches. Reaching the furthest parts of the abyss, it stopped at a great barrier—a boundary designed by the Son, a place where he locked away the vilest of beings. Now the messenger of God stood outside, prepared to open it. With a thrust, the cherub pierced the supernatural obstruction. Smoke billowed out, intense heat stoked the air. The transparent wall shattered. A surge of rotating gas bubbled through the crevice. Smoke pushed into the sky, the dense mixture turned the air darker than black and thicker than tar. Out of the vapor rose silhouettes of abominable figures, shapes upon shapes protruding from the point of disturbance. Disfigured beings that appeared like locusts, because so many funneled out. They were angels of old who, for eons, had watched men. Out of the pit, they came along with a king superior to the rest. Known as Samyaza to the angels and Azazel to men, the watcher emerged from the pit with a title true to its nature. In Hebrew, they called it Abaddon, and in Greek, Apollyon, both words translated as destroyer. It was an appropriate description for an angel bent on extinction.

However, freedom came with a cost. The Son agreed to release the most vile if they harmed neither the grass, trees, or vegetation. Nor could the fallen touch humans sealed with the mark of God. A condition for their release, the dark angels had to comply or risk confinement. For the first five months of their liberty, they had to keep the obligation. However, the angels could torment the beast and those who did not exhibit the light of God. On earth, the only illumination came from the children sheltered from persecution. Angels of heaven and angels of separation could see the spiritual auras; all knew where God hid his first fruits. Their glow shined like beacons, and powerful angels hedged them. Although the unseen could see the protected ones, men could not locate them. Yahweh allowed the fallen their power, but they hated the limitations of the agreement.

Stipulation exact; the sandglass tipped, Apollyon and his angels immediately attacked. Having crowns of gold placed on their heads, the circlets signified power over men. With countenances like scorpions and human-like faces, the army of angels descended on the world. Riding upon the lost like steeds in battle, the demonic army stung, tortured, and tormented. Men reeled in agony. With stabbing teeth jagged and sharp, the angels gripped like piercing lions. Exhibiting unyielding aggression, they swarmed both beast and man. Their speed streaked through the air. Quick movements blurred vision; the angels appeared to flow like the windblown hair of women. Iron breastplates decorated them, and angel wings jarred as they flapped. Their sound, heavy in the air, the vigorous fluttering emitted a muffled rumble. *Homo sapiens* thought horse-pulled chariots were mounted against them. Men begged for death, but the agreement was specific: Angels and demons could harm, but they could not kill. The screams brought pleasure to the angels of old. In contrast, the angels in heaven hid their faces. Their sorrow paled in comparison to the pain they sensed.

In heaven, words began to flow from the four horns on the golden altar. Horns of mercy, symbolic of refuge, the altar had one placed at each corner. A voice spoke from heaven. "Blow the trumpet and loose the four angels who are bound in the great river Euphrates." Immediately, the angel that held the sixth trumpet sounded. Four strong angels gushed out of the riverbed. From the earth of Babylon, they appeared, free to befoul men with their stench. Abaddon and his four great angels strategized against the conditions of the fifth trumpet. The four, forced into incarceration, held immense pent-up rage. Time magnified their scorn; the captains over the demon legions wanted to kill. Ratcheting up the assault, iron breastplates ignited into a fiery reddish-orange. Blazed in jacinth, the demonic army burned like brimstone. Their hostility fueled their mounts; the steeds began to bellow smoke out of their nostrils. Clouds of smoke swirled around the crowns of the angels. Flowing hair changed to gray smoldering tufts; the filaments of the fallen moved like the manes of lions. Scorpion tails transformed into serpents with many heads. With each swipe, the hydras struck multiple times. Teeth punctured to the core; the holes reached the souls of men. The pattern of the fluttering wings drummed a paralyzing dirge, driving men crazy. The fallen angels formed a horde of unhinged men. The demon-driven army reached a number of two hundred million. Apollyon instructed the fallen and their demon offspring to destroy the people of Yahweh. The supernatural army, comprised of demons and possessed humans, positioned themselves around the nation of Israel.

The timeframe gave Satan a great opportunity. Knowing the details of the agreement, Lucifer used it to secure power for his prophet. Throughout the fifth and sixth trumpet, men tried to end their lives but could not, because angels interceded. Humanity was subjected to endless torment. However, no part of the mutual understanding prevented men from killing one another. A minute seemed like an hour, and an hour a day; throughout the chaos, the prophet called out, "Repent and look to the One, and I will stop it." Men

ANGEL'S INFLUENCE

remained unrepentant as they wailed and gnashed their teeth. The prophet of the Antichrist relentlessly chanted that he alone could stop the madness.

Finally, the long season came to a close, and the time of the trumpets came to an end. None were spared from the nightmare of blood and despair. The false prophet shouted, "Demons begone!" Abaddon, his legion, and the four great angels stopped. As quick as a snap of the fingers, the madness ended, and men regained control of themselves. The world witnessed the prophet cast away the great evil. All over the world, people fell on their knees, crying and thanking the holy man. The world marveled at the power of the man of God. Men, women, and children everywhere bowed to the prophet. The prophet said, "Blessed is the messiah who gave me the power to stop the demons and return stability to the world." At the word of the prophet, the great and small believed the Antichrist to be the Messiah. The Jews stood stunned. Cries rang out; the Jews praised the God of Abraham, Isaac, and Jacob for bringing the long-awaited deliverer. The people of Judaism became servants, and their temple became the center of dragon worship. The Antichrist had to be the messiah since the prophet paved the way for his coming.

In heaven, the Lord watched the angel instruct John the Apostle to measure the temple. Ascertaining the dimensions of it and its altar, John counted the worshipers. However, the angel restrained him from gauging the activities of the courtyard. Yahweh gave the courtyard to the Gentiles, and the Antichrist allowed the Jews to rebuild their temple. The trauma of recent days swayed the Jews and Gentiles; both remembered the recent terrors. Salvation from the torment moved them to set aside past differences. For the first time, both believed in one man and one prophet. The time of the fifth and sixth trumpets caused a third of men to die. The power of the prophet proved legitimate, and the world believed. All fell into deception, and the Antichrist arrested complete control over the minds of men. The first woe spoken by the angel had passed.

173

CHAPTER 24

Never Before Did the World Need a Witness

In a world of filthy dreamers, the Lord nurtured two witnesses. Two tender olive branches were set aside to expose the prophet and his church. God made them strong, meaty, and full of substance. Imbued with the Spirit, Yahweh anointed them with thought-provoking tongues. Their power was unending since oil flowed from the golden pipes into them. For the sake of prophecy, God held them back through the time of the demons. They had to wait for the realization of the false prophet. It was the purpose of the evil; the trumpets enabled the prophet to implant fear and delusion. From his miracles, hearts turned cold; the world had to fall into a resistant state. Deep trickery, along with an artistic stratagem, pulled truth out of the hearts of men. Yahweh wanted Lucifer's minister to parade his power. The wonders of the fake prophet held men in an illusion, a false reality that only equal magnificence could break. With the command, the anointed ones rose from the depths of humanity. Their objective was to shatter the veil of blindness. The two witnesses set themselves to deliver great miracles on par with the false prophet.

The fallen angels noticed them. Unable to touch the witnesses, they focused on moving men against them. The two witnesses represented all who had been martyred and persecuted for the name of Jesus. God gave them a specific assignment: to expose the false prophet. Through their words flowed truth; from their lips mani-

ANGEL'S INFLUENCE

fested the Spirit of God. In heaven, Yahweh proclaimed, "Not by might, nor by power, but by my Spirit." It was their time; the favor of God began their three-and-a-half-year ministry. The world heard salvation from their mouths but rejected it. At every turn, the witnesses looked through darkened eyes. Their very presence incited hatred; the Jews harbored intense hostility against them. Two more prophets made no difference, as their words did not matter to the Jews. The false prophet thirsted for their blood, and both he and the Antichrist stirred volatility against them. Both men stood in direct defiance of what Lucifer had the world believe. The dark angels wanted to destroy them and the elect Yahweh hid, but the angels of Yahweh would not allow it.

Knowledge is a most genuine thing, and real understanding is a most treasured gift. The cries of the witnesses did not dissuade Satan and his plan. The prophet instructed all, great and small, to receive a mark. All walks of men—the strong and the weak, rich and poor, free and bonded—complied. Oblivious to the connotations of taking it, none realized they were being marked by Lucifer's spirit. It symbolized his essence; once inside, Satan ruled them. With the marvels of technology, the prophet commanded a chip to be placed within the right hand or forehead. A chip meant to go into the forehead of children, while adults received it in the palms of their hands. Electronic pulses stimulated the nervous system; the microchip became a control mechanism. The mark tracked activities; all aspects of living became scrutinized by the system. Through it, the Antichrist controlled central banks, the economic engines that made the world move. Global networks tracked everything from health to prosperity. The secret circles of the kings switched economies to consolidated banking.

Along with world banking, international courts partitioned law and order. Elite lawmakers divvied up rewards or punishments, freedom or incarceration. Taking the mark was a total conundrum. Some men resisted it; they refused to allow anything foreign within their bodies. To not have the mark meant instant alienation. None could partake in commerce; dissenters became outcasts of the Big Brother society. Retribution faced them; the system would not allow anyone without a mark to buy or sell. Daily activities that sustained life were shut out; those who declined the chip found themselves abandoned. Men left to their own devices quickly succumbed to the pressure. Fear enveloped their senses; the welfare of their family outweighed the toils of resistance. Opposition was harsh; the cashless fiat system had no place for sentiment or opinion. It kept countries under its thumb, and controlled poverty, and servitude. The method became the foundation of the beast system, giving Satan's circle exclusive autonomy. As with any new technology, the ease of use seemed exhilarating. With a scan, men handled money, managed personal issues, and purchased goods and services.

Miraculously, a small number remembered the tales of the mark. Trapped by their lukewarm ineptitude, they kept their ideas silent, their ways separate. No one was trusted, not friend or family, because the false prophet taught the worship of the Antichrist and none other. Satan attached his number to his prophet. The false prophet had a number, and it was the number of a man. Placed on his vestige, he brandished it like a weapon. His number, six hundred sixty-six, was a cryptic number of the most vile of rulers. In Hebrew, the number translated to Nero Caesar, who hated Christians. The false prophet held the same sentiment; he too despised the people of God. It was a mystical triangulation; the one who wore it represented the mindset of the one it described. The prophet shared the same state of mind as the name of the numerical code. Both Nero and the prophet were bent on the mastery of men. The number was Nero, and the prophet set the beast number on his attire. Both men played roulette with lives. However, the false prophet became a calculation, a riddle, a greater beast. More dastardly than any Caesar, the prophet commanded control over the spirits of men. He became a better monster because he took away the word of God. The most possible of insults, Satan used the prophet to replace knowledge of Yahweh with centralized worship.

Using the Jewish temple as his base of communication, Satan ordered his prophet to set an image in the most holy of holies. An AI with the appearance of the Antichrist, a lifelike image to present to the world. Televised to look real, the prophet gave life to it. Through artificial intelligence, all saw and heard the messages from their messiah. The prophet moved men to worship the image; both Jews and Gentiles bowed to it. The world marveled; all leaders of the counterfeit churches followed and believed. Ministers of the multitudes left festering cankers in the hearts of men. They taught lies like Hymenaeus and Philetus, who declared the resurrection had already passed. Many believed life under the Antichrist was the foreordained kingdom of God. Deceived to believe the resurrection held an allegorical spiritual meaning, men felt it had already happened.

Still preaching Christ, the two witnesses did not deter the progress of the prophet. The world population loved their lascivious and lustful lifestyle; they enjoyed their revelings and banquets. Excess filled men; none wanted to listen to contrary words of repentance. Abomination fulfilled salvation; strong drink paired itself with busybody speech. Thievery made for merry hearts, as long as they were not at the brunt of it. The world stood proud, full of bouts of evil against anyone who challenged their ways. The witnesses brought out hatred; all wanted to kill them. Men held an invincible aura, believing nothing could stand against them. Yet for all their efforts, none could dispose of the two men. The Son of God protected them as they preached truth to a rebellious world. With each encounter, hostility grew; no one listened to the inklings of the spirit.

The witnesses had power from God and the faith to wield it. Their countenance was likened to Moses and Elijah; with a word, they stopped the rain and brought down fire. Any who tried to harm them were met with fire proceeding from their mouths. None could best them because they devoured enemies with their words. Men who tried to silence them found themselves useless. Whatever malice came their way, they rebuffed it. The witnesses brought miracles against the world of Mystery Babylon. Plagues of old, water to blood, frogs, locusts—all were at the power of the men of God. The Son commanded an angel in heaven to open a scroll. Meant to be seen by Satan and his angels, the scroll measured about thirty by fifteen feet in length and height. On it, taunting judgment discernible to the unseen, it floated freely in the air. On it, a proclamation came from the testimony of the witnesses. The words indicting, the judgment clear, Yahweh left no doubt that his two men were there to expose deception. It became clear the standard of judgment would come from the same scriptures Lucifer diligently tried to pull up by the roots.

Squelching attacks of violence against them, they escaped the sword, waxed valiant against resistance, and even turned away armies. The false prophet could not best them. The witnesses of God became a thorn in the side of the prophet, the Antichrist, and those who coveted the system. Every word a testimony against them, leaders came at them but could not destroy them. Their actions and words plagued the prophet. At the end of their testimony and their message complete, protection around the witnesses fell away. After suffering their message for three and a half years, Satan commanded his men to lay hold of them. Using the men of the spiritually bankrupt city, Abaddon took the olive branches of God and killed them. Hope for the Jews had been lost long ago; Jerusalem had become as dead as Sodom and Egypt. Both witnesses died in the same city that crucified the Son. For three and a half days, their bodies lay untouched in the streets.

Men cheered as televised media replayed the visual feed of their deaths. Over and over, news outlets displayed them, commenting on how no one was above the great prophet. Declaring the men blasphemous, correspondents cited how foolishly they spoke when they called the image an abomination of desolation. Men loved the system the Antichrist and the prophet created. Unlike the witnesses who called on men to reject sin, the prophet blessed the desires of the heart. Happiness rang out across the world. In many tongues, they applauded the prophet. All nations praised the beast and his victory over the two witnesses. Everywhere, people gave gifts to each other. Gifts of joy, celebratory gestures because it was the end of the troublemakers. Many made merry with strong drink. Parties sprang up all over the planet. Their deaths prompted such elation that festivities flared up everywhere. The merriment continued for three and a half days.

All the while knowing their fate, the witnesses faithfully carried out their mission. After three and a half days of revelry, while the world watched the rotting bodies, Yahweh breathed life back into them. Suddenly, without warning, breath filled their lungs. Chests began to move, and blood coursed through their veins. Both sat up and worked themselves to their feet. Shock and disbelief overtook the world. As suddenly as the men revived, the fun and frolicking stopped; men stared at television screens dumbfounded. The sight ran shivers down spines because the false prophet had taught there was no resurrection. All heard a great voice shout down from heaven. "Come up hither." In disbelief, the world witnessed the men of God ascend in a cloud. Within the same hour, a great earthquake fell upon Jerusalem. The earthquake destroyed a tenth of the city and killed seven thousand inhabitants. Those left fell on their knees and gave glory to God. The miraculous revival and the voice that called them opened eyes. The scales of deception fell off men. The remnant of the Jews realized that the prophet and his church were a lie.

Afflicting themselves, mourning and weeping, faces everywhere cried out to God. Immediately, people began tearing at the mark; they wanted it out. The Antichrist moved his system to crush the awakening. Satan purged many through death; the cleansing sterilized society. From this, the great mystery had been exposed; the usefulness of the prophet had run its course. The false prophet and his dark religion lost credibility. The sleepers had been awakened; men cried out to God instead of the prophet. Unfortunately for them, the fire in their lamps had gone out long ago. Still, Yahweh intended to give them a chance at redemption. Spiritual blindness made it a righteous gift because they were caught up in the most evil of days. The second woe the angel had spoken of had passed.

As the Lord called the two witnesses, he instructed the seventh angel to blow his trumpet. After the angel sounded, great voices in heaven began to speak. Like a choir, they said, "The kingdoms of this world have become the kingdoms of our Lord, and of his Christ, and he shall reign forever and ever." All could hear the souls under the altar rejoice.

The twenty-four elders fell and worshiped Yahweh as he made ready his return. As the elders bowed, they said, "We give thee thanks, O Lord God Almighty, who art and wast, and art to come, because thou hast taken to thee thy great power, and hast reigned." Thus began the time of the dead.

CHAPTER 25

The Rapture that Cemented Prophecy

A dark hostility pervaded the nations. Those who made no effort to repent found bitterness. They loved the lifestyle created by the Antichrist and delighted in the precepts of the prophet. Hearing of looming judgment did not sit well with them. Despite the testimony of the witnesses, they did not fear God. The Son stood in heaven, watching their hearts become pitiless and rigid. With a gesture, the Lord commanded the temple doors to open. Misty smoke pushed out from the entrance; the world trembled as heaven disclosed its secrets. Inside stood the ark of his testament, the solemn oath made by God for men. Surrounding the temple, lightning and thunder rattled the air. Among the flashes, voices whispered the vows and accomplishments of Yahweh, spoken words that gave record of how Christ took past, present, and future burdens. Every drop of precious blood was an affirmation. The calling of the two witnesses began the expiating process. Voices rumbled; the words of authority shook heaven and earth. An angel appeared from the temple and positioned itself on a cloud. Traveling to earth, it carried a heavy, imposing sickle. Adorned with a golden crown, its task was to make known the resolution of the Son. Crying with a loud voice, it shouted, "If any man worships the beast and his image and receives his mark on his forehead or in his hand, the same shall drink of the wine of the wrath of God. It is poured out without mixture into the cup of his indignation, and

ANGEL'S INFLUENCE

he shall be tormented with fire and brimstone in the presence of the holy angels and in the presence of the Lamb." It was the judgment the nations abhorred, the sentence they refused to accept.

After the angel on the cloud finished the message, it readied itself. Pulling the harvest tool firmly back, the cherub waited for the order. Shortly thereafter, another angel came out of the temple, crying with a voice to the angel on the cloud, "Thrust in thy sickle and reap. The time has come for thee to reap, for the harvest of earth is ripe." The voices in heaven reverberated the testament. Sound echoes from the vocals bombarded the Earth and cracked open graves. Headstones fell, mausoleums separated, crypts severed; everywhere, graveyards crumbled. The worthy ones of the dead woke from their slumber. Flesh reformed, what had dissolved renewed; the dead emerged from their graves. All over, believers awakened and glorified the One who resurrected them. Servants, prophets, all great and small, listened to the command to come. Light bathed souls; the faithful rose like the sun. No longer did they consider time, as darkness no longer threatened them. Lastly, those hidden during the time of trouble saw Jesus on a cloud. The Son beckoned them. No longer did the 144,000 stay nestled from the Beast. Yahweh plucked them out; none in the wilderness experienced death. All became the Sons of God, heirs with the right to say, "My Daddy," to the Father. In a twinkling of an eye, the bridegroom met his bride; they assembled in the sky.

In the light of day, as the sun moved from east to west, a splendorous event took place. Above Mount Zion, the saints stood on a translucent barrier, a firmament clear as glass. It was large, vast as the sea, and able to hold many. Creation rejoiced at the sight of the risen. The children cried for joy because they were in the presence of God. Still human, their flesh held natural enmity; the bride needed purification. Yahweh prepared them for reconciliation. Without warning, the Son lit up; his feet burned like pillars of fire. The flames ignited the glass that kept the bride. Fire consumed all that stood on it. Blood mingled with fire; it was a transforming blast that changed the elect from mortal to immortal.

A rainbow arc drifted above Yahweh, reflecting pastel colors off the sea of glass. Dressed in a cottony cloud, the Son stepped down from the sky. Planting one foot on land and the other in the sea, Yahweh covered every part of the earth. In his hand, he held a little book. Inside the book were smaller books; it was the inspired writings. Divinely revealed from the hands of prophets and disciples, the words set the standard of good and evil. Opening the books, his eyes glowed, and the illumination swept to all corners of the world. The Son cried with the intensity of a roaring lion. The voices of the seven thunders echoed with the same passion. The seven thunders, angels of the churches, testified on behalf of those assigned to them. Sealed words, their utterance accounted for the secret things between God and men. Yahweh lifted his hand to heaven. The Father of Spirits, the Son of God, presented himself to his Ancient Father. Swearing by his Father who lives forever, Christ announced the judgment of his first fruits. Using the book of books as the principle, believers on the sea of glass began their trial by fire. Life works and ambitions burned on the Bema seat. Straw and gems, selfless and self-serving, all actions stoked hot in the flames. Worthless deeds made of straw, sticks, and stubble burned to ash. Thought and conduct found with lasting value caught ribbons of tint off the bowing rainbow. Life decisions, choices that did not succumb to the fire, refracted like beautiful gems. Those raptured felt their bodies surge in wisdom. Unknown mysteries channeled their thoughts; believers on the glass received rewards based on how they lived. Some received thirty-fold, some sixty; the merited recompense reflected the quality of their life. Blessings to be received in the future kingdom, the immortals were to become kings and priests. However, for now, the White Horseman and his army had to prepare themselves for battle.

The purification was complete, an angel flew by holding the everlasting gospel. The same writings of the little book flowed like a banner over the earth. Holding the flag, it spoke to every nation in every tongue. The angel shouted, "Fear God and give glory to him, for the hour of his judgment has come, and worship him that made heaven, and earth, and the sea, and the fountains of waters." The final plea did not warm hearts; men on earth remained defiant. Hearts thick with rebellion, those under the Antichrist cursed God.

ANGEL'S INFLUENCE

Dread fell across the faces of those on the clear glass. Once part of the human race, many held familial connections on earth. Loved ones and acquaintances faced judgment, and the saints knew what that meant. Perceiving the groaning, the angel said, "Be not perplexed. What has happened was already revealed to those left behind." Knowing the defiant chose Lucifer over Yahweh did not ease mourning; the children on the glass prayed and wept for them. They afflicted their souls, hoping judgment would be swift and merciful. Those left in the world faced troubling days never thought possible.

Of those still in the grave, only the blasphemous and second harvest remained. All had opportunities; the dead ran their races and made their choices. Evil waited for damnation. Believers not worthy of the first selection waited for the second. Those innocently blind lay in a state of repose. All on the sea of glass heard the angel exclaim, "Thus says the Lord God. They are not worthy to be part of the first resurrection." Turning to the Antichrist and his prophet, the angel cried, "Babylon is fallen…is fallen…that great city because she made all nations drink of the wine of the wrath of her fornication." The beautiful city of the prophet became worthless. The accounts of the witnesses and graveyard destruction brought on a hefty psychic tension. Lucifer needed to nullify recent events.

The Antichrist used everything at his disposal to explain away the inexplicable. Media sources spun grave openings as robberies. Video feed of the ascension was altered. Reporters played revised footage, breaking it down to a hypocritical stunt. Remastered into a magnificent ruse, earthly devilish tongues sold it as a fool's day ploy. Advances in audio technology explained away voices heard in the air. As the mages of Pharaoh, they used trickery to deceive an already confused populace. Fear subsided; the citizenry wanted an answer and accepted the reasoning. Recent circumstances caused a purging; the nations blamed the prophet for the upheaval. The centralized point of operation for the false prophet, the city within a city, had been defamed. Men no longer wanted to listen to the prophet. The media compounded their duties by adding that the miracles attributed to the prophet were fake. The Antichrist had no more use for the false prophet. The false church transformed into a social setting with the image of the beast at its center.

No longer did men believe in spiritual things. The world made an oath to worship the man of sin. Satan achieved the unthinkable; he destroyed all semblance of Yahweh on earth. His vision realized, Lucifer had his kingdom. Those left on earth housed dead souls; it was a godless world full of godless men. Lucifer designed a beautiful catalyst; men followed what served them best. Deaf and hard, those left in the world loved themselves unto death. This is the final woe proclaimed by the angel.

CHAPTER 26

How Lucifer Built His End-Time Church

The beast that rose from the sea gave the prophet the ability to speak. He was a different beast, a priest who spoke like a dragon. Wearing two horns like a lamb, he was gentle in demeanor but cruel in spirit. Through great miracles and prophetic language, the prophet united both Jews and Gentiles. A great overseer of a den of fornication, the supreme cleric led a church that had been passed down many times. She was a loose woman that the kings of the earth knew. A church that soiled herself, her intercourse was widespread. She made all in the world drunk with her erotic beguiling. Her message was intoxicating, she was a whore that sat on many waters. Nations and cultures felt her presence. With her help, the Antichrist turned the world into a place of desolation.

The woman adapted to any belief, any system, any ideology. She was the church built by Lucifer, and she earned the title, "Mystery Babylon the Great, the Mother of Harlots and Abominations of the Earth." Dressed in purple and arrayed in scarlet, the luminosity of her gems made her alluring. She was a beautiful woman who held a golden cup filled with abominable and filthy deeds; the cup overflowed with atrocities. The woman proudly paraded her title, Mystery Babylon, on her forehead. Straddling a blood-red beast, the Harlot rode it as though she owned it. She built her controlling influence on the souls of a blood-soaked world. Her lewdness impaled her subjects; the false church bastardized and debased men. She used her marionettes to make a beastly religion. As her title implied, the woman began in Babylon, where the mysteries housed the dragon. The dragon, known as Lucifer, knew her conception because he nurtured the whorish woman from her youth.

The dragon the woman loved had seven heads, each representing a kingdom controlled by him. Kingdoms in history were used to further his goals, each one ruled in the name of blasphemy. From the loins of Nimrod, the father of Babylon, she grew. Babel, the city of the religion Baal, was where Satan formed his great mystery. Baal worshipped Lucifer as the sun god. It was Nimrod who forced the reverence of creation. Pantheism became sacred; Lucifer wanted men to worship the creature more than the creator. The things of Babylon infiltrated the great dynasty of Egypt, famed to be the empire that killed the Hebrew children. It was the second kingdom Lucifer used. Every Egyptian god had a task; the gods of the Pharaohs exhibited traits of both men and creation. The Hebrews allowed Egyptians to leave with them. Taking their pagan ideas, the Egyptians of the Exodus weaved the mysteries into the chosen people. Lucifer's third king, Shalmaneser, the king of Assyria, laid siege to the ten tribes of Israel. Assyria swept them away, never to be seen again. The dragon used Medo-Persia to model the Nation of Islam. The fourth kingdom gathered and organized the enemies of Judah. Lucifer influenced the fifth king, the ruler of Greece, to refine pagan mythology and spread it across the world. Satan stood behind these five kings; each kingdom contributed to a greater purpose. They were five fallen kings that paved a path for the sixth king. From the sixth, the woman would become the catalyst of defilement and deception.

Lucifer stood behind the great empire of Rome. It was the sixth kingdom where the dragon received a deadly wound. Ruled by iron, it birthed the woman who sprawled herself before the nations. By the time Rome came to power, Babylonian ideologies had been reinvented under various deities. The mystery of iniquity had reformed itself many times, opening minds to seducing spirits and doctrines of devils. It is from these numerous gods that Rome built her church. Beginning with seemingly harmless rites, the birth of the counterfeit church paired rituals with the teachings of Christ. Declaring itself Christian, the woman fed Mystery Babylon to an innocent, unsuspecting people. By the time of the seventh kingdom, the deadly wound dealt by Christ at the cross had healed.

Although the Rome that bore the woman had fallen, it was not completely gone. The woman of the sixth kingdom survived. Following the pattern of pagan practices, the whore reconfigured mother-child worship. Throughout time, civilizations and cultures adopted mother-child deities. China had Shingmoo, Germany had Hertha, and the Scandinavians had Disa, all gods that held babes in their bosoms. Through every kingdom, and every empire, Lucifer planted a mother goddess with a child. The Greeks worshiped Aphrodite, the Sumerians Nana, and Egypt introduced Isis, mother of Horus. Israel knew of the mother deity Ashtaroth, known to them as the queen of heaven. Even Rome embraced Venus and her son, Jupiter. Satan flooded the world with mother-child gods, knowing at some point Yahweh was destined to come. His goal was to diminish the uniqueness of the Son and desensitize the minds of men. It was because of the birth of Christ that the woman designed her mother-child deity.

The false church gave their mother god many names: Madonna, from the Babylonian goddess Semiramis; Baalti, or "My Lady"; Mea Domina, or "Lady of the Sea"; goddesses with halos and stars over their heads. The mother god of the church became the mediator to heaven. Statues were made of her. Men counted beads, and hailed blessings to her. Repetitive prayers of praise, such as "Blessed is the womb that bore thee and the paps that thou hast sucked," lifted the mother above the son. The immaculate conception, the dogma of the mother god free of sin, preserved at the moment of conception. The church explained the hereafter as the Celestial Paradise and the Apostles' Creed as the statement of Christian faith. She turned pagan obelisks into ziggurats filled with rooms of prayer. The cross became her symbol; followers displayed it on roofs, towers, walls, and furniture. The priests sprinkled the sign over babies, and members ashed the cross on their foreheads. Parishioners signed it over their hearts and blessed themselves with it. The scarlet woman planted the symbol everywhere she went; it became an emblem, a charm of protection against dark forces.

The popularity of the cross brought relics into worship. As with the cross, other items promulgated lore, legends, and superstitions. Anything associated with Jesus became a relic. The crown of thorns, created wine, and even the clothes of the Christ child were attested to hold supernatural capacities. The foreskin, the cup of the Last Supper, and anything touched by Jesus held mystical powers. The woman claimed to possess Pilate's basin, the purple robe, a sponge of vinegar, and even a collection of nails from the cross. The church asserted to have pieces of the hair of Mary and relocated her childhood home to Loreto, Italy. Relics became holy; trinkets from martyrs brought great value. Sacred bones of saints buried beneath churches consecrated the ground. Bones of martyred men became a requirement for dedication. To be properly sanctified, daughter churches had to possess a relic under it. The woman called the worship of relics the Holy See, and peddling it made her prosperous.

Taking the sale of consecrated items motivated the woman to find other means of wealth. In no time, her priests began the custom of charging for religious rites. To have an "Extreme Unction" required estate donations. The selling of indulgences went far toward cleansing sin. To pay before death curried favor in the hereafter. Money became a high component for the woman; her leaders became indulgence sellers. Traveling from place to place, priests went to towns with bull documents in hand. Holding official letters from the church, they fleeced believers. On the crest of the documents, "*Sobald der pfenning im kasten klingt, kie seel' aus dem Fegfeuer springst*," which translates to "as soon as the money in the casket rings, the troubled soul from Purgatory springs." A greedy enterprise, the rich gave much while the poor had little. No money meant no intercession; the poor deceased became known as "forgotten souls in Purgatory." But the woman had a solution for the insolvent. Her leaders set up a purgatory society, a payment plan for the less affluent. A practice originated from Zoroaster, a religion of the Persian people of Babylon.

The overseer of the harlot church became a priest-king. His titles were many, the world knew him as Supreme Pontiff, Pont-Maxx, and Pontifex Maximus. He became the Peter, the interpreter of the mysteries. Followers referred to their church leaders as Vicar, Holy Father, names that elevated the minds of men. Her servants, prideful, believed no activity was out of bounds. Drunkenness, adultery, sodomy, even priests justified acts of murder. Assassinations, brothels, stealing offerings to support lavish means, leaders of the church became as abominable as the woman. The king priest declared *Unam Sanctam*, translated as "the only true church, outside of which no one can be saved." Parishioners believed the high priest held the keys of heaven and earth. Said to be mystic keys, the priest-king of the whore became the bridge-maker. Wearing seasonal purple and splashes of scarlet, he sat on a throne etched with mythical animals. Called the "Chair of Peter" with the fabled words "labors of Hercules" inscribed on it, followers kissed the chair the priest sat upon. Pomp and circumstance of Baal mimicry, subjects carried their beloved priest as he sat on his diocesan throne.

The special obeisance given to the priesthood created superiority complexes. When men rejected the church, it did not sit well. In response to this, the order *Ad extirpanda* decreed those who resisted divine authority were heretics. Heretics faced fire at the stake. Wayward believers were excommunicated and eventually labeled heretics if unable to find redemption. Campaigns began. The Spanish Inquisition, the massacre of Huguenots, the world witnessed persecution on a major scale. Power over life and death made the whore drunk; she bathed herself in the blood of saints. Holding the cross in her left hand and the cup in her right, the cross gave her divine right, and the cup, executive authority. She perfected tyranny, her voice resounded through the men who wore the miter. The miter, a headdress of the king-priest, inscribed on it the words *Vicarius Filii Dei*, interpreted "Representative of the Son of God." The words equaled the number of a man; it tagged the priest-king with the cryptic code of the original beast. Numbered in Hebrew as 666 and in Greek as 616, he was greater than the Caesar of old Rome. He was the beast who lifted the woman into a power worthy of the seventh king.

The seventh kingdom, the man called Antichrist ruled over, was made partly of iron and partly of clay. It was a kingdom that revamped the attributes of the sixth kingdom. Hidden within the seventh king dwelled an eighth king, Lucifer, the last king, possessed the seventh. Men did not know of his presence; it was the eighth king that gave strength to the seventh. Lucifer used the voice of the seventh to speak great things. Antichrist blasphemed God in heaven; he desecrated any semblance of Christ. All the actions of the past empires led to a final, most tragic kingdom. A beast system that declared war against the children of God and held the dragon as their deity. A world filled with men whose names were not written in the Book of Life. A most powerful and abominable kingdom, it reigned for forty-two months.

Along with the seven heads, the dragon had ten horns. The woman desired to beguile the horns. She loved the power of the horns; she lusted to share authority so none could challenge her. These ten kings, poised to influence, changed the world. They were men not mainstream but substantial, the ten kings blended within the sea of humanity. Their purpose was not to be known but to pledge devotion to the Beast. The woman saw their greatness and thought she could rule them.

Her point of operation centered around seven mountains: Coelius, Viminal, Aventine, Esquiline, Quirinal, Capitoline, and Palatine, the seven hills that surrounded the counterfeit city of Babylon. The scarlet woman, who sat on the mountain tops, helped the man of sin. Her false prophet became the final piece to complete the beast system, a wild system, as wild as the little horn that rose among the ten. The church whored herself out to Satan's Antichrist, blessing him over the pulpit. She seduced a frightened world and adjusted her doctrine for the benefit of the system. With her purple-clad robe flowing in the wind, she trained her daughter churches in the ways of the dragon. For her homage, Satan allowed the whore to believe in her significance. The kings gave her support; they allowed her to bask in the thought of her indispensability. It became a tolerated relationship, a convenient pact that allowed the whorish woman to overpower peoples, multitudes, nations, and tongues.

From the moment of her conception, she reigned unabated for 1,260 years. Her time of dominance ended when until Lucifer found use of the woman. Her resurgence fell within the grand scheme; the

ANGEL'S INFLUENCE

fallen angels and demonic horde influenced the harlot. Her prophet and the magnificence of her churches mesmerized people. It was a monumental lure on an international scale. Speaking lies in hypocrisy, having their conscience seared with a hot iron, the prophet got both Jew and Gentile to unwittingly follow. Once the two witnesses exposed her mysteries, Antichrist used the power of the kings to end her. The prophet who called down fire and achieved amazing miracles was exposed as a charlatan. The Lamb with two horns, the priest who gave life to the image and caused the mark, was stripped of importance. Antichrist left the whore barren. Any that clung to her or resisted her desolation was met with the rage of demon fire.

Her ending became her judgment. The host in heaven rejoiced, saying, "Alleluia. Salvation, and glory, and honor, and power, unto the Lord our God. For true and righteous are his judgments, for he hath judged the great whore, which did corrupt the earth with her fornication, and hath avenged the blood of his servants at her hand." Unbeknownst to Lucifer, God set it in his heart to hate the whore. He riled over the prospect of sharing power with her and the men in her clergy. The dragon always believed her undoing his; she was no more than a tool for Satan and the kings. Disdain for men fueled his narcissism. Lucifer's arrogance and pride unwittingly fulfilled the word of God. The prophet was a beast, the Antichrist a beast, the system and everything that came with it fell under the name Beast. But Lucifer, the author of everything, was the true Beast. Having crowns on his horns and blasphemy on his heads, the beautiful angel morphed into an unrecognizable monstrosity. The whore and her prophet were his stepping stones. With the false church gone, Lucifer took delight in his kingdom.

CHAPTER 27

Seven Golden Vials Filled with the Wrath of God

Yahweh gestured to the angels to prepare their vials. Known as bowls, each vial packed judgment for an ungodly world. Above the beast system stood the immortal army on the sea of glass, a glass mingled with fire because it hovered barely into the ozone. The saints held harps of gold and sang the song of redemption. Singing the song of Moses in one voice, they praised, "Great and marvelous are thy works, Lord God Almighty. Just and true are thy ways, thou King of saints. Who shall fear thee, O Lord, and glorify thy name? For thou only art holy; for all nations shall come and worship before thee, for thy judgments are made manifest." When the worship ended, the tabernacle opened in heaven. Seven angels came out of the temple, clothed in pure white linen and armored with breastplates, a golden girdle wrapped around each messenger. One of the creatures under the throne handed each angel a saucer. Filled with the wrath of God, smoke began to fill heaven as the last angel received a vial. The vapor circulated from the temple. The temple filled around the altar where the angels stood. Thick and impenetrable, it was the sweet aroma of the glory of God. Yahweh did not allow anyone to go into the temple until the last pouring of the vials.

The great earthquake set the sequence of events. The trumpets unfolded the effects of the seismic activity. Fire, hail, a falling mountain, a tumbling star—the damage tipped the balance of an already fragile ecosystem. Earth was slowly dying; the planet could not recover. Seven angels readied their vials, in them an exhibition of how a world dies. An angel that preceded the others held a sickle in its hand, a sickle similar to the first except this cutter had a different purpose. Waiting for instruction, the angel held it with intent. The messenger with the power over fire called out. "Thrust in thy sickle and gather the clusters of the vine of the earth. It is time, for the grapes are ripe." With an immense backswing, the angel thrust the sickle into the earth. It was a machete designed to cut down. Seven angels, one by one, commenced to pour. It was time to gather and squeeze until nothing remained.

God filled the vials with plagues, widespread afflictions short in duration. Each bowl compounded upon the next; the saints wept for the world. Yahweh knew his bride lamented for the lost souls. Right after the children finished their song, a great voice out of the temple beckoned to the angels, "Go your ways, and pour out the vials of the wrath of God upon the earth." The first angel that had power over mankind departed. The angel flew over the heavens and poured its vial over the earth. An infectious bacteria overcame men. All on earth developed noisome, grievous sores. Sensitive to the touch, the foul wounds festered wherever the mark had been placed. Painful, disgusting, and noxious, God made the body reject the foreign chip. Skin lesions boiled around hands and foreheads; painful ulcers oozed pus. Men reeled in pain.

The angel that held authority over life poured its vial over the earth. An unrecoverable ocean could not sustain itself. Heat from the falling mountain triggered a microscopic chain reaction. Tsunami waters receding off the land and sunken ships filled the ocean with toxins. Contamination on a high scale meant that men did little to arrest the killing tides. The sea became as a dead man. Within a short time, oxygen deprivation had spread to the four corners of the earth. Dead creatures from the shallows and from the deep washed up everywhere. It became difficult to breathe near coastlines. Red as blood and lifeless as a corpse, the vial took life from the deep.

The third angel flew over the heavens and poured out the vial it was holding. Like the ocean, the rivers and fresh waters turned red like blood. Although the ocean affected the mouths of rivers, it was not the reason the waters met their fate. The great star that fell from heaven contaminated aquifers. Fountains of waters, saturated with bitterness, and the blood from dead fish and creatures contaminated streams, rivers, and lakes. The tiniest of microbes could not sustain themselves. The angel over water shouted, "Thou art righteous, O Lord, which art, and wast, and shall be because thou hast judged thus. For they have shed the blood of the saints and prophets, and thou hast given them blood to drink for they are worthy." The impact from the massive meteor drove deep into the earth. Clean water could not be found; no water table escaped the bitterness. Freshwater had been given the death knell. Like the oceans, the water became dead. Mammals, birds, and even humans succumbed to the toxins. The bitterness of wormwood spared no living creature.

Another angel shouted from the altar, "Even so, Lord God Almighty, true and righteous are thy judgments." With that, the fourth angel took flight and poured its vial. The power within the vial gave the angel authority over the sun. The burning and accompanying meteors of the falling star weakened the ozone layer. Intense heat followed, unveiling unfiltered rays of the sun. Fire fell down from heaven. The angel with power over fire mercilessly scorched men. People everywhere hid themselves in the shadows. Many bodies lay in the streets, some dead, others suffering from third-degree burns. The watchers were terrified as the lofty mountains burned and the world melted like a honeycomb. Men all over the world cursed the God in heaven. Repentance was not on their lips; those on earth were thoroughly possessed. Blasphemy rang out everywhere; no one would bend their knee to the God of the plagues. The cursing reached heaven. The angel of fire who cried to thrust in the sickle did not ease its judgment.

Unfortunate beauty burned to ash; creation ended by the heat of the sun. Deciduous trees planted from the times of old found no mercy. Heat scorched everything, making it impossible to walk on the ground, touch rocks, or any man-made object. All the wonders and spectacular loveliness disappeared. Yahweh allowed his design to end in fire because he promised to never again destroy it with water. The obedient seas and rivers completed their operations. Nature did not deserve judgment; fault landed squarely on Lucifer, who maligned the Son. The curse and current plagues landed squarely at the feet of the dragon and his rebelling angels. Shock and disbelief hit Lucifer; he thought the catastrophic words of the writings had been fulfilled. Now he ruled over a world wasting away and subjects destined to die.

The angel over darkness took flight and poured its vial over the seat of the beast system. Darkness covered the Antichrist and the dragon. It was a looming indistinctness, a foreboding sense of isolation. Irreversible darkness, it was filled with anxiety and eternal separation. The vials spun his worshipers into an unnatural torment. Sores with no drink to subdue the heat ratcheted up greater blasphemy. Men gnawed at their tongues, their mouths parched and sandy, dry like a desert. Unrepentant, the world begged the Antichrist to relieve their pain. Unable to rectify the vials, hatred inside Lucifer grew deeper and more sinister. His hatred burned brighter and brighter; he seethed at what the bowls had done. Indignation burned him to the quick. What remained of the Jewish state captured the ire of the dragon. Those Jews left in his kingdom gave the Antichrist obeisance; they took the mark and set the image in their temple. Despite their obedience to the Antichrist, the Jews were still remnants of the chosen people. In the kingdom of Lucifer, they were the last connection to Yahweh. Enmity in Satan wanted them gone; the dragon decided to destroy what was left of the people of God. The fifth vial magnified the darkness; it pushed Lucifer to place blame on the Jews for the pain and suffering caused by the vials.

Crying to the world, the Antichrist stirred nations against them. Through the man of sin, Satan blamed the state of Israel for everything that plagued men. The sixth angel, who had power over the land, poured its vial. The essence of the bowl merged with the waters of the river Euphrates. The seven streams that fed the Great River were no more. The topography of the land had changed; the scenery had been altered by the effects of the trumpets. Movement of the ground rerouted the tributaries, and the heat from the vial turned the riverbed to dust. The great river that was from the beginning was no more. Men could walk on its riverbed; the disappearance of the Euphrates opened a path for the kings of the east to converge on Israel.

Three spirits plunged boldly from the dragon, the Antichrist, and the prophet. Spirits of devils, working miracles before the kings of the earth. Unclean spirits that agitated the souls of men to fight. Across the world, any that could fight were summoned. Out of men, the greatest concentration of warriors came from the east. Lucifer was glad to see the riverbed dry; it made for easy passage for the great army of the east. The spirit that came out of the dragon drove the nations and their governments. It moved all in the world to contribute their power and technology to the army of Satan. Through the command of the second vile spirit, the Antichrist assembled a massive coalition. The unclean spirit that came out of the mouth of the false prophet provided divine providence. Although the prophet had lost power, he still obeyed the Antichrist. To do so gave the prophet an outward semblance of importance. The prophet cursed the Jewish nation; he blamed Judah for recent calamities. The three unclean spirits moved like frogs; they fueled energy into the army. They sprang up strongly, assembling men at an unbelievable pace.

The preparation for that great day was set. Filled with fornicators, unclean, and covetous men, Satan formed his army at Mount Megiddo. Legions possessed men; heightened pain and agony drove them crazy. Gathered at the place of decision, the army positioned itself with blood-lust in their hearts. At the head of the valley lay the plain of Esdraelon. Esdraelon, in the Hebrew tongue, translated to Armageddon, the site of the final and conclusive battle between good and evil. It was here souls amassed to annihilate. Above, Yahweh and his bride watched the consequences of the vials. The saints accepted the bowls, knowing all too well they would provoke evil. Those on earth profited nothing because the God of the plagues readied himself to come as a thief. A horrid correction was about to come down because Satan refused to yield.

CHAPTER 28

Final Battle Between Good and Evil

A great apostasy had occurred. The army that surrounded Israel was composed of sons of lawlessness. The curse of the bowls aroused an already hostile world against God. Lucifer and his spirits roiled men into believing that the people of God caused their misfortune. Wearing the sigil of the dragon, the godless army positioned themselves. Above them stood the saints adorned in breastplates of faith and helmets of hope. Son versus interloper; a revelation of the true King.

The seventh angel, who had power over the air, poured its vial. The army on the glass heard a voice from the temple say, "It is done." Shortly thereafter, more voices muttered from heaven. Indiscernible words, garbled utterances; men felt the energy of the voices. With each reverberation, the sounds concentrated in magnitude. Echo upon echo, the compounding voices boomed like thunder. All saw evidence of the sound compilation flash across the sky. The reecho shook the earth. A mighty earthquake divided the unnatural city. Split into three, the great city of commerce tore asunder. Every human resource passed through it; it was the Antichrist's world economic hub. Along with it, cities all over the world fell from the power of the voices. Words that thundered judgment, bringing into remembrance Babylon the Great. It was time for the world to drink from the cup of wrath. A cup overflowing with bitter wine, a deserving swill for the dragon and his Antichrist.

Smoke from the temple flowed down to the saints. It was a smoke that rose continually. Gently swirling, caressing the virtuous, the essence of the Father saturated them. The twenty-four elders and the four beasts fell down and worshiped. With them, the army on the sea of glass bowed to the God sitting on the throne. All cried, "Amen. Alleluia." Heaven rejoiced at the sight of the blessed, "Praise our God, all ye his servants, and ye that fear him, both small and great." The praise resonated like thunder, "Alleluia for the Lord God's omnipotent reigns. Let us be glad and rejoice and give honor to him, for the marriage of the Lamb has come, and his wife has made herself ready." Great voices in heaven, too many to count, praised the army of the Lord of Spirits. Comprised of many nations, the saints rose to their feet. Mighty vocal expressions reverencing like thunders; they were those who participated in the marriage supper of the Lamb. Adorned in fine linen and ready, the bride and groom completed their sacred dedication. Straddling white horses, the army stood behind the One called Faithful and True. Eyes burning with fire, the Son displayed a regal legitimacy. The White Horseman held many crowns. Known from the beginning as Yahweh the Omnipotent God to Word of God, then Savior to High Priest, a new name appeared on his apparel. On the girdle around his waist, the Father gifted a new title to his Son. Obscured by blood, it was a befitting name for One worthy to judge and make war on this day of the Lord.

In front of the dark army stood the Beast, the Antichrist. Next to him were the kings of the earth along with the warriors they had gathered. Driven by the hatred of the dragon, the alliance warred against the One on the white horse. Men, frothing for flesh, attacked the tiny state of Israel. The dome of defense that protected the Jews faced its greatest challenge. With a great shout, the army of God responded. Plummeting off the glass, innumerable horsemen with chariots fell down to earth. Coming from the east and moving to the west, the day riders rode like the wind. With a great rumble and a mighty roar, the pillars of earth shook at their descent. Untouchable, the immortals of Yahweh jumped and leaped like uninhibited impalas. Saints climbed walls like stout men of war. Swords could not stop them; no known weapon could pierce their armor. Pain crossed faces, and the hearts of men failed. Fear ran through them because, for all their efforts, they could not kill the army of God.

The clash of the forces pulled most of the godless from the borders of Israel. Like a flash of lightning from the east as it moves to the west, the Son appeared in the sky. All combatants witnessed Yahweh in the clouds; his unexpected arrival startled men. As the two armies collided, the Son hovered over the skirmish. Yahweh shouted at the beast army. His words were quick, sharp, and piercing; the Word ripped apart all in its path. With a shout, Christ slew men where they stood. Those within the direction of his voice melted to the bone. With one cry, the Lord slew many. Eyes dissolved, tongues struck, and men became smitten with astonishment. Warriors of Satan began to strike one another. Enraged and amazed, their faces turned red with fright. They killed each other. Yahweh continued his descent; he floated closer and closer to the peak of the mountain.

By this time, the beast army had broken through the Jewish defenses. Vicious men murdered any they could find. Children were bashed in front of mothers; men brutally ravaged women. By now, half the city of Jerusalem had been pillaged. It was the time of Jacob's trouble. Voices trembled, men labored in pain, and everywhere they held their bellies. Faces drained, great was their distress because Judah had allowed the abomination of desolation in the temple. Now they ran from impending doom. The weak could not run; men forgot the day of rest; in desperation, the people of Israel cried out to God.

Yahweh and his army responded to the pleas of Judah. The saints pushed the dragon and his men backward. The holy army gave chase, and evil men fled for their lives. The coalition of the godless found themselves trapped at the hindered parts of the sea, a desolate place along the shore. The skirmish continued until the Son finished his descent. Lower and lower Yahweh drifted, closer and closer he neared the mountaintop. As his feet touched the peak, the mountain exploded. One side flung to the north and the other to the south; the once mountainous land turned into a plain. From Benjamin's gate to the corner gate, leveled. Once hidden by hills, the tower of Hananel had been flattened. Along with the army of Lucifer, all beasts in the way perished. The power of the Son dissolved the mountain. Boulders shot in every direction. Stones hailed down on the godless army. About the weight of a talent, sixty-six to one hundred twenty pounds fell on men. The rubble squeezed them, and blood percolated through cracks. Vital fluids seeped into the streets. A stream of blood ran through the city of David. The Son squeezed the army of its life essence until the blood reached a depth of four and a half feet. Deep enough to touch the bridles of horses, the Red River meandered two hundred miles through the streets. As the angel proclaimed, the army of the dragon had been pressed through the wine press. Not a tenth of them survived. All in heaven heard men curse God with their last breath.

This mountain that men could touch burned with fire, fiery tempest, veiled in shadow. Mountains suspended over mountains, hills sunk under hills, and the elements of the planet melted. Islands sank below the surface; astral bodies hid their light. The earth dissolved because the power of the Son moved it out of its place. Of the people left, they stood from afar, amazed at what took place. Kings thought of themselves and shook in fear. Their idol works no longer carried meaning because all was incinerated from the cleansing fire. Yahweh shattered the image and severed Jerusalem into three parts. Two-thirds of the men of Judah died; a third miraculously survived. Of the remnant, they fell on their faces and cried out to the Lord.

The saints shouted a victory chant; their voices pounded like thunder and flashed like lightning. An angel stood with the sun at its back and cried, "Come and gather yourselves together unto the supper of the great God that ye may eat the flesh of kings, and of captains, and of mighty men. Also, the flesh of horses along with them that sat upon them. All flesh yours to feast, both free and bonded, both small and great." The birds in the air descended upon the dead. As commanded, fowls covered corpses like a net. Eagles pecked out eyes, and all sorts of beasts gorged themselves. God covered the carnage with smoke from the burning pitch. A never-ending fire consumed the stench; the upheaval laid open a flaming abyss. A hot cauldron that burned continually, it became a place none could pass.

God gave the place to the cormorant, the owl, and the raven. An empty place where land once fruitful became lifeless.

Scattered around the cavity were the broken weapons of the dead. God made a pit, a place to discard rebellious angels and unrepentant souls. Whatever fell in it burned to ash. The pit became a lake of fire that could never be extinguished. Around the lakeshore, ravenous lions paced, waiting for food. Without miraculous intervention, the world faced a similar fate. The planet lost its ability to sustain life. Yahweh stretched out his mighty hand, pulling the land masses together; he reverted Earth back to its former state. Healing the air and cleansing the water, the Son brought life back from the brink. Of the few left, shame overwhelmed them. All peoples, great and small, fell to their knees. The battle against the antagonist decisive, the blood on the girdle evaporated. With the victory, a new name appeared on the sash of the Son. King of kings, and Lord of lords, a title earned for a triumphant God. On this day, Lord Yahweh saved the world. His adversary, Lucifer, received his just reward, a befitting outcome for the master of lies.

CHAPTER 29

The Great City on the Sea

The world envisioned by Satan was a place where taboos became reality. A vision that began with the acquisition of power and ended with a godless society. Founders Adam Weishaupt, Albert Pike, and Giuseppe Mazzini never saw the fruition of their labor. These men were part of a lineage that paved the way for the kings. It was the kings that gave Lucifer his pinnacle achievement, his great city of commerce. The city was the foundation, the working mechanism for Mystery Babylon.

Located on a peninsula nestled between two continental crusts, it was an economic marvel in the midst of the seas. Jewish merchants wanted to be part of the city of commerce. Prospective riches— their desire for profusion took priority over the new moon. Some of Judah subleased shops during the holy seasons. Keeping the Sabbath became an inconvenience. Making the bushel small and the shekel great carried the utmost priority. Barters of worldly pleasures, the once children of God eagerly wanted to be part of the system. The angel begged them, "Come out of her, my people, that ye be not partakers of her sins, and that ye receive not of her plagues. For her sins have reached unto heaven, and God hath remembered her iniquities." As foretold, the city became a center that offered everything imaginable. A cold place that balanced worth with usefulness and discarded men who did not have a purpose.

Godless men loved the city that Lucifer built. Outwardly wealthy, inwardly vile, the power of the kings flaunted its intrigue.

ANGEL'S INFLUENCE

It was a place that sold anything conceivable. Elaborate woodworks in cedar, fir, oak, the finest craftsmen inlaid ivory upon carvings. Carpenters crafted vessels outlined in precious woods. Brass, iron, marble, beautiful materials made way to lovely homes and furnishings. Silky linens, eye-popping embroidery, pricey gems set in costly jewelry; women loved the spa treatments, makeup, and clothing that enhanced femininity. Countries sent their cargo; all wanted an affiliation with the port town. Freight shippers from afar desired to invest their names into the city. Kingdoms sent artisans. Their smiths sold precious metals, silver, iron, and tin in the marketplace. Vessels of brass, handmade trinkets, the commercial hub paraded all manner of goods and services. Fresh spices were abundant, sweet ointments spilled into the air. Wine, oils, and fine flours gave way to delectable culinary cuisine. The city catered to the selling of exotic beasts, sheep, and horses, some paired with chariots, some packaged with slaves.

The hub had an advantage over the lowly. Pride laid the foundations of fraud and oppression. It was a city where the haughty preyed upon the weak. The influential stole innocence; women, children, and even men were reduced to playthings. Human trafficking brought lucrative royalties. Unspeakable sexual pleasures awaited those who could afford it. Even the souls of men were for sale, some as servants and others as prostitutes. Night-lights illuminated men decked in elegant array. Their desires insatiable, their hearts filled with inconceivable fantasies. Leaders proudly boasted about the greatness of their debauchery. Unholy, unnatural acts, the red-light district touted the worship of physical erotics. The heart of the city pumped like a queen; she sat high, married to her seduction. The streets had no regrets and no conscience. Citizens of the city obdurately lived in unrepentant sin. Quilted with beautiful buildings, the great city harbored a dark underworld.

All in the world brought gifts and paid homage to the city. On land or sea, on islands and mountains, none on earth could live without help from its merchants. Kings, gleefully complacent to its charm, accepted the port as a centralized hub for military logistics. As before, the angel Azazel taught men alien skills. The fallen cherub opened minds to new inventions, improved machinery, and scientific achievements. Unknown armaments and newly acquired abilities accelerated men to god-like statuses. The city of commerce built weapons, and the cherubs used them to perfect the army of men. An angel passed sentence over the city: "Therefore, shall her plagues come in one day, death, mourning, and famine, and she shall be utterly burned with fire. For strong is the Lord God who judged her." Heaven recorded the crimes of the city; the vials became the means of punishment. The marketplace, district, and home of commerce met its destruction by the pouring of the bowls.

Men stood afar, dazed and afraid. The city that made them rich was gone. Mountains of iron, copper, silver, and gold melted away. There was no more music because there were none left to play. Parties ended, songs silenced, ceremonies forgotten, the craftsmen and their millstones ground to a halt. Its entrance fragmented to powder, men took up a lamentation for the commercial city: "What city is like Tyre, destroyed in the midst of the sea?"

Kings lived luxuriously within its walls, people cried for its trappings: "Alas, alas, that great city Babylon, that mighty city! In one hour is thy judgment come." Men did not weep for it but for the lifestyle the city gave.

They wailed: "Alas, alas, that great city that was clothed in fine linen, and purple, and scarlet, and decked with gold, and precious stones, and pearls! In one hour, our riches have come to naught."

Shipmasters, along with employed sailors, distanced themselves. The owners of trade stood afar, crying as they saw the burning smoke: "What city is like unto this great city!" They mourned and cast dust on their heads: "Alas, alas, that great city wherein were made rich all that had ships in the sea by reason of her costliness. In one hour is she made desolate!"

A mighty angel took a great millstone and cast it into the sea, crying with a loud voice: "Thus, with violence shall that great city Babylon be thrown down and shall be found no more." Yahweh destroyed Babylon, the port of commerce, and the angels in heaven rejoiced over it.

With the defeat of the dragon, his city lay in ruins. A very powerful angel appeared over the earth. Casting the light of glory,

ANGEL'S INFLUENCE

it hovered over what remained of the metropolitan marvel, crying mightily: "Babylon the great is fallen and has become the habitation of devils and the hold of every foul spirit and a cage of every unclean and hateful bird. For all nations have drunk of the wine of the wrath of her fornication, and the kings of the earth have committed fornication with her, and the merchants of the earth have waxed rich through the abundance of her delicacies." Fear gripped kings. They trembled and suffered great anxiety since rulers all over had fornicated with the city. They cried for her; her destruction was grievous.

Heaven did not mourn; the city of Babylon received the reward it was due. The Son gave it a double portion because the commerce town had the blood of prophets and saints on it. The place of the great mystery was broken; none could venture to it. The destruction of it shook Lucifer and his angels. Almost all on earth expired in sorrow and in darkness. No more lies crossed their lips. The desire for meat, drink, and plunder left their thoughts. With the acquisition of wealth and good days gone, men perished. The kingdom of robbers and extortioners fell away. The world of self-gratification became a thing of the past. Judgment doused the rebellion in men. The fallen angels considered their fate. Their stiff necks and proud edification did not deter the Son and his divine position.

CHAPTER 30

For a Thousand Years, the Lord Reigned

The conflict was over; the battle was decisive. The holy army ground the evil kingdom into dust. In front of Yahweh stood the two faces of the beast system. Their arrangement with the dragon turned the world into an unrecognizable place. The Son reached down and ripped Satan out of the man of sin. The man, known as Antichrist, willingly became the face of the Beast. Next to him stood the prophet who worked miracles for the sake of the Beast, the supreme leader of the whorish religion. He pushed the mark and encouraged the worship of the image. By divine command, the angels cast both alive into the lake of fire, a consuming inferno burning with brimstone, where Antichrist and his false prophet burned until there was nothing left.

Turning to the dragon, Yahweh gestured to heaven. Out of the clouds came a great angel. In its hand were chains, unbreakable bonds meant for Lucifer and his minions. Infused with the power of God, the angel snared and wrapped the links around them. Below the deep valleys of earth lay an accursed place. Out of the sight of men, it reached far beyond the terrain surface. Lucifer heard God speak to those men left: "O my people that dwell in Zion, be not afraid of the Assyrian. For a little while, he shall smite with a rod and shall lift his staff against you after the manner of Egypt. Then the indignation shall cease, and my anger will be their destruction." The words haunted Satan; disbelief crossed his gaze. He saw the key in

ANGEL'S INFLUENCE

the hand of the angel, the key to the abyss, the bottomless pit where fetters held the angels of Noah. Shackled among them were the half-human, half-angelic demon offspring. They, too, were caught up with their fathers. By order of the great cherub, all were cast into the pit. The angels hurled massive stones upon the cavity entrance. Bound by a transparent barrier, the Son ensured all witnessed the future of men. Of those left alive, they looked narrowly upon Lucifer. Seeing a small, insignificant angel, they asked themselves, "Is this the man that made the earth tremble and the kingdoms shake?" The Son sealed Satan and his horde in the abyss for a thousand years.

Impure and dirty, the world had to be cleansed. From heaven, the sun peered through the pitch. Warm rays cut through the darkness, and the moon found itself. Like the other stellar bodies, the stars fought against the dusky sky. God opened the fountains above and below; water quenched the torrent flames. Once an instrument of destruction, now a tool of healing, Yahweh resurrected life. Molecules captured toxins, and the air began to clear. Land and water reverted, and the planet returned to its former beauty. The Lord made the heavens and earth anew, declaring to the world, "In the day that I shall have cleansed you from all your iniquities, I will set up all nations together." The Son began to gather, starting with the chosen people. God raised the Jews out of their slumber. Tearing the Hebrew people out of their graves, he replanted Israel into the promised land. There were no more struggles, no more threats, no more foolish dividing questions. The Jewish state found a better dominion than the first. King David ruled over Jerusalem, and the people of Israel awoke in the land of milk and honey.

All walks of men rose from their graves. God never desired to condemn the innocent, especially if he intentionally blinded them. Mingled within the risen were Christians, believers who took their relationship with God for granted. They followed Christ thinking their meager efforts were good enough. Both the blind and lukewarm gathered before the Son. Above the revived stood the saints, spaced on mountaintops. The Bride sat on lesser thrones in lofty places. Blessed to be part of the marriage supper, they had been granted the rights to judge men. Among them stood the ones beheaded for the witness of

Jesus. They became martyrs because they shunned the image and did not take the mark. Therefore, like the first fruits, the second death had no power over them. The Son assigned them sections of the world to monitor and instruct. The Bride of Christ became kings and priests over the nations of the world. Their task was to watch over men and teach them the true intent of the Word of God.

Throughout the kingdom of God, men were no longer tossed back and forth. There was no strange doctrine to turn them, no tongue lured them. Sleight of hand deceptions, cunning trickery, the Lord dissolved all vain deceit. The elect edified the whole, and utopia sprang forth. The people truly loved one another. Men esteemed others, and labor between brothers established bonds. All prayed to Yahweh and gave thanks for their existence. The Spirit of God was never quenched again. Disasters ceased, and dreams filled the hearts of young men. God sanctified the people and made their past blameless. The Son gave mankind a second chance.

Men rejoiced. Dropping to their knees, they cried, "This land that was desolate has become like the garden of Eden." In God's great kingdom, there were striations: immortal and human, both experiencing the wonders of God. One shined in faith, the other schooled in charity. The kingdom of Yahweh became an age of enlightenment, a world where all learned the new covenant. Christ put his laws into their hearts. The Bride drilled the people, clarifying the mysteries. Humans still struggled with the natural pulls of the flesh. Carnal thoughts constantly conflicted with the lessons of the teachers. With no Lucifer to fuel passions, men became innocent. Pliable like those in Eden, they became childlike, and easily influenced. For millennia, they learned right from wrong and how to love. In the kingdom of God, none were punished with condemnation because everything relied on the gift of choice.

Men loved the world the Son made. Sweet spice smells wafted through the air. Lovely trees oozed thick sap, every flower bloom loaded with nectar. A picturesque sight, men loved to lie beneath them. Soothing aloe plants clustered in bunches, and plenty of almonds bent the branches of sturdy trees. Bitter gum resin sprayed its distinctive smell along varieties of tropical and subtropical shrubs. All sorts of fragrances overwhelmed the senses. Delightful, intoxicating flowering plants dropped fruit and their edible leaves. Wolves played with lambs, leopards with kids, calves lay next to lions. Children led all manner of animals by the hand. Nothing in the world of God thirsted for blood. No snakes waited to strike because the earth became full of the knowledge of the Lord. Weaponry became useless, men no longer warred against each other. Swords became plowshares and spears were repurposed into pruning hooks.

God built houses—lovely, clean, beautiful cities. Stone walks drizzled in fair colors, and home foundations sparkled in sapphire. Window trims crafted with translucent quartz and gates built out of oval-shaped garnet. Many pleasant stones, and unbelievable patterns of colors ran along house walls. Magnificently structured abodes aligned pristine, translucent streets. Colors reflected off thoroughfares. The people of the world felt at ease because God became their stabilizer. All thrived; the spiritually poor rejoiced. Those of the second resurrection found an earth full of plenty. All lived in peace; none were homeless. No strife, fighting, or contention; the kings kept order, and the priests taught spiritual harmony.

Out of the upper parts of the east mountain, torrents gushed through cracks in the rock. Trees surrounded waterfalls, and mineral-filled springs turned lands fertile. Running east to south, the life-enriching aqua cut through the mountains. Too steep to venture, the crevasse set a barrier between mortal and immortal. A second ravine ran to the west. A meandering stream served as a guide to another mountain. At the base of the second summit, the stream turned into a winding labyrinth. Its intricate course made it impossible to navigate. God allowed only one path to the holy place. The two tributaries worked their way down until both merged into one. The tree of life stood at the base of the second peak, the mountain where men lived. Standing at the bend of the west stream, its roots began at the holy point. Roots weaving from east to west, God placed the tree where the people could see it. Emitting moisture from its leaves, the tree formed a cloudy dew. The dew covered the east mountain and encircled the base of the western peak. Mist particles sprouted rainbows in all directions. From mountain to mountain, bands of colors refracted light; it arced like a crown in the sky.

Then there was the valley that cut to the north. Trees along the path gave off smells of frankincense and myrrh. As the valley continued, the vegetation thinned. The crevasse opened into a desert. Arid and barren, life could not sustain itself in the wilderness. Within the uninhabited place lay the door to the pit. Also, under the desert slept those doomed by the unpardonable sin. Mixed within the blasphemous were those who once loved Yahweh but for different reasons turned away. Once called saints, they dipped into the saving blood of Jesus. Children of God who bore good fruit; however, within their walk, something happened. The cares of the world, seeds of temptation, burrowed through their armor. Minds became reprobate, and disloyal thoughts dulled their senses. Their love faded, and they lost their way. They turned away and trampled on the shed blood. To reject the sacrifice was akin to rejecting God because to save such would require crucifying Christ anew. Believers who forwent their first death found themselves incarcerated among the abominable. As deprived as Dan, the son of Jacob, who introduced idolatry to the people. His blasphemous lineage fell lower than a viper biting at the heels of horses. In the same manner, believers who turn away cause many to tumble backward.

There was no more stumbling because the Bride could read the intent of hearts. Anger, clamor; the kings and priests replaced evil speaking with tenderheartedness. The Son lifted the scales; he unified his elect with a pure language, an exclusive, accessible tongue. Telepathic speech between the Groom and his Bride; the saints could speak internally with Yahweh. God opened all human dialects to the saints; nationalities did not matter. Unashamed, the Lord blessed men. "Behold, I lay in Zion for a foundation a stone, a tried stone, a precious cornerstone. This stone is me. I will be a sure foundation." The people saw a holy city come down from heaven. Touching the top of the mountain, those who changed from mortal to immortal could go into it. The world was ready for Yahweh to live among them.

CHAPTER 31

New Jerusalem, the Most Beautiful City

The Son promised His people a city full of mansions. Inside, residential dwellings were stacked one upon another, creating an amazing and splendorous place. Yahweh bathed every part of its construction with tongues of fire—flickering, lapping tongues. The city burned with the Spirit of God. Called New Jerusalem, the Son hid it within the lights of the universe. Now disclosed for all to see, stones of many colors dotted its slightly tinged pavements. Stars lit the floors, and fire streaked over rooftops; all manner of light bounced throughout the city. There was no longer a need for an altar, because the martyred no longer cried for justice. In New Jerusalem, there was no temple, because angels no longer prepared instruments of wrath. The Son of God became the temple. Located above the city sat a throne. The seat of it touched the holy mountain and faced west toward the mountain of men. Looking westward, Yahweh declared to the people on earth, "I dwell in the high and holy place with those of a contrite and humble spirit." Finally, both groom and bride resided together. They cohabited in New Jerusalem, the city at the feet of the throne.

The throne to the east faced the footpath to the west. Connecting God to men, the trail ended where the far west mountain began. Bordering the holy mountain to the east were six mountains—a column of three mountains farther to the east and three more lined the south—majestic, interwoven towers. Each alp supported the next, on them the kings and priests held their positions. Their seats sparkled like frost; the peaks glistened with their presence. Running out of the base of the main throne, a river of fire was triggered by the Son. It set the holy mount ablaze and baptized the city. The great mountain, with its lesser summits, cast their light on men and their cities. Everything basked in light; it drove away darkness and enlivened the tree of life.

Centered in New Jerusalem stood a tree. The scent of the tree was fragrant and sweet; its bark, leaves, and flowers were always eternally fresh. On it grew cylindrical clusters of fruit, an identifying feature only seen on the tree of life. Another tree flourished at the base of the west mount. An elaborate root system connected the volunteer tree to the one in New Jerusalem. Both immortal and mortal enjoyed the bounty of the tree. The fruit in the holy city overflowed with spiritual energy. The tree with men emitted fruit good for the body. Filled with restoring enzymes, it healed bones and invigorated spirits. The sacred path began at the tree. No longer strangers or foreigners, men followed the root system down to the entrance of the city. Everything connected to the tree of life, because it was the foundation of creation. Its roots firmly entangled around the foundation of the city. Twelve footers supported it, three to the north, three to the south, east, and west. Inscribed on each one the name of an apostle. A strong base with the cornerstone as God, it was a place the people aspired to enter. A city fitly framed, its structure climbed into the atmosphere.

With a golden stick, an angel gauged the dimensions of the city, measuring twelve thousand furlongs square, equal in length, width, and height. Beautifully translucent walls surrounded its exterior. New Jerusalem stretched 1,500 miles to the east, 1,500 miles to the west, north, and south, forming a cube-shaped city accessible only to angels and those with crowns. The Son held a royal diadem, distinct from the rest. Crowned with a superior headdress, Yahweh proclaimed with a great voice, "Behold, the tabernacle of God is with men, and he will dwell with them, and they shall be his people. And God himself shall be with them, and be their God." Sitting on his throne, the Lord was pleased with the design of his city.

ANGEL'S INFLUENCE

Made of all manner of precious stones, New Jerusalem lit up like a colorful prism. The streets of gold and city bulkheads emitted an ambient yellow glow, while walks and paths shimmered like Vaseline glass. Everything in the city beamed rays of gold. A clear quartz foundation refracted waves of colors, and the wall around the city consisted of twelve layers of gemstones, each color subtly shifting with the changes in light. Above the jasper foundation, a horizontal layer of sapphire ran end to end, followed by a line of greenish-blue agate. The green emerald proved more dominant. Above emerald lay sardonyx, an onyx with red and white stripes. A brownish-red line of sardius complemented the sardonyx, followed by chrysolite, a thin yellow lava rock. Braids of all manner of beryl topped the chrysolite. Topaz superimposed the chrysolite, and an apple-green chrysoprase ran above the topaz. Red jacinth streamed over the chrysoprase, and purple amethyst capped the uppermost parts of the wall. The foundation absorbed reds, greens, blues, yellows, and shot browns, purples, and other colors straight up. Clouds bounced opaque tints; the colors amplified the beautiful city. Measuring two hundred sixteen feet in height, the wall secured New Jerusalem from those not worthy to enter its gates.

Twelve gates outlined the city, each seven or eight feet in height and big enough for a man to enter. Over each gate, Yahweh inscribed the names of the sons of Jacob—one name for one gate; three to the north and three along the south, three gates to the east and three more to the west, each gate fashioned from a large pearl. Cherubs monitored the gates, their iridescence changing to match the hue of the angel guarding them. Treading on flaming fire, the angelic host left contrails when they finished their watch. Dressed in white, the cherubs created faint tracks from heaven to earth, twinkling violet streaks of hyacinth. Men could spot multiple ropes entwining the sky, vines stringing to heaven, the lines resembling tree branches with hanging star ornaments.

Within the walls of New Jerusalem, both the saints and the celestial walked, talked, prayed, and worshiped. It was a society full of supplication and praise. Only those written in the Lamb's Book of Life had passage, and the Lord knew every name. Righteousness flowed from the throne; men witnessed the tabernacle pitched not by hands. Kings of the nations honored the great God of the city. Through the mountain path, men walked to the holy place, celebrating holy days and sabbaticals with God. The Son put his name on their foreheads. Inhabitants of earth marched in groups saying, "Let us go speedily to pray before the Lord, and seek the Lord of hosts." Ten representatives of the people interpreted for the nations.

With glee and in different languages, the nations cried, "Come, let us go up to the mountain of the Lord, to the house of Jacob." Now all knew the true God. To honor the Lord, men inscribed the words "Holiness unto the Lord" on the bells of their horse bridles. All felt the Spirit of God in the mist. The people rested because the Lord cared for them. The world no longer needed the aid of luminaries. The concept of day and night disappeared. All nations walked in the light, no longer dependent on the sun or moon.

God allowed the Jews to build a tabernacle. Measuring a mile square, the outer walls had massive gateways. Each entrance featured a guard chamber with windows above the gateposts. Yahweh wanted the golden rays of New Jerusalem to shine through the temple windows. Palm trees and detailed cherubim woodwork lined the halls. Each utensil and every bowl in the temple was sacred; the altar had a horn attached to each corner. Through millennia, the Son allowed Jewish sacrifice as a remembrance. Even in the face of their "I am," they struggled to let rituals go. Some desired to continue the prestige that came with ceremonies. The custom comforted their souls, reminding them of a past when they were special. Even in the face of grace, the people of Abraham could not part with the law. The law was their clarifying agent. Correction could not erase what had been drilled into them. The Jewish people heard the hosts of New Jerusalem praise God. From their temple, they listened to the cries. "The Lord is good. His mercy endures forever. Praise the Lord of hosts; we bring the sacrifice of praise into the house of the Lord." New Jerusalem was a holy place, not exclusive to them; the Jews needed their own peculiarity.

Healing waters flowed out of the city, running beneath the threshold of the Jewish temple. The Son split the waters at the door;

half the water diverted southeast to the Dead Sea and the other half continued west to the Mediterranean Sea. Large trees bordered the river, and smaller trees followed the streams. The therapeutic trees cleansed and nourished everything they touched. Bearing twelve types of fruit, the sweet pulp matured monthly. Medicinal leaves, compatible with steeping, water, fruit, and foliage brought longevity to the people. The waters healed the Dead Sea and its surrounding lands. The southern part of the sea held life, but the northern part, which harbored the pit, remained marshy and heavy with salt.

God had made life perfect; for a millennium, people on earth shouted, "The holy, holy, Lord over all, praise to the God that fills the whole world with his Spirit."

Joyful words hung on the lips of men; praise ran off grateful tongues. "Blessed be thou, and blessed be the name of God forever and ever."

Likewise, the angels, grateful that the Father sent his Son, shouted, "O Master, great and perfect are your ways. Blessed are you and blessed is the One who gave himself upon your request."

Led by another angel, the four great angels shouted homage to the Son, "We beseech your love for your sacrifice for those below. Your precious self, so that the accuser could no more charge the inhabitants of the earth." The first, Michael; the second, Raphael; Gabriel; and lastly, Phanuel—these angels resided over the house God made. Spreading their wings, they watched from the four corners of the earth.

Over time, memories of the past faded. The world never compiled the times of darkness. Only the Son kept the secrets of the lightning and thunder. Whispers in the thunder spoke of looming peril. Young men woke from their slumber, sweating over horrible glimpses of future events. The prophecies troubled men because they conflicted with the lessons of the teachers. Yahweh gave the people every blessing, except for the right to enter New Jerusalem. A deep envy crept in. It became hard to accept the difference between those on the mountain and the rest below. The unknown stirred many, questions grew in the hearts of men. Some queried about the relationship between God and the saints. Others felt they had proved

D.S. BOYCE

their love. Watching from their prison, Satan and his angels saw the weakness in men. Knowing Yahweh had imprisoned and released them before, Lucifer and his fallen anticipated a day when the Son would free them again.

CHAPTER 32

The Looming Darkness

For a millennium, Satan watched through the cage of the abyss, full of maddening darkness, with no firmament above or solid ground below. Seven stars guarded the pit, and they were great angels kindled in flame, each of them fiery mountains. Amid the dry wasteland, the seven stood watch over the opening filled with stones. Each angel had a name, monikers that defined them: Uriel, known as the angel of clamor and terror, struck fear in the ungodly; Raphael, the custodian over the spirits of men; Raguel, the dispatcher of punishment, a surveyor of humanity and the luminaries; Michael, the keeper of virtue and observer of deeds; Sarakiel, the comforter of the innocent who experience transgression; Gabriel, head Archangel over paradise; and finally, Remiel, the caretaker over risen spirits. These seven guarded the pit until the time of realization.

For a millennium, judgment froze. Twice God imprisoned the most wicked of angels, first during the flood and again after the trumpets. In the pit, the lawless ones waited. Just as the host of heaven, these angels earned specific surnames: Yekun, the master of seduction, lured a great number of the angelic host; Kasbeel, the provider of evil counsel; Gadreel, the expert of instruments of death, taught men how to kill; Penemue, cultivator of ideologies, tempted the world with supercilious philosophies; and Kasyade, the angel of enumerating spirits, through whom the art of the fermented grape became known. These lofty angels ranked above scores of inferior spirits, under them lay captains of fifties, subordinates that studied the skills of their superiors. Legions upon legions followed their elders, imparting their innate talents throughout mankind. Angels in opposition to God were the sorts of spirits sealed within the pit.

Many times, Lucifer and his army fought Michael and his angels. Both sides, once kindred spirits, now eternal enemies. Yahweh knew each name of those in the pit. The imprisoned hated him because the Son hindered their desires and thwarted their dominance. Seeing the world God made deepened their resentment. The confinement overflowed with contempt; the disdain of Lucifer, the angels, and their demon off-spring escalated. God kept them there until the fulfillment of under-standing ran its course. Once all flesh grasped the will of God, the great angels withdrew from the entrance of the pit. Weakened and unguarded, the Adversary and his cohorts freed themselves. It did not matter to them why God loosened their chains. Their animosity feverish, the bindings unbearable, the fallen of Lucifer flurried from their prison. Moving like locusts, they swarmed and overwhelmed mankind. The angels attacked the souls of men, covering the world with a looming darkness.

The moment of decision presented itself, teetering in the balance, the future of men. Like a roaring lion, Satan did not waste the chance before him. Covering the four-quarters of the earth, he posed a question. As he did in the garden when he asked Eve about the prohibited fruit, he queried: Why can't all enter into the beautiful city? The Old Serpent knew the people desired something forbidden. For millennia, he listened to their curiosity concerning the city of God. Envy served as a simple tactic—undetectable and untraceable. The kings and priests did not teach about the wiles of the devil, an intentional decision because Yahweh wanted men to choose without provocation. So for a thousand years, the teachers exhorted the doctrine of the Lord. They moved the people to say, "The Lord is my helper." But the words did not endure time; truth became fables, and lies became truth. Forgetting the difference between them and the elect, men coveted before the Lord. Exposing their inner ambitions, the people demanded to enter the great city, New Jerusalem.

Satan gathered an army. Men retooled their plowshares into swords and their pruning hooks into spears. Climbing up on the breadth of the earth, the army walked the path between the mountains. To the threshing floor, they marched, believing themselves worthy to take part in the glory of God. Parents, children, friends, and brethren all charged toward the great city. Numbered as the sand of the sea, the army bordered the holy mountain. Among them, angels and demons prodding and spurring the emotions of the people. The first fruits sat quietly as Satan swept his tail. None engaged the army; the immortals did not form any opposition. Neither did the Son summon them; instead, the Lord faced them. The presence of Yahweh met the disgruntled at the gates. Peering at the beguiled, he knew they had no zest for him. Lifting his mighty hand, he commanded fire from heaven. In an instant, all that challenged God, his great city, and their occupants perished. The resistance had been grave, but the response was quick, God destroyed all that turned away. There was no more deception, no blindness; the deceived succumbed because they chose the coveting cherub. This was their second death and the end of the second resurrection.

Those men left heeded the inklings of the Spirit. They embraced the teachings and did not adhere to temptation. Their hearts flourished with a healthy hunger for God and his covenant. They were people who developed a strong love; they retained the Lord's name on their foreheads. From afar, the worthy watched the might of the Lord. The remnant lamented, and the elect stood somber. As promised, the Son removed iniquity. Righteousness prevailed over the angels that brought darkness. Knowing their condemnation, they begged for prayers. The Son rebuffed them because prayers were meant for men and not for them. Taking hold of Satan, and his angels with their demon spawn, Yahweh cast all into the Lake of Fire. A fire burning like brimstone, the same place where the Antichrist and the false prophet met their fate. A space of eternal separation, an emplacement made for Lucifer and his angels. However, the important things, immovable things, still remained. Those who held on received rewards on par with the saints. Called the second harvest of God, the people waited to be counted among the sheep. But those that fell became numbered with the goats. Both are destined to stand before the throne. The great white throne where God will judge the quick and the dead.

CHAPTER 33

There Is No Other Judgment Than Righteous Judgment

The breath of God funneled down from heaven to the portals of earth. Moving through one gate and out another, the gentle breeze soothed the angels. A current filled with affection, the draft covered the host and strengthened their resolve. It was this kind of touch that kept the angels firmly devoted. That same tenderness comforted believers in times of rest and times of need. From two other gates, a cold, bitter headwind loaded with hail froze hardened angels and defiant men. Two flows wafted over the throne outside New Jerusalem, one sweet, the other rotten. With the defeat of Lucifer and the end of the dispensation, the winds of grace abruptly stopped. There were no more chances to reflect; both good and evil faced judgment on the great white throne.

The divine seat between the mountains began to shine. Brighter and brighter, it glowed until the throne turned white-hot. Heat radiated from the One who sat on it. Extreme emotions electrified the air; heaven and earth hid from the presence of the Lord. Everything stood motionless, waiting for the command from the Son. With a nod and edict, the dead, small and great, came back to life. Every man in his own order, Christ, the first and second, then those who still slept. Lastly, God regathered all that rejected him in the final deception. Whether buried, dispersed at sea, or scattered in the wind, all souls returned to their former selves. Two sets of people stood

ANGEL'S INFLUENCE

before the throne. On the right, the ones of the second resurrection who held their faith. On the left stood the blasphemous, men who trampled the blood and unbelievers of the second death. God the Father felt profound conviction within his Son. The judicial process was certain, the outcome hinged on the gift because choice dictated predestination.

From two books lay the fate of men. The Son held one in each hand, the first contained volumes of smaller books and the other the book of life. Calling all at his disposal, the cherubim, seraphim, along with the ophanim who led the eyes, all assembled around the throne. Angels of the garden, cherubs of the doors, keepers of the gates, all that fought and obeyed, witnessed the trial. Standing before the holy seat, the nations of the world. To the right stood the people called sheep, to the left those defined as goats. As instructed, the angels sorted the two groups by their conduct. The Lord looked to the right and called the sheep, "Come, ye blessed of my Father. Inherit the kingdom prepared for you from the foundation of the world." Wisdom poured forth, and the books were opened. The kings and priests gave testimony to the people. They testified of their hearts, weighed their works, and opened the mysteries of their minds. Secrets laid open; Yahweh judged the memoirs of the sheep. The Lord opened the other book. Inside the book listed the names worthy to be in his presence. Penned within the book, all those on the right were found listed within its pages.

In front of the goats, the Lord tried the sheep. As he did the first fruits on the glass, the activities of their life burned in fire. Actions of substance seared brightly; the worthless things disintegrated to ash. Those on the right found favor and reward. They remained faithful and remembered the words of the prophets. The Son said to them, "Come, you who listened. Come, you who thirsted, and take of the water of life freely." Around the throne, the host whispered a serene melodic chant. Encircling the throne, the angels sang, "Alpha and Omega, the beginning and the end, the first and the last. Blessed are they that do the commandments of the Lord." All found worthy had rights to the tree of life and the beautiful city.

The Son turned his gaze to the ones on the left. The goats shook in fear. After witnessing the transformation of the sheep, their hearts sank. Understanding their folly, the condemned wished they had never been born. Once again, the books of the written word opened. At the great white throne, the saints brought into remembrance the feats of men. Kings, princes, and other blasphemers failed the testimony of the book. Shepherds who deceived their flocks were found guilty; their condemnation doubled because of their falsehoods. Then there were the people who lived with the Son only to be snatched by Lucifer. Souls begging for mercy, men who killed saints and stepped on the divine blood. The Son rebuked them, "Verily, truly, I say to you, inasmuch as you have done unto one of the least of these my brethren, you have done unto me."

Declaring his authority, the Lord addressed the audience of witnesses, "Therefore, fear not for my name shall be a son of righteousness that will rise with healing in its wings." The goats knew their future lay in the hands of the living God. Their shame played out before the author and finisher of all things. There was no redemption for the goats.

Looking back to the judged, the Lord said to the ungodly, "Depart from me, you cursed, into everlasting fire prepared for the devil and his angels." The books weighed their hearts and found them wanting. Judged guilty, the Lord opened the book of life.

The Son prepared a proper compensation for the wicked. The ones on the left were filled with sorcerers, whore-mongers, murderers, and idolaters destroyed souls and polluted hearts. They were dogs that instinctively reveled in the power of lies. Now their artful disruption brought terror to their souls. No wealth could relieve the stress; anguish became their lot. In life, they spoke hard against the God that held the books. Now that God searched for their names and could find none in the ledger.

The condemned saw the burning place, filled with pillars of fire deep and unending. The Son threw the unworthy into the lake of fire. Unlike Lucifer and the angels who burned for an eternity, men died in an instant. The lake of fire was not designed for humanity. The grace of God did not let any of his image suffer. Those of flesh

ANGEL'S INFLUENCE

burned until consumed, they lasted as long as the condition existed. With the completion of judgment, death had no more meaning. Never again would men feel its sting; the grave no longer held control over them. Death met its end; the lake of fire consumed it. Its conclusion was written within the volumes of the books. Authored through the Spirit, the Lord fulfilled every promise he made in it.

God made a perfect plan and created it with a perfect purpose. After the end of death, there was no sorrow or crying. Heaven had been purged from the great apostasy. The former things had passed away. The angels in heaven learned their place. Those of men left became Sons of God. Yahweh was their God, and they inherited the earth and the city. Illuminated with joy, angels danced up and down the long ropes between heaven and earth. Up and down the ladders they ran, stringing lines of white light. Witnessing the movement and glee of the host, both Father and Son were pleased with the quintessence of the angels.

CHAPTER 34

How a Cherub Influenced the World

In the north, a thin stream fed an inland sea. Flowing through the mountains, the running waters skirted the borders of the desert. There lay a waterway secured from sight; the little basin housed seven islands. Over the isles floated a barrier, an enclosed bubble full of portals. Opening and closing, the winds of the Spirit blew through the island gates. Cherubs rode the currents, and the whirlwind of the Lord drove them along. They were chariots riding on the sentiments of God. Agents of blessings and dispensers of judgment, the host dutifully carried out the will of their Father. Some blew through narrow passages, and others crossed vast entries. Back and forth on the stones of fire they traveled, leaving footprint impressions on the paths. Stationed over the throne, the covering cherub never walked the fiery stones.

Fixated in one place, Lucifer never entered the gates. Purposely made with a distinctive motif, he was an angel meant to cast light. His Father embedded all manner of gems within his feathers: ruby, topaz, emerald, onyx, every stone a refraction of radiance. Gold sockets set the jewels, and the furrows divided the colors. His light produced multiple pigments around the throne. Beautiful ornaments with beams of jasper, sapphire, and turquoise, his wings paraded every shade combination. The tints panned when Lucifer moved, each shift altered the prism. Flat feathers absorbing light, the gems

ANGEL'S INFLUENCE

brightened when the angel arched. Lovely tones of sardius, diamond, and gold, his feathers slightly curled for maximum contrast. Designed with hollow pipes at the tips, his wings hummed when the Spirit filled the tubes. A calm, alluring, fluctuating sound, his translucent feathers tinkled like glass. Wings that swayed like chimes in the wind, he was a most magnificent angel. All in heaven enjoyed his beauty and the serene thrum Lucifer made.

For eternity, he watched Uriel, the angel over the luminaries, manage the gates. Overseer of the cycles of heaven, Lucifer noted how the stars marked the seasons. Watching angels monitor the winds, the covering cherub envied the power Uriel had over the gates. Lucifer marveled at how the host navigated the fiery stones. The gates fascinated him. They were conduits between the heavenly places. Through them, the angels aligned the orbs, fixed the periods, and kept the movement of days constant. Led by the chief angels Melkel, Helammelak, Meliyal, and Narel, the four of them shared watch over a quarter of the year. Subordinate watchers Adnarel, Jyasusal, and Jyelumeal assisted the stars of the seasons. Melkyas and Helemmelek cared for the sun, Tamani surveyed the abundance of the cosmos, and Barkel, Zesabel, and Heloyalef oversaw the shortfalls of the universe. All fell under the leadership of Uriel, the gatekeeper. His captains commanded thousands; the display of discipline impressed Lucifer. Amazed at the collective, he knew whoever controlled the angels held the power.

It was the secrets of the lightning and thunders, the mingling of words that lifted Lucifer. Above, he discerned the inaudible language, the God speak not privy to others. The confidentiality swelled his pride; almost from the beginning, he plotted against God. His scheming, the first sin, the beautiful angel concentrated his efforts on the cherubim. Thus began the secret agreement between the angels and the covering cherub. Darkness crept beneath the light; the ego inside Lucifer distorted him.

On the day heaven shook, myriads of angels conspired against God. A complete agitation, the division began the cycle of corruption. At the epicenter, the anointed cherub, Lucifer. Stationed in the heights of the clouds, he staged his coup. Heaven fell into a state of

225

confusion because the angels never considered their place. The tempest pitted angel against angel. Of those who rebelled, all were cherubim of the lowest rank. None had the power to reach the throne because the seraphim guarded it. Lucifer and a third of the angels lost. The Lord cast the insurgents out of heaven. All were denied access to the stones of fire. However, Lucifer became a special case because he stole the souls of men. Transferring his curse, the covering cherub won the right to walk the stones. But he could not stay in heaven; his presence upended the rest. In the first week of the era of sin, Lucifer became known as Satan because he was now an adversary.

The second week brought on great wickedness. Evil rose on earth. The angels that left their first estate decided to create. Michael and Raphael took hold of two hundred stars that dared to change men. Set in chains, the most vile were locked away. Satan and his followers became promoters of sin. Men became infested with corruption; their fleshly state developed enmity. Jealousy, strife, hatred, and pride, mankind lost interest in God. Satan replaced God with the big bang theory and the missing link. Men accredited the origins of life to a primordial ooze. From this, life evolved from simple microbes to complex creatures. Human thinkers scoffed at the possibility of any divine source. Instead, men worshiped advances in technology and believed in humanistic systems. Satan created Kabbalistic doctrines that embraced occult mysteries within sacred texts. Through utterance and knowledge, men pursued enlightenment and wondered after paranormal superstitions. It was this conflict between spiritual and material, divine and human, that Lucifer blurred.

With that came the third week. A man of righteousness appeared. Dropped in the sea of humanity, a God-man walked the earth. Unscrupulous kings and leaders of men moved people against him. However, the Father sent angels to intervene. Satan had to do more than destroy his nemesis; he had to take his crown. If Yahweh were to only kneel, Lucifer would win, but he could not expose a weakness. So the fallen angels stirred a spirit of contention within the Jewish leadership. They constantly pursued Christ until the Son finished his purpose. Once done, the angels lowered their hedge of protection. Seeing the shield gone, Satan seized the opportunity. Using the Jews as his weapon, he moved them to kill him. Through death, the Son took on sin. Stripping men of the curse, he placed it upon Satan and his angels. The Son of God could not remain with men; he had to return to his Father. In his place, he set forth angels to aid the churches and spread the Word.

The fourth week brought a time of testing. The death curse now on Satan, the world faced persecution. Lucifer intercepted the righteous and destroyed the innocent. Martyrs begged for justice, and souls waited for judgment. The angels said, "These sayings, faithful and true, and the Lord God of the holy prophets sent his angel to show unto his servants the things which must shortly be done." The Comforter, sent by God, inspired men to take the little book. A book of faith was sweet to the taste but bitter to the stomach. The mysteries of God lay within its contents. Never once did God lift the gift of choice. Men who decided to be unjust, he let them be unjust. Any that desired to be filthy, he let them remain filthy. Souls that lived to be righteous, the Lord let them stay righteous. And for those who sought holiness, he allowed them to be holy.

In the fifth week, the grave kept hold of the souls. Resting and waiting for the appointed time, the ground dripped with pangs of transgression. Then Yahweh picked his first harvest. The first chosen rose from the grave and returned to life. Very few Jews were found within the first selection. Many rejected the Talmudic interpretation of an adversary. They separated from their orthodox counterparts who regarded Satan as legitimate. Reforming Judaism, they embraced Satan as a symbolic metaphor, an aspect of human qualities. Jesus said of the children of Abraham, "You were chosen by me, but in truth, you are the children of the devil." The Jews could not accept an invisible enemy because they were a people constantly targeted. When it came to an adversary, all the Jewish people could see were men.

Darkness thickened in the sixth week. Lucifer and his angels stirred the world against the Son and his saints. Angels became locked in combat, and men annihilated each other. The vilest of angels, freed from prison, pushed humanity to war. The Son and his holy army defeated the dragon, his man of sin, and prophet. Victory assured, the angels of God took hold of Satan and his horde. All were locked away for a thousand years. Yahweh restored the earth and revived the innocent caught in the chaos.

The bondage of Satan opened in the seventh week. Seeing New Jerusalem and the greatness of the Son plunged Lucifer into anguish. Men created lesser than the angels had been exalted over him. He saw a most lovely and beautiful world. Mountains that reached heaven, receptacles of light and of thunder. Pristine waters filled with healing and balanced seasons swirling with energy. Sturdy foundations put the stars at ease. Their pathways of stones now lay nestled in the mountains with the gates that had fascinated Lucifer. God returned men to flesh; it was their second resurrection. The first death was physical, the rekindling full of grace, God brought them back to obtain spiritual understanding.

In the eighth week, the second harvest faced an insurmountable test. The treachery of Satan planted dissatisfaction within the utopia of God. He exploited the envy in men. Ministering words fell short, and many disobeyed. They allowed their natural selves to take over. Once again, Satan created an army of angels and men. This time, spiritually imperfect, unworthy mortals demanded to partake in the wonders of New Jerusalem, the beautiful city. Rebellion became their choice, and the Son stood alone against them. Angels gathered; the kings and priests gave witness. With the power of the Almighty, Yahweh destroyed the last bit of corruption in heaven and on earth.

The ninth week opened the books. Sitting on the throne, he gave guardianship to the righteous and judgment to the wicked. Continually, Satan toyed with the volume of books. Through time, he tampered with it and made the writings difficult to know. For all his efforts, Satan could not completely destroy the little book. Using haughty men, he moved them to alter its message. Indifferent to consequence, men desecrated the volumes and altered the words. But now, all before the throne understood the book. It revealed the intent of hearts and spoken words, all deeds unraveled before the Son. The angels attested; the kings and priests recorded the testimonies. Standing next to unbelievers and blasphemers, those of the sec-

ANGEL'S INFLUENCE

ond resurrection. The men who rejected the covenant were sentenced to death, a spiritual demise that ripped them out of the book of life.

The tenth week ended the cycle of sin. The spiritually damned were cast into an everlasting lake. Within the fire lay Satan and his angels, burning for eternity. Corruption had run its course, and the cycle of weeks cleansed everything. Satan had stolen and thought himself the strong man. In the end, he endured a fate worse than death. Death, too, had been abolished, and the agreement of the grave stood no more. Men felt no more stings because the Son made all things new.

New Jerusalem in comparison to Earth

ABOUT THE AUTHOR

D. S. Boyce grew up in Granite City, Illinois, and graduated with a BA from Southern Illinois University, Edwardsville. After a distinguished career in the military, she worked for the United States Postal Service while continuing her education. Since her teens, she has always strived to understand and grow nigh to God. Through life experiences and deep conviction, her desire to find a way to honor God revealed itself through writing. Writing became her venue to glorify Christ, and the Spirit led her to explore and understand God's prophecy.

www.ingramcontent.com/pod-product-compliance
Lightning Source LLC
Chambersburg PA
CBHW021510291224
19645CB00007B/36